Winner of the British Fantasy Award for Best Newcomer, D'Lacey is best known for his shocking eco-horror novel *Meat*. The book has been widely translated and prompted Stephen King to say 'Joseph D'Lacey rocks!' A film adaptation is in progress. Joseph lives with his wife and daughter in Northamptonshire.

JOSEPH D'LACEY

BLOOD FUGUE

CROMER

© Joseph D'Lacey, 2012

The right of Joseph D'Lacey to be identified as the author
of this work has been asserted by him in accordance with
Section 77 of the Copyright, Designs and Patents Act 1988.

Salt Publishing 2012

Printed in Great Britain by the Clays Ltd, St Ives plc

Typeset in Paperback 9/10

ISBN 978 1 907773 37 2 paperback

For my dad, Richard, who showed me the magic of books.

1 3 5 7 9 8 6 4 2

PART I: FOUNDLING

'Real freedom lies in wildness, not in civilization.'
CHARLES LINDBERGH

CHAPTER 1

Dusk comes early to Hobson's Valley.

The sun slips behind the crest of Bear Mountain at about two thirty in the afternoon during the winter and just before five in the summer. For an hour or more after, the valley lives in a purple twilight that casts its silence out with the mountain's lengthening shadow. Something about the haze that lingers over the pine trees makes the landscape look as though you're viewing it through a violet filter. The temperature drops the moment Bear Mountain becomes a silhouette.

It doesn't matter where in the valley you are at this time, you always notice the change; everyone does, locals and strangers alike, no matter how long they've lived here. You pause at that moment each day to mourn the sun's passing and steel yourself against the premature birth of night.

The creature watched. It sensed.

No light came from the vehicle, except for the spark and flash a match that gave rise to a single red glow before dying. In the darkness the red ember periodically burned brighter as it moved from one position to another inside the car. Within a couple of minutes, a flick sent the smouldering end through a rolled down window to the moist ground where it sizzled and died.

Instead of light, there was sound. What began as whispers and stifled giggles became chatter and laughing—occasionally, high-pitched screeches of delight followed by more laughter. Soon, the rear door opened and a girl spilled forth. A young man staggered after her, slamming the door shut behind him.

'Wooo. I am buzzing. Buzz, wuzz, wuzz.' The girl's voice was lilting, the words over-emphasised.

'That buzz came all the way from Acapulco.'

The girl giggled.

'Well, I love a south of the border buzz. But right now I need a north of the border whiz.'

The young man stumbled in the scant glimmer of starlight from above.

'Wait for me.'

'What?'

'I'm coming. I need to go too.'

'David, you are not gonna pee with me. You might get it on me.'

She dissolved into sniggers and had to stop while she recovered. David caught up to her.

'Okay, then let me watch you do it.'

'You can't see a fucking thing out here.'

'Come on, Gina. You owe me.'

She walked away from him, whispering back as she went: 'Take my hand.'

David reached out and found her trailing palm. It was warm and smooth in the cool of the night. They were already twenty yards from the car but she squeezed his fingers and drew him on.

'Hey, Gina, isn't this far enough?'

She led him into the trees where they had to duck beneath the lowest branches. A willowy pine branch caught on her sleeve but she pressed past it, determined. The branch bent, but did not snap and as she left it behind, she released it. It whipped back towards David. He heard the swish and felt the sting at the same time.

'Jesus—Fuck it.'

He stopped and held his hand to his cheek. The skin had parted and raised like a second pair of tiny lips. He felt the warm wetness of his blood, slick and sticky on his fingers. The pain made his eyes water and the saline dripped into the wound making it burn.

'What is it? Are you okay?'

'The branch fucking cut me. It cut my face.'

'Here, let me see.'

'You said yourself, you can't see a fucking thing out here. I'm going back to the car.'

'Wait. Just let me make sure you're all right.'

She was next to him now, pressing close. It was enough to make him want to stay a little longer. She put her hands to his face—

'Shit, Gina.'

—and touched the ridged welt there. Touched the fluids that had so recently been inside David's body. She kissed the damage. When she withdrew, she licked her lips silently in the darkness. She tasted him. She swallowed her saliva, tinged with David's tears and blood, ingesting him.

'Don't go back yet,' she whispered.

Lifting up the hem of her short skirt, she hooked her thumbs into the elastic waistband of the thong she wore and pulled it down, stepping free and placing it in her denim jacket pocket. She hiked her skirt up and as she squatted, she pulled David down with her to the ground. There beneath the trees, the earth was covered with pine needles that were tinder dry. With David kneeling beside her, she began to urinate. He listened until she had finished.

'That was beautiful, Gina. Amazing.'

'Shh. Lie down.'

He turned over and lay on his back expecting her to squat over him but she didn't.

'I've got Trojans,' he said.

'You won't need them.'

Looking up, David could not even see the stars through the canopy of trees. The darkness was intimate, pressing against his face like a mask. He smelled pine and dirt and Gina's sweet piss.

His blindness lent power to every sensation. He felt her unbuckle his belt and unbutton his fly. She yanked down his jeans and boxers well past his knees. In the dark, free air, his skin was alive to every sigh of wind, every scratch of the pine needles against his behind. He knew he wouldn't be able to hold himself back for long. As soon as Gina touched him he would shudder his pale sperm into the night.

He felt heat then, the moist heat of her breath against his thigh. Her lips not just warm, but hot. The contrast with the chill in the air was exquisite. Her cheek brushed his penis and then the heat was there, right there around him.

'Gina, I'm gonna—'

'Not yet you're not.'

And from then on she used only her tongue. With no more pressure than a feather lain against his taut flesh, she caressed his beating totem.

Gina, her skirt still pulled up over her hips, swung her ass from side to side in the darkness and ground her hips against the nothingness of night. With her hands on either side of David's hips she bobbed her head up and down, licking and circling and flicking; the contact so light it could last forever.

He didn't feel it when her tongue divided into three writhing, snake-thin, shafts. The central one continued to work away at him, twitching and sliding over, under and around, keeping him on the very edge of explosion. The other two shafts of tongue-flesh stretched away towards the joint of his groin where they began to gather and push at his skin. They released a fluid through tiny orifices in each tip, numbing David's skin in the places where they touched it. They pressed into him in muscular spasms; they elongated and sharpened and wormed against him and the skin beneath. It weakened and thinned and stretched at their insistence, finally splitting.

The two warm shafts burrowed into him and all the while he moaned on the precipice of his orgasm. The snakes of wet pink flesh tunnelled into the vulnerable softness where his legs joined his pelvis. They separated the tissues and muscles beneath and David ached there, believing it was his intense arousal causing him such pleasurable pain. He cried out, a yielding sound devoured by the night. As he submitted, she pushed further until the two outer tendrils of her threefold tongue found both his femoral pulses and breached the arteries.

Gina moaned as she drew on him. David moaned too. When she had taken enough, she stopped and withdrew the two wormlike spikes of lingual flesh from inside him. They fused once more to become one with her tongue and the wounds she'd made in his flesh sealed up. Finally she closed her mouth over David's penis and gave him what he wanted, that which he had begun to beg for, his pleas gaining volume in the otherwise silent forest. She gave him that pleasure and he gave more fluid in return. She wasted nothing.

And while he lay, panting, recovering, her trifurcated tongue tunnelled into the earth and reabsorbed the urine she'd spent there minutes before

The creature watched it all, sensed it all. It was aroused.

The shop bell jangled and the door slammed behind a slim, weathered man. The shopkeeper's greeting was dismissive, as usual.

'Hey, city boy.'

'Hey, Randall,'

The rugged man mooched along between the partially stacked shelves looking for anything he could use.

'Got any brown rice this week?' he asked.

'Sold out.'

'Sold out? You said you'd call me when the rice came in.'

'I didn't get the chance. Jeff Katz came in and bought it all.'

He knew what that meant. Randall had shifted the whole batch to the chef at Segar's Cabin so that he didn't have to worry about the product going over its sell-by date. If he wanted rice now, he'd have to eat out or drive thirty miles through the pass into Saracen, the town in the next valley.

He picked up some canned fruit and frozen meat, the kind of things he couldn't grow in his own yard and placed them on the counter. Randall avoided eye contact as he tallied up the goods.

'Eleven fifty.'

The man placed a well-worn hundred and Randall tutted to himself.

'Ain't you got anything smaller?'

'Sorry.'

Randall made him wait while he counted out the change nice and slow. The 'city boy' watched the shopkeeper's hands as he molested the coins and bills. He had spatulate fingers; the kind that splayed out at the ends making them look like a frog's pads. The nails were broad, thick and grey. The 'city boy's' name was James Kerrigan. He had read a book on palmistry years before; fingers shaped like Randall's were called Murderer's Fingers.

'You seen your folks this week?' Randall asked.

'I see them every week.'

'I heard Burt hadn't been too good,' said Randall with some satisfaction.

'Burt's just fine.'

Randall appeared to lose count of the change and started over.

'You still writing for them magazines?' he asked.

'Sure.'

Kerrigan wanted to keep the conversation to a minimum. He knew what was coming next.

'You should get a real job, Kerrigan. Get out of that cabin

more often. Spend some time with your folks. A guy could go crazy up there on his own.'

'It is a real job, Randall.'

'What is it about those woods anyway? If you had more sense, you'd live right here in town like the rest of us.'

The inevitable flush of anger that accompanied any trip to Randall's flooded his face with heat. He kept quiet, not wanting an open quarrel. Randall looked up and smiled. He leaned towards Kerrigan like a man about to share a dirty joke and, even though they were the only people in the shop, dropped his voice to just above a whisper.

'I don't know what it is you do up there all day but people don't like it. They talk about you, Kerrigan.'

'Randall, I really don't think—'

'No, Kerrigan, you don't. That's your problem. I've lived in this valley all my life and I know how it is. Things happen in those woods sometimes. Bad things. When they do, you'll be the one who gets the blame.'

Kerrigan was careful not to touch Randall's hands as he passed him his change. He didn't even check it, just stuffed it into his pocket. He wasn't going to allow the meddling geezer to see him lose control, but right then he wanted to smash Randall's face down into the antiquated cash till and keep pounding until there were no more sounds from him. Kerrigan took a couple of deep breaths and paused before speaking. His voice sounded alien in his ears.

'Thanks for the advice.'

'It ain't advice, Kerrigan. It's a fact.'

He didn't know why Randall had it in for him so bad. He wasn't the only one, though. Kerrigan had left Hobson's Valley for just a couple of years but it was a bigger insult to most locals than being an ordinary stranger from out of town. Three years after returning, they still expected him to crawl and eat shit.

CHAPTER 2

Reminders. August 15th

Left arm sore and heavy this morning. Took four Tylenols. Couple of hours before the pain eased off. Thought there was some kind of scar on my wrist. Stood outside to get a better look but couldn't find anything. Could have strained it hoeing yesterday. Maybe time to get a new computer keyboard. Remember: get doctor to check it out if it hurts again.

Got to stop getting groceries at Randall Moore's place. Guy's a fucking reincarnated Nazi or something. Way he looks at me, I can see him breaking in one night, putting a bullet between my eyes. So don't forget: go to Olsen's from now on.

Important: Visit Burt and Kath. Take goodies and a treat for Dingbat.

Call Amy. Maybe.

Kerrigan tore the top page from his reporter's notebook and stuck it to the door of his Westinghouse with a banana-shaped magnet. He frowned at the previous note for a few seconds, screwed it into a ball and threw it into the trash, shaking his head.

It was a shock when the Jimenez family trooped single file into his back yard as he was picking beans for his dinner one afternoon in late August. In that moment, the temperature had sharpened a degree or two and a little of the late summer light had retreated from the sky. The vapour in the air took on the faintest shade of lavender. Kerrigan noticed, as always, that the silence deepened in that first moment of change and any sounds that followed it seemed louder.

Hikers often stopped to ask directions through the woods to favourable camping spots or to find out the best way to the higher trails beyond the tree line. But on that day, even though he heard their footsteps and their rhythmic Latin chatter, he still jumped a little when he turned to see them standing there. They all wore bright, new outdoor gear; their boots still shiny from the box. It was poor quality stuff; none of it worth a damn if the weather got nasty.

Holding a plastic bag full of freshly picked beans and with dirt all over his hands, Kerrigan spent a moment in each of them and discovered something about them that they did not yet know. It was a wild feeling, both savage and wise; like slipping on a glove still warm from someone else's hand. There was an urge to caress, the urge to make a fist. The moment he acknowledged it, the sensation was gone and he was left staring at them, not quite sure what to say.

Holidaymakers usually knocked at the front door. This was the first time anyone had made their way so boldly into his vegetable patch.

'Hi there,' he said, dispersing the silence. 'Can I help you with something?'

The head of the family held out his hand and the others spread out beside him.

'I am sorry to scare you like that, sir. My name is José Jimenez. This is my wife Maria and my children Luis and Carla.'

His English was accented but easy to understand and he held Kerrigan's gaze as though he felt no shame over their intrusion. Kerrigan took them to be wealthy Mexicans. After dusting the crumbs of soil from his fingers he grasped Mr. Jimenez's hand, measuring him in the contact.

'Jimmy Kerrigan,' he replied.

The family looked on, approving of the unspoken machismo in the exchange. Jimenez let go first.

'We are looking for a trail in this forest,' he said. 'I have asked others in the town but none of them knew the way. All of them said you would.'

Most of the folk in Hobson's Valley disguised their dislike of outsiders and treated them with a grudging respect. They usually told visitors the way if they knew it. Perhaps these Mexicans were a little too far from home to be made welcome. It would be just like Randall Moore or one of the other old timers to feign ignorance.

Sensing the racial implications of what Mr. Jimenez was telling him, Kerrigan softened. Despite a few knock-backs in town they were still determined enough to ask yet another stranger for help.

He grinned.

'I can help you find just about any trail around Hobson's Valley and I know every path on Bear Mountain. Do you have your own map?'

The parents exchanged a flicker of a glance before Jimenez answered.

'Yes.'

'Come on inside and I'll mark the trail on it for you.'

Kerrigan led the way to the back door. It felt like a long walk with them all following him. He imagined them taking in everything around them; the rows of beans and corn and onions, the wooden fence separating the forest from the garden, the rusty porch swing. Even the sound of the crickets that had intensified in the moments since the sun had fallen beyond the peak of the mountain and the water that plopped from the high gutters into the collecting barrel below, still dripping intermittently since the afternoon's rain. The qua-la-la, qua-la-la of turtle doves pecking and sifting through the fallen pine needles, the fragrance of the moist air, the leaning tools visible through the open shed door, the smell of creosote, the creak of the hinges on his back door.

Instinct swelled within him; he didn't like them being out of his line-of-sight. He was relieved when he faced them once more across the kitchen table and snapped on the overhead lamp. It seemed bright in the afternoon gloom.

'Are there really bears on this mountain?'

The girl's question scattered thoughts of darkness and delighted him.

Carla's speech was different from her father's. It was schoolgirl English; precise but with other accents creeping in. She sounded sophisticated, somehow European. Kerrigan found it hard not to stare at her. Her breasts were petite, the curves of her body coltish and athletic. Her look was in one moment adolescent defiance, in another Hispanic feminine mystery. He guessed she was sixteen or seventeen. Before he could censor them, images of a taboo courtship filled his vision.

'Some of the older folks say their parents shared this land with bears, but I'm not sure I believe them,' he said, breaking the moment. 'As far as I know, the bears have been gone for a hundred years.'

'Maybe some of them could have hibernated like they were frozen in time,' said Luis. 'Maybe someone could wake them up again.'

Kerrigan chuckled until he saw that Luis's parents weren't fazed in the slightest by their son's flight of fancy. To them it seemed a reasonable question. He cut his laughter short.

'I think all the bears died out a long time ago, Luis. You might find their bones, but I doubt it. I've lived here almost all my life and I've never seen a single trace of a bear, living or dead.'

'They should change the name of the place then,' said Carla.

Kerrigan had to smile.

'They should at that,' he said.

Silence filled the kitchen. Kerrigan let the space between words stretch out.

BLOOD FUGUE

Mr. Jimenez reached into the pocket of his colourful all-weather jacket and drew out a large brown leather wallet. He laid it down on the table with practised care and Kerrigan noticed the four dark ribbons that held it closed. Mr. Jimenez slipped the knot on each ribbon and opened the wallet like a book. Protected inside was a single sheet of well-preserved paper or parchment that had no creases to suggest it had ever been folded.

'Wow. That's not the sort of map I see too often.'

'It's an heirloom,' said Mr. Jimenez. 'Unique in every way.'

Kerrigan sensed the man's pride and something else too; a hint of melancholy.

Everyone moved closer for a better view. The map was hand drawn in black ink and showed a large area of Bear Mountain, including the land upon which they all stood. Kerrigan wondered if the cartographer had drawn the images free hand or if he'd traced them first in some way. Whatever the case, he had a skilful, if amateur, hand. Much of the scale was inconsistent and there were artistic flourishes that made features of particular trees and rocks along the marked trails. In some places wild animals were depicted in rampant poses. The embellishments reminded him of mariners' charts with spouting whales and Kraken hauling ships into the deep.

'It's a work of art,' said Kerrigan. 'Not exactly accurate, but it's close enough to follow. Some of the trails it shows are abandoned. And some of these aren't on any of my maps.' The chart went some way to explaining why the family had no luck when they'd asked for directions. 'I suppose it's one of these disused trails you're looking for, right?'

Mr. Jimenez smiled.

'Well, I can take a look for you. I've got some pretty good maps. I can't guarantee anything, though.'

'We appreciate any help you can give.'

'Which trail are you after?' asked Kerrigan.

'This one.'

Where Mr. Jimenez was pointing was one of the more

14

unusual places for a trail to have existed. It was a branch of an old track that ran parallel to the tree line and just far enough inside the forest that the mountain wouldn't be visible. The primary track was remote enough; it appeared to skirt the mountain for several miles before stopping. But there was no logic to the one they were looking for. It wasn't circular, it didn't lead to a place of particular beauty and it didn't relate to anything else on the map. It led away from the old track and the mountain, and down into the forest. At the end of the trail there was an icon; a man whose legs had become roots and his arms branches.

Kerrigan laughed a little too loudly.

'What does this signify?' he asked.

When there was no answer, he looked up at Mr. Jimenez and the faces of his family. Their expressions were guarded.

'We are not sure,' said Mr. Jimenez.

A shadow was all the creature required to be safe. As the sun fell beyond the peak of Bear Mountain, a colossal gloom engulfed Hobson's Valley, bringing not nightfall, but its presage. Revelling in the chill of the early twilight, the creature flitted between the pines, silent and swift. When the sun no longer touched the town, it became the creature's playground.

Long before it reached the outskirts, a scent came to it and the creature halted to sample the air with its tongues. It chose a new direction, moving slower now, stalking. Its gaunt, pale body slipped between the trees like mist, leaving no trace. It came to a fence, beyond which was a small dwelling made of stone. A warm glow lit its windows.

The creature paused and tilted its head, as though the scene were familiar. It shuddered but could not hesitate. It leapt the fence and followed the scent through the neat rows of vegetables, padding silently towards the house.

CHAPTER 3

Kerrigan frowned.

'So why go there?'

Again the silence.

'I'm sorry,' said Kerrigan, 'It's none of my business. I'm just curious.' He smiled and their expressions relaxed. 'I have to admit I've never spent much time hiking in that part of the forest. It's quite a distance.'

'If you could show us the way we would be most grateful.'

'I can do better than that. I'll mark it on a waterproof map and let you use it until you finish your holiday.'

Kerrigan saw the relief and simple excitement on their faces as everyone stepped back from the table.

'Can I get you some tea? Coffee? Something cold?'

As he stepped out of the kitchen to get the right map Mr. Jimenez replied in embarrassed tones.

'We have troubled you enough already.'

Kerrigan poked his head back into the kitchen.

'The kettle's there, the cups are on the drainer. You set it up and I'll make the drinks. How's that?'

'Luis, do as Mr. Kerrigan says.'

Kerrigan left them to it.

His maps were laminated and he kept them rolled up and stacked in an old umbrella stand in his pantry. He'd spread them onto the table more times than he could count, for

16

every kind of visitor. He'd seen young couples looking for excitement in the wilderness, recently divorced mothers taking their children into the woods while they mourned a split home, teenagers looking for a quiet spot to eat psilocybin mushrooms and solitary men who disappeared into the woods in search of themselves to return days or weeks later, bearded, gaunt and crystal-eyed with the harsh peace they'd discovered. He'd advised them all, marked pathways on their maps, explained where to find clean water, told them what to avoid.

He pulled the light cord in the pantry, flooding it with a dim yellow glow. He reached for the maps but his hand was drawn to the carved walking staff rising above them in the umbrella stand. His fingertips fluttered over the dark wood and he drifted for a moment. His eyes wandered along the racks of tinned and dried goods, drawn downwards. Beneath the lowest shelf, nestled in the shadows was a wooden chest, layered with dust. He tried to remember what it contained and made a mental note to check once the Jimenez family were safely on their way.

'Here we go,' he said, walking back into the kitchen.

He rolled the rubber band down the tube of encapsulated paper until it sprung off into his hand. Mr. Jimenez folded his leather wallet closed and made space. Kerrigan unfurled his map across the table and used four heavy grey stones to hold it flat. He'd always believed a rolled map would last a lifetime or longer.

Solid paperweights were a necessity for every map inspection. Years before, Kerrigan had selected four smooth rocks from Singing River, the waterway that had created Hobson's Valley over millions of years. The slate grey stones were the size of ostrich eggs, speckled with sparkling flecks of mica. A sun-ray catching them just right would release a glitter of cobalt sparks from their surfaces. The four he'd picked all had the same 'feel'. He liked to think he'd found four stones that had once been part of a single boulder.

He set a stone on each corner of the chart.

'If you put your map down over here,' he said, 'I can use it to estimate the position of your trail.'

With reverent care Mr. Jimenez placed his leather bound map once more upon the table and with a red marker Kerrigan inscribed his directions over the contour lines of the new map, creating a dotted path on the plastic coating.

'This is where you are now. You can drive another two or three miles but the road finishes at a picnic area called The Clearing. You can leave your vehicle there for a few days, even a week or two if you want. From The Clearing you'll take a trail known as the Eastern Path. It's not popular because there isn't much to see. You'll be hemmed in by pines, so it's kind of a gloomy walk.'

He glanced up at their faces but they were intent on the map. All but Carla who held his gaze for a moment.

'About five miles along, the path forks. The left fork is called Trapper's Trail and it's well signposted. It leads out of the tree line and up towards the summit over a lot of loose shale.

'You'll be taking the right fork, into dense pine forest. That's the continuation of the Eastern Path and it's not so well trodden these days. It could be overgrown and there may be fallen trees. Slow going, believe me. Eventually, it leads to a pass that goes into the next valley but you're not going that far. You need to follow the trail for about another twelve miles. Then you'll be at the start of the trail you're looking for.'

He looked up again. They were staring at the map, absorbing every word he said.

'This is a long hike, folks. Are you sure you'll be OK?'

'Please don't take us for stupid tourists, Mr. Kerrigan. We are not strangers to the outdoors.'

Kerrigan frowned.

'Okay. Well, that's good. So, around the twelve mile mark, should be the start of the trail on your map. How you're going to find it, I don't know. Maybe there'll be some kind of marker or sign but I doubt it. If this trail is as old as your map looks, I doubt you'll even find it. I'm expecting you to come back tired and disappointed.

'If you do find it — and if you can re-break it — it's eight more miles before you reach this . . . whatever this place is. And when you're done, you've got to come all the way back knowing exactly how the scenery will look. I think it will take two or three days to get there. I'll expect you back here in a week at the outside.'

There was silence around the table. Maria's expression tightened. What he'd taken for excitement was, in her case at least, trepidation.

'Now, up by Trapper's Trail, there's a spring for collecting fresh water.'

'We will work it out, Mr Kerrigan.'

'Okay, sure, but have you got enough food such a long—'

'We have everything we need.'

The water had been boiling on the gas stove for some time and the steam was beginning to fog up the kitchen. As Kerrigan turned to remove the kettle, Buster, his Siamese cat, leapt on the map for a closer look at the latest batch of strangers. The Jimenez family all jumped at the same time as Buster skidded to a halt at the centre of the stones. Mr. Jimenez snatched up his map and backed away.

'Yeesh, he won't hurt you,' said Kerrigan, 'Will you, Buster? You like visitors, right?'

Buster perused the four faces above him. He padded towards Carla and stared at her with his paws right on the edge of the table. She reached out her hand as if she thought he'd bite her. Buster stretched towards her. She touched her fingers to the top of his head, giving him a little scratch before pulling away. He waited for her to do it again and when she did they were friends.

My choice too, buddy.

Kerrigan finished making the tea and handed the mugs

around. They looked uncomfortable, unsure what to do.

'Here, sit down.'

He gestured to the four rickety chairs around the table, all damaged by him leaning back on two legs and stressing the joints. He pulled up a stool and, with the map no longer the focus of the discussion, silence was king once more.

'I can't help wondering why you're going all the way out to this trail. I mean, what are you hoping to find there? Treasure?'

He laughed but no one else did.

'We have come to find the last resting place of my grandfather, Raul Rodrigo Jimenez,' said Mr. Jimenez.

Kerrigan was intrigued.

'He came here too?'

'He lived in this place.'

Kerrigan flicked his gaze across all their faces.

'In Hobson's Valley?'

'In this house.'

Kerrigan realised his mouth was open. He shut it.

'You're kidding.'

José Jimenez shook his head. The others were quiet, solemn. Buster jumped from the table onto Kerrigan's lap and he stroked his fur as he thought about what this piece of information implied. The notion that their ancestor had lived in this house, *his* house, stabbed at his root. He'd been undercut, preceded. Negated. The strength of his reaction frightened him.

'It is okay, Mr Kerrigan,' said Mr. Jimenez, 'we are not here to evict you. We merely wish to take my grandfather's bones and return them to the land of his birth. If we cannot find them then we are here to pay our respects and see the land where he made his life. We are fulfilling his wishes, as stated in his will.'

'But why now? Why after so much time has passed? Couldn't he have arranged to have his body returned to Mexico for burial at the time of his death?'

'My grandfather was from Spain, Mr Kerrigan, as are we.'
Kerrigan blushed.

'God, that was stupid of me. I'm sorry.'

'No matter.'

Carla and Luis made a show of studying the map. Their parents sipped his tea.

'I ask too many questions,' he said.

'No. I am glad to speak of it,' said Mr. Jimenez, 'and you were good enough to help us before you asked your questions.'

He placed the leather map case on the table.

'This was left to me in his will. We received it two months ago by mail with a letter from Symmons and Sons, a law firm in Boise, and a copy of the will. They were instructed to keep the map in a safe deposit box before passing it to a Jimenez at a time specified by my grandfather. I am the only Jimenez left. In the will, he asked that his remains be brought home to San Sebastian to be cremated and scattered in the Pyrenees, the beautiful mountain range of our region where he spent his childhood. He has left us quite a task.'

'He sure has,' said Kerrigan. 'But why wait all this time?'

Mr. Jimenez looked embarrassed.

'It is superstition. He believed that any descendents who touched his remains within a generation would be cursed.'

Kerrigan had never heard of such an elaborate will, or such long lasting paranoia.

'Sounds like he was a little — eccentric,' he ventured.

'There is no doubt of that, Mr Kerrigan.'

'How will you transport his — remains?'

'Let us first see if we can find them.'

Another silence bunched up in the small kitchen. Kerrigan had stopped stroking Buster. The cat jumped up onto the table again and then into Carla's lap. She accepted his advance with more confidence this time and began to stroke him in the same way Kerrigan had.

Mr. Jimenez placed his mug down on the map.

'What are those?' he asked.

He nodded his head towards a mobile that swung idly over the kitchen sink. Each piece was hand crafted from polished pine and withy strands to create a simple X shape within a circle. The handiwork was rough and ready.

Kerrigan cleared his throat.

'Those are, uh—binders.'

'What are binders?' asked Mr. Jimenez.

'That's a good question.' He groped for an answer and found, as always, that it was difficult to explain. 'They—well—I always used to notice the shape in the stained glass windows of our church when I was a kid. Round windows with even-armed crosses in them. I'd kind of stare at them and daydream when I was meant to be singing or listening to the preacher. I started carving them out of fallen branches and reeds from the edge of the river. I make a couple of new ones every day. I've got a whole drawer full.'

He laughed, embarrassed by the admission.

'Why do you call them binders?' asked Maria.

'I don't know, I just do. Probably it was the name I made up for them when I was a boy.'

'I like them,' said Carla.

'Me too,' said Luis.

The kids looked fascinated. José frowned.

'You fashion these from pine, no?'

'That's right,' said Kerrigan.

'Why does the wood look so old?'

Kerrigan's eyes defocused for a moment. He blinked.

'Uh, that's typical of Idaho pine. The sap is very dark.'

Maria wore a look of mild concern.

'They are not occult, are they?' she asked.

'I don't think so. I mean, the idea came from the church, so . . .' Kerrigan shrugged his shoulders. 'I give them to everyone who stops to ask for directions.'

What credibility this might give them, he didn't know.

'How much do you charge?' asked Mr. Jimenez.

'Nothing. I give them away.'

'But why?'

'To make the journey through the forest special.'

Out of nowhere, that was as close to the truth as he had ever come. He watched the binders turning and turning on their nylon threads and began to drift the way he always had when looking at them. An X within a circle, a nought and a cross, a kiss and a hug. Four slices of a pie. Simple. Beautiful—

'Weird,' said Luis.

'Cool,' said his sister.

'Can we have one?' they both asked.

'You can all have one. Like I said, I give them to everyone that passes this way.'

He stood up to fetch a few from the kitchen cupboard.

'Thank you, Mr. Kerrigan,' said Maria, 'but I don't think the children should have such things.'

'They're for all of you to have, not just the kids.'

Maria was adamant.

'We do not want them.'

Mr. Jimenez placed a hand on his wife's wrist.

'I do not see any harm in it. Mr. Kerrigan is a good man. He has tried only to help us.'

Kerrigan watched their personal politics play out. Maria was going to give in without a word being spoken. That didn't mean she was happy about it, of course.

'If it is no trouble,' said Mr. Jimenez, 'we would gladly accept your gift. It will give us a way of remembering this journey that we have made together.'

'It's no trouble at all.'

The binders he made to give to strangers were on thin strips of cowhide so that they could be worn. He took four from the drawer and handed one to each of them. Carla and Luis put theirs on immediately. Maria handed hers straight to her husband who placed them in his coat pocket.

'Thank you, Mr Kerrigan. And now I think it's time for us make a start. We have a lot of miles to cover.'

'You're not thinking of hiking now, are you?'

'Of course. The day is almost over and we need to make progress.'

'You won't get far before dark. Take a look outside.' They all turned and saw the hazy gloom pressing in at the windows. The electric light in the kitchen was warm and bright next to the bruised purple shades of the early dusk. 'You ought to be pitching camp right now.'

'We will see.'

Mr. Jimenez stood and the family followed his lead. Kerrigan knew there was no point trying to dissuade them now. They'd soon wise up to the realities of Hobson's Valley and Bear Mountain.

'Come through this way,' said Kerrigan.

He led them out to the front entrance and held the door open for them. Parked out front was a white Land Cruiser. The damp scent of pine was everywhere and the crickets chirped, much louder now, from their hiding places. José Jimenez turned back and held out his hand.

'Thank you again for your help. Completing this task will mean a great deal to my family.'

'No sweat.'

Kerrigan took his hand and held it, not wanting them to leave. Maria watched but didn't speak.

The children seemed excited and carefree. With their binders around their necks they looked like converts to a strange religion or child soldiers ready to crusade against the unbelievers. Kerrigan let go of José Jimenez's hand and the family trotted to the car, eager to be on their way.

The doors of the Land Cruiser slammed shut and the engine started easily. As it moved off up the track into the pines, only Carla looked back, waving a pale hand through the glass before the car disappeared from view.

Kerrigan sat down in the rocker on the porch and listened

to the engine being swallowed the deeper into the trees it went. A minute later and the sound was gone but still he listened for it, hoping to hear one last note or grumble wafted his way on a breeze. He didn't rock in the chair. Instead, he touched his fingers to the binder that rested against his chest beneath the fabric of his shirt.

Trees limited the view from his porch but the air was always sweet and that was why he liked to sit there. Now that the car was gone he could hear the forest sounds again and beyond that he could hear the Singing River smoothing the rocks in its currents.

He didn't stay out for long. The night's arrival was swift and cunning, the thought of it enough to calcify his joints. He retreated inside before its blackness paralysed him.

CHAPTER 4

The morning was dry and chilly.

Kerrigan assessed the sky as he walked, a deep, cloudless blue. It would be warm once the sun rose high enough to shine into the valley. A mile beyond Randall's store Kerrigan reached Hobson's Valley's main road, known simply as The Terrace.

The wide street was well kept and clean. There were a few souvenir shops, a gas station, post office, hiking shop and small grocery market, all within a few yards of each other. Oak trees lined the sidewalk and beyond the small commercial area, there were houses, mostly wooden, many of them with two floors. Towards the edge of town were a few trailer homes and smaller properties. The road wound along beside the river for several miles before twisting up into the hills, away toward the flatter land on the other side and civilisation. Hobson's Valley was a cul de sac and Kerrigan's stone cabin marked the very end of it.

In Olsen's Grocery, there was a better selection of food than in Randall's store. The trouble was that Kerrigan generally shopped in the afternoon when he'd finished work. He went to Randall's because, if he was quick, he wouldn't be outside when twilight came. Seeing all the varieties of cereal on the shelves in Olsen's he resolved, yet again, to go shopping in the mornings. He bought a box of Lucky Charms; a bag of cookies and a few other items that seemed like treats and went to the checkout.

He didn't see her until it was too late.

'Hey, Jimmy K.'

He tried to keep the startled look from his face.

'Hey, Amy.'

'Why haven't you called me?'

'I've been working.'

Amy smirked.

'Writing isn't work, it's laziness.'

'It's work. If I don't write, I don't get paid.'

'That's so lame. Are you working all night too?'

'No, but—'

'So call me. A girl could get to thinking you didn't like her any more.'

He looked at Amy's dyed blonde hair, dry and brittle from too much attention. He looked at all the cheap gold rings she wore and her heavy charm bracelet. He looked at the layer of make up she used to hide the generous helping of plainness she'd been dealt at birth and he looked at the bulges where her store uniform clung to her. She ate too much and didn't get enough exercise. Soon she'd be wearing pantsuits and sneakers for every occasion. Right now, though, there was still a little allure left in her. Mostly it was in her eyes; eyes that promised anything in return for a little company, some good food, a few compliments.

Beside her was a romance novel, its spine cracked open, its pages curled and splayed. Under the cheap, drip-dry Olsen's uniform, Amy's black underwear was just visible. She wasn't smart, she wasn't interesting but Kerrigan's response to the hint of her bra pressed so tightly by her breasts against her clothes reminded him that it wasn't smart and interesting he needed.

Dry-mouthed, he said:

'Why don't you come over on Saturday? I'll make a picnic and take you on a mystery walk.'

She pouted.

'Will we have to go far?'

He laughed.

'Just far enough to work up an appetite and no further. Deal?'

'I'll think about it.'

Even a dead-end-town chick like Amy couldn't be seen to say yes too easily. He knew she'd call him later that day.

'Great,' he said. 'I've missed you.'

She checked to see if anyone was listening but the store was almost empty.

'Really?'

'Really.'

He took his sack of junk food and strolled the hundred yards or so to number forty-eight, The Terrace.

His childhood home was falling into the clutches of decay. The battle to keep it young looking with coats of paint, replacement frames for the doors and windows and regular work in the yard was a battle his folks were losing. He shook his head, scolding himself for not coming down more often to keep the place tidy, but he'd made the same gesture a hundred times and his behaviour never changed. He was too busy to look after a second house.

Occasionally, he paid a boy to mow the lawns and cut back the weeds but not often enough to do any good. The house, with its green roof and bare wooden porch, with its green and white cushioned porch swing, now too mouldy and rusty to use, was quietly dying.

Kerrigan walked along the cracked paving stones bordered by shin-high grass and clumped up the dry boards of the front steps to the door. The bell hadn't worked for years. He hammered three times as hard as he could with the edge of his fist on the frame of the door and stood back to wait.

Now that he was closer he could see how the paint was flaking off. White scales littered the porch. He poked his finger into a bald spot on the doorframe; the wood was soft and rotting. The place was turning into a health hazard.

He heard shuffling in the passage and saw the grey figure of Burt approaching with his walker. Every time Kerrigan saw him he seemed smaller, thinner and slower. It took the old man a long time to open the locks.

Once Burt had managed to unlock and open the door he reversed a shuffle at a time to make way. He was still in his pyjamas. Kerrigan closed the door and let his nose adjust to the mustiness and decrepitude that lingered heavy on the trapped air. It wasn't the smell of the house, it was the smell people make as they waste away.

Burt grinned and Kerrigan gave him a hug, trapping the walker between them. Despite his eighty-one years, Burt's grip was wiry and fierce. In his youth, he'd been a natural strong man and some of that force remained, hidden beneath the stained pyjamas and slack, wrinkled skin.

'How're you doing, Burt?'

'Laughing it up, as ever, I guess.'

'You sleep late this morning?'

Burt looked confused for a moment, before glancing down at his attire and shrugging.

'I was just about to shave and get dressed when you knocked on the door.'

'Well, don't let me interrupt you. I'll see you in the kitchen when you're done.'

From the smell of Burt he'd been wearing the same outfit for a month.

Kerrigan left the old man, taking the paper sack of treats into the kitchen. He was relieved to see Kathleen doing a crossword at the table instead of watching crap on breakfast TV or scaring herself with the news.

'Hello, sweetheart.'

'Hey, Kath, good to see you.'

He set the shopping down on the table. Kath stood, a little

stiffly, and Kerrigan hugged her for a long time, placing a kiss on top of her head.

'You want some coffee?' she asked.

'You sit down and look at what I brought you. I'll make the coffee.'

'Burt won't have any. He's depressed.'

'Burt'll do what he's told.'

As he filled the kettle to make filter coffee, he heard Kath rustling through the paper bag and crooning over what he'd brought them.

'Chocolate covered cherries flavour ice cream. I don't think we've had that one before.'

It was one of her favourites. He decided to ignore the comment.

'You seen Maggie this week?' he asked.

'Yeah. She brought us a spaghetti Bolognese and salad. Didn't stay long, though. Said she had an extra visit to make.'

'How was the food?'

'Well, Burt covered his in ketchup and Tabasco just like he does with everything, so I don't think he noticed. I gave most of mine to Dingbat. He seemed to think it was pretty good.'

'Maybe the church should concentrate on feeding stray dogs instead of you old folks.'

'There's nothing wrong with the food, as such. But the way Maggie Fredericks cooks it makes it inedible.'

'I feel sorry for her family.'

'She hasn't got any family, James. That's why she runs around after the needy. She's no saint, she's just bored and lonely.'

'Common problem in these parts,' he said.

Kathleen's response convinced him she'd been kidding about the ice cream. She didn't miss a trick.

'Oh, don't be such a dope, James,' she said. 'You made this life for yourself. You were the one who left us for the big city and then refused to move back in when you came home to the valley.'

'Jesus, Kath, I couldn't move back in. I was almost thirty. Everyone leaves home. It's natural. Anyway, I'd never get any writing done if I lived here. You're like a pair of spoilt teenagers.'

'You'd know about that. You were the most ruined child in this town.'

'Don't remind me.'

Burt appeared. A couple of steps, a push on the walker. A couple of steps more.

'I can smell fresh coffee.'

'No you can't,' said Kerrigan, 'I haven't made it yet.'

'Well, I'll have a cup when you do.'

The old man had on a pair of jeans held up by a belt that Kerrigan had punched extra holes into. He'd put on the Nike trainers Kerrigan had bought him too, but he still wore the smelly pyjama top. Next to the clean blue of the jeans and the almost unworn white of the trainers, it looked truly filthy.

'You won't have anything until you start acting like a civilised human being. If you don't change out of those pyjamas you can make your own coffee and you can drink it alone. I'm serious, Burt. What the hell has gotten into you? Where's your self-respect?'

Burt said nothing. Maybe the old man knew better than to argue with him. Maybe he was too hurt to reply. Kerrigan watched Burt turn himself around and walk, six-legged, back to the bedroom.

Maybe he's had enough.

He could understand how Burt might feel that way, especially when he thought back to the man Burt had once been, bending iron bars around his neck and lifting giggling ladies over his head like they were made of balsa. As a young lumberjack, he'd split thicker logs than any of the other local men and felled mature pines with an axe in seconds. Everyone had admired him for it. Now he could barely stand up after taking a dump. Kerrigan spooned the coffee into the filter and placed it over the cracked jug they'd used for making coffee since before he'd started drinking it.

'I'm sorry, Kath,' he said.

'Don't be. Someone had to say something and he doesn't listen to me any more.'

'When was the last time he changed clothes?'

'Four or five days maybe.'

Kerrigan shook his head.

'If he does this again, you remind him what I said.'

He poured the boiling water over the rich brown heap of coffee and stirred it as it seeped through the paper into the jug below. He poured until the jug was almost full. While they waited for Burt he put some of the groceries away.

'How've you been doing, James?' asked Kath.

'I like it up there.'

'But you want for company, don't you?'

'Yes and no. I get a lot of articles written and they pay well. Means I get time to write my stories. It's good to have no distractions.'

'Have you ever told the truth for any of those magazines?' she asked.

'I save the truth for my fiction.'

'Maybe that's why no one's interested in publishing it.'

Kerrigan chuckled.

'There's more to it than that,' he said, 'but you're probably right. I ought to write romances or something.'

He set three cups on the table along with sugar for Burt and milk for Kath. As he poured coffee, Burt returned. He was wearing a white shirt with a collar and he had combed his wisps of fine white hair across his head. He'd shaved too.

'My God, who *is* that man? He looks like someone I married. Will you give an old lady a kiss and make her happy?'

Burt smiled. It was hesitant at first, like he was embarrassed to be capable of happiness. The smile was followed by a look of pure mischief.

'I'll give you a darn sight more than that when I get over

there, lady. I just need to accelerate to my cruising speed. Might take a few minutes.'

Again the smile, ragged and careless like the smile Kerrigan remembered. When he eventually arrived, Burt leaned over and gave her the kiss he'd promised her and Kerrigan saw in that brief exchange their spirits flying colours bright as banners. A part of them would always be young.

Outside there was a sudden scratching before Dingbat catapulted through the dog flap in the back door. After two years, Kerrigan still hadn't worked out what breed Dingbat was but he had a lot of energy. The dog barked like there was an army of cats in the kitchen. He ran to Kerrigan, wagging his fluffy tail in recognition and turning in excited circles. Finally, he collapsed onto his back in submission and growled for attention. Kerrigan gave him a treat from the glass jar on the counter and rubbed his tummy. Dingbat tried to chew the dog biscuit upside down, half choking himself on the shattered crumbs.

'You should see a doctor, Dingbat,' said Kerrigan, 'You need Prozac.'

'Don't you talk to my hound that way, boy,' said Burt, 'He'll bite your nuts off before you can say crossbreed. Ain't that right, Dingbat?'

Dingbat leapt to his feet. He stood with his head cocked to one side, his tail swishing in expectation as he waited to be addressed again.

'You catch any squirrels today, Dingbat?' The dog turned his head over even further as Burt spoke then flicked it to the other side, whining a little.

'I swear that dog understands every word I say.'

'You both show similar linguistic abilities,' said Kerrigan. Kath smiled.

Burt said, 'If I was ten years younger, James Kerrigan, I'd tan your hide,'

'I think we're both a little old for that, don't you?'

'A boy's never too old to appreciate a good beating.'

'How old a 'boy' do you think I am, Burt?'

'Not old enough to avoid a darn good switching.'

'Settle down, you two,' said Kath.

Kerrigan saw a little colour in the old man's cheeks. He was glad to see it.

For a while Burt and Kath talked about the little details of their lives and the things they saw on the news each day. They hardly ever went outside the old house and although Kath used Burt as her excuse, Kerrigan knew the real reason was that they were scared of the world now. They no longer understood or trusted it.

'Why don't you two come over to my place one time?' asked Kerrigan.

'We don't have a car,' said Burt.

'So what? Maggie would give you a ride.'

'Oh, we couldn't ask her,' said Kath. 'And anyway, it isn't safe for Burt to be out, he could take a fall.'

'You should come. It's only three miles. You'll feel good for doing it. I'll make sure you're well looked after.' Kerrigan smiled at them. 'There's nothing to be afraid of.'

'If we come over,' asked Burt, 'will you return the favour and visit us for supper?'

The old man was staring at him. Kath looked down at the table. Kerrigan glanced at Dingbat who wagged his tail. He searched for a response.

'I'm not exactly—I mean, I'd love to, but I usually do my best work in the evenings and—'

'Come on a Saturday, then,' said Burt. 'You don't work Saturday nights do you?'

'Well, sometimes,' said Kerrigan.

'You mean you wouldn't take one Saturday night off to come and visit the only family you have?'

'Of course I would but I . . .'

'What, James?' Burt demanded. 'You what? Don't tell me you don't have a car. We could get Maggie to give you a ride down.'

'But I'd have to walk back. She's in bed by nine.'

'That's right. But like you say, there's nothing to be afraid of, right?'

'Go easy, Burt,' said Kath laying a hand on his forearm.

'No,' said the old man. 'No way. One of the 'big' reasons he gave us for moving up to the end of town was that he wanted to get over his fear of the dark. Have you done that yet, James? Can you take a walk after sundown? Can you sleep right through the night without waking? Or do you still piss the sheets?'

'That's enough, Burt.' Kath's voice was icy. 'I won't hear you speak to our boy that way.'

Burt was breathless. Kerrigan saw real anger in his eyes.

'It's okay, Kath. He's right. I *should* be able to do it. And I have been out walking when the sun goes over the mountain but just—not after dark.'

Kerrigan sat quietly for a time. Burt stared at the chequered pattern in the seersucker tablecloth. His breathing slowed and the fire left his cheeks. He looked ancient and exhausted again, no better than when Kerrigan had arrived.

'Okay,' he said, 'I'll do it.'

'What?' Burt was incredulous.

'Now, James there's no need to go making rash promises after a few heated words,' said Kath in a hurry. 'Burt didn't mean it. Did you, Burt?'

The old man didn't have any fight left in him.

'No, I didn't mean it. I just wish sometimes that things were different.'

'So do I,' Kerrigan said, 'and that's why I'm going to do it. You let me know when you can come up and we'll have lunch. I'll cook us something really good, whatever you want. If it's warm enough I'll do a barbecue. And the following Saturday I'll walk to your house for supper and then walk back. How's that?'

Burt looked shocked.

'You serious?'

'Absolutely.'

'Well, that's just great, son. Just great.' Burt's expression lifted. 'Why don't you barbecue some corn on the cob and we could have those special chicken wings Kath used to make.'

'I'll bring them with me,' she said.

'Can you make a decent potato salad?' asked Burt.

'Of course I can,' said Kerrigan.

'Maybe Kath should do the potato salad,' said Burt.

'Listen, this is my barbecue and I'm doing the cooking. You can bring the wings but that's all. Okay?'

'Okay.'

Kerrigan lifted the battered jug.

'Who wants more coffee?'

Kerrigan stayed until he noticed Burt tiring again and he left to let the old man rest.

As Kerrigan said goodbye and walked out into the late summer sunshine, the threat of darkness was distant, the fear of it childish.

CHAPTER 5

A Candle. Matches. An earthenware bowl. Silt from the Singing River in a chipped coffee cup. A tightly bound bundle of Sweetgrass. A vial of water. A craft knife.

Kerrigan places the items on a large mat of woven rushes and kneels before them. The only light comes from a propane lamp. He glances at the windows, each one a black square pressurised by the gathering night, and shudders.

Hands trembling, he lights the candle and snuffs the lamp with a twist of its valve. Darkness leaps in from all sides. Kerrigan cowers.

Please.

He lights the Sweetgrass bundle and stands it in the river silt before blowing out its flame. Only when its redolent smoke reaches his nostrils does he feels the surge in his veins. His trembling ceases, the tension falls from his shoulders, he raises his head.

He uncorks the vial and washes his left forearm in its cool water, the moisture absorbing into his skin. He takes the craft knife, places its tip between the tendons on the inside of his forearm and thrusts. Something bursts within his wrist and a spray, black in the candlelight, jets from the wound. He lengthens the incision by drawing the blade towards his elbow and the spray becomes a dark tide.

Positioning his wrist over the earthenware bowl, he

watches his fluids, dark as molasses, cascade from the wound, his palm, his fingers. With his right hand, he passes the blade of the craft knife through the candle flame and quenches the hot steel in the river silt. He waits for the level in the bowl to rise. Long before it is full, the flow recedes and the incision begins to close. Soon the cut is no more than a long, angry scab.

By the light of the candle, Kerrigan sets to work.

Kerrigan woke at first light, a flutter of anticipation in his stomach at the thought of what the day would bring; something a little different from a sore back and tired eyes sustained at his keyboard.

After washing and sitting quietly for a while on the porch, he smudged himself with the smoke of sage and cedar: He placed the crushed leaves in an abalone shell and set fire to the mixture with a match. The flame soon died leaving a smouldering pile that he could work with. Standing naked at the back of the house, he used an eagle feather to waft the smoke towards himself making sure it touched every part of his body. He paid particular attention that day to circulate the smoke around his genitals. Only when he was satisfied that he was cleansed did he tip the ashes from the shell and into the soil beside the back door; a dark place where nothing ever grew.

Buster watched like he did every morning. Kerrigan had the feeling that if he didn't smudge, Buster would find a way to remind him. After breakfast, he sat on the porch once again and fashioned a binder using his goat horn lock knife. The blade was so keen it could pare away shavings thinner than Bible paper. He used withies softened in water from Singing River to bind the two shafts of the cross. He laid curved sections of pine into grooves cut at the outer ends of each shaft to surround the cross in a ring. Once the circle was in place, he secured it with further strips of damp reed. When the withy dried, it shrank, clasping the binder tight.

He made two that morning, entering a pleasant trance in which time ceased to exist. When they were finished he put them aside and sanded down the two he'd made the previous morning until the surfaces were as smooth as the skin of a child's face.

Amy was due at eleven thirty and the morning had almost disappeared without him noticing. He'd bought ham and salami for her sandwiches but in his own he used mushroom pate and a piquant bean paste made from his own crop. He slid a bottle of white wine into a chilled sleeve and made a salad. Everything went in his backpack with a couple of candy bars and some water.

Before Amy arrived, he stood outside the back door and removed a binder from his pocket, testing the weight of it in his right hand. The wood was ruby dark. It felt like a good one. He twisted to the left, curling his index finger around the binder, and snapped his posture open, flicking his wrist at the last moment. The binder breathed a single sighing note as it flew, clear as a flute. It spun towards the compost heap and disappeared deep into the compacted organic material, its song cut short with a soft thump.

As he went to retrieve it, he heard Amy's Honda pull up out front. Not wanting to meet her with dirt all over his fingers, he decided to dig the binder out later.

Knowing she wouldn't want to walk far, Kerrigan let Amy drive them to The Clearing to begin their walk. The place he had in mind for the picnic was secluded but if she didn't have the energy to get there, the privacy it offered would be worthless.

Amy drew the Honda up to one of the squat wooden posts forming the circular boundary of the car park and picnic area. She'd barely pulled on the park brake before Kerrigan was out of the car and sniffing at the air. Amy spent a moment inspecting her make up in the rear-view mirror before joining him.

Noticing he'd left the passenger door open, Kerrigan gave it a push. It slammed, rocking the Honda on its suspension.

'Shit, Jimmy, be careful.'

'Oops. Sorry.'

'You don't know your own strength, sometimes.'

'I'm excited,' he said. 'Come on, lets' go.'

He pulled his pack on and adjusted the straps.

'This way.'

He set off at a gentle pace towards the Eastern Path.

As he walked past the Jimenez's Land Cruiser, parked a few yards from the path, he glanced into the covered bed of the truck and saw they'd laid a canvass tarp over whatever they'd left behind. Each of them must have been carrying a heavy pack. He'd expected them to turn around when they found out how rough the trails were; that they'd be back before the weekend, contrite, but having enjoyed a challenge nonetheless. They'd already been gone four days.

'Hey, slow down. You said this was a stroll.'

'It is a stroll, Amy.' He waited for her to catch up and took her hand. 'I'm sorry. I love it out here. I get—revved up.' He grinned at her. 'You set the pace and I will guide you.'

The urge to pull away and forge ahead was difficult to resist. Kerrigan wondered how the Jimenez's would be coping. By now they'd be footsore, hankering after a decent meal and a soft bed. His thoughts turned to Carla, in her sleeping bag in the depths of the forest at midnight. He walked faster but Amy's hand held reined him in.

'Why did you come back?'

For a moment, Kerrigan thought she meant to Olsen's to ask her for a date. Then he understood.

'You don't have to tell me if you don't want to,' she said.

'It's not that, Amy. I want to give you a real answer but it's hard to pin down.'

'Take your time. We've got all day, right? I want to know more about the mysterious Jimmy Kerrigan.'

His laugh was hollow.

'The city didn't need me,' he said and regretted his choice of words immediately.

'What's that supposed to mean? Is Superman turning his back on the citizens of Metropolis? Come on.'

The sneer in her voice cut him. He tried to let it go.

'What I mean is, I didn't feel I was adding anything. The things I did there, I could have done them anywhere and, in the end, the city's a far worse place to be than here. It's dirty, it's loud, and it's dangerous. Actually, from my point of view, it sucks.'

'That wasn't how you thought it would be?'

'No, of course not. I thought it would be fast and exciting. I thought it would be different every day. But every day was the same.'

'Were you lonely there?'

No need to pause for that question.

'Sure, I was lonely. But most people are lonely if they're honest about it.'

'You didn't have a girlfriend?'

'Oh, I had girl*friends*. Several. But that just made it worse somehow.'

He saw Amy's expression tighten.

'And no one was honest,' he continued before she could get angry, 'Everyone played games with your head. Never said what was really on their mind until after they'd taken what they wanted and dumped you. I got used to that real quick.'

For a while she was quiet. Walking at her pathetic pace took all his willpower.

'How come you never left Hobson's Valley?' he asked, more to slow himself down than anything else. 'Must have been plenty of places you could have gone to. You got family any-where else?'

'No. Just my brother, Mark—he's real sick right now—and our mom and dad. My grandparents lived right here in the valley but they've been gone a long time. Mom and dad are only children so no aunts or uncles either.'

'I didn't know that. What's wrong with Mark? I thought he was working up in the motel at Segar's Cabin.'

'He was but they laid him off. And it wasn't because the season's nearly over, either.'

'So what was it?'

'He had some kind of . . . episode.'

'Oh yeah? What kind?'

For a while there was only the sound of their footsteps scuffing over the dirt of the trail. Amy's dumb 'flat shoes, for walking' and his Meindl hiking boots.

'They've got him over at the Pine's unit in Saracen.'

'He was sectioned?'

'Yeah.'

'What did he do?'

'He, uh, attacked one of the housekeepers at the motel. Tried to bite her neck open.'

'Jesus. Was she hurt?'

'Just shaken, I think. She had a broom handle across his throat. She said all she could hear was the click of his teeth as he strained towards her. He kept screaming, 'I'm one of them,' over and over. He was still yelling it when the police took him away.'

Amy stopped walking and turned towards Kerrigan. She couldn't hold his gaze. Looking down she said:

'I signed the papers.'

'What papers?'

'The ones that allowed them to lock him up for his own safety and the safety of others. I betrayed him.'

'No you didn't,' he said, giving her as much sympathy as he could force from himself. 'You did what anyone would have done in the same situation. I would have done it too.'

He put his hands on her shoulders and looked into her eyes to make the statement stick. To make it real. At the same time, he tried to push the vision of Mark's assault away, the sound of her brother's jaws snapping,

'You would?'

'There'd be no other choice.'

She managed a smile.

'Thanks.'

He pulled her close, loving the feel of her plumpness against him and hating himself for it. About a mile further Amy's breathing became louder and more laboured. Her pace slowed.

'Almost there now.'

'Really?'

'Yeah, really. I don't want to say too much about it, but it's a nice secluded spot. I don't think anyone knows the place, so we can enjoy our picnic in peace.'

They'd been walking along a corridor of pine trees. Sometimes the trees were close on either side, other times it was a wide avenue with plenty of light entering from overhead. The forest itself was dense, though. It wasn't possible to see more than a few yards into trees. To their left, it looked impenetrable.

'In here,' he said.

'In where?'

'You can't see it, but there's a way through. After about a hundred yards it opens up again. Trust me, you're going to like this.'

Bending down to avoid getting branches in his eyes and face, he took Amy's hand and drew her into the forest.

'Make sure you keep your head down.'

Twigs of pine and fingers of fern caught at them as they walked, bent double. Every few steps Kerrigan glanced up to check his bearings.

'How much farther?' she asked.

'Not far now.'

He squeezed her hand.

Up ahead light broke through the canopy splashing into

bright mottled patches on the ground. A flash of green. They were heading in the right direction.

After a few more yards they were able to stand a little straighter, though the trees still pressed in close against them. Amy was panting hard. The walk from the cabin to this spot was a warm up for him; on any other day, this was a place where he might stop for a moment to drink a sip of water and taste the air before continuing.

The world was silent but for the crunch of dry twigs beneath their feet. Suddenly they broke out of the forest and into a tiny clearing. Amy took a sudden breath in surprise.

'Oh my God. It's beautiful.'

CHAPTER 6

The clearing was carpeted with grass that belonged in some rich pasture far out on a well-irrigated plain. Near the centre of the clearing was an array of rounded boulders, all of them covered in a delicate fur of moss. At their heart was a small pool of dark but perfectly clear water. It was a place of purity and hallow. Kerrigan had missed its peace and welcoming stillness and the moment he connected with it, he regretted bringing Amy.

Silently, he greeted the stones and the trees and the grasses of that place, asked permission to play among them for a while and when he sensed their concurrence, indeed their welcome, he laid down his pack and placed his palm against the cool earth through the soft grass.

'What do you think?' he asked.

'I've never seen anything like this,' said Amy. 'What is it?'

'It's a spring. Thousands of years old. Men and animals have been coming here to drink or bathe since long before the birth of Christ. The minerals in the water make the grass grow like this. You won't see grass this healthy anywhere else in this state.'

While Amy looked around, he spread the rug out over the grass and placed the Tupperware boxes and wine nearby.

'How deep is this?'

She was standing looking down into the spring. There was a hint of trepidation in her voice.

'It goes all the way to the bottom, I think.'

'Seriously, Jimmy, how deep?'

'I don't know, but it's a long way down. We can go in later if you want.'

'Swim? In there?'

'Sure. Why not?'

'Is it safe?'

'I'll go first and you can decide for yourself how safe it is. Come and have some wine.'

The eating and drinking part of the afternoon was over quickly. Kerrigan didn't mind. Amy enjoyed the wine and the sandwiches he'd made her. She ate her Snickers bar in less than a minute, even though he'd intended the candy as an emergency supply.

When they'd finished, they lay back saying little while their food settled. He was beginning to fall asleep when he felt Amy's hand on his chest. He opened his eyes and she was leaning over him, her hair falling around her face, her cleavage pressing though the open neck of her blouse.

She smiled in that way that meant the moment had come; it was a familiar smile to Kerrigan, born of simple needs; no words necessary. He smiled back and she leaned in to kiss him. The swelling curves of her breasts were warm and heavy against him and it was that feeling of weight and fullness more than her kiss that made him hard. He was a bad kisser and always had been; he reached his hand behind her head and pressed her face to his until their teeth clashed and their tongues stretched into each other's mouths. Clearly Amy liked bad kissers. She pressed her body closer to him, her sighs the loudest sounds in the forest.

Then she pulled back.

'How safe is it here?' she asked.

'What do you mean?'

'How private?'

'I'd say it was as private as my bedroom. Or yours. That's why I picked it '

'Mm hmm. In that case, why don't you show me how safe that pool is? Maybe I'll join you.'

Kerrigan stood and stripped quickly. He wasn't ashamed of his body and he knew his physique had an effect on Amy. His erection sprang free as he pulled his shorts down.

'At least you're well armed,' she observed.

'This is no weapon.'

'Sure it is. It's your love-club.'

'Jesus, Amy. Sometimes you say the weirdest things.'

She slapped his bare, sun-deprived butt.

'Go get in that water. Take your torpedo with you.'

He walked across the cushion of grass, feeling it give beneath his soles and felt the power of the earth below him — either that or the power of the wine. The pool was still except for a disturbance near its centre where a small upward current made gentle domes and ripples on the surface. No more than fifteen feet across, the pool formed a ragged circle. Around its edges the rocks were heaped up as if a cairn-making giant had rolled them there to mark the spot. Kerrigan climbed to a perch on one of the larger stones. The moss was damp emerald velvet beneath his feet.

Amy watched, still clothed.

'Ready?' he asked.

'Ready for what?'

He bent his knees and sprung up and out as far as he could. In mid air he piked and aimed straight downwards. He hit the water and was swallowed by its chill-shock. Keeping his body rigid and straight he let himself sink. When his momentum ceased and the current threatened to push him up, he swam down hard, pausing mid-stroke a couple of times to blow against pinched nostrils and equalise the pressure. Thirty feet down, he swam sideways and clung to the rocky wall of the spring.

It was dark but for the blurred forest light glimmering

above. Chilled updrafts of spring water made him shiver. The darkness became too much for him long before he ran out of air. Kerrigan had no idea how far down the flooded shaft really went. What might be down there waiting to take a slimy hold of his ankle and draw him into eternal night?

He let go of the side and swam upward to the light. The halo of brightness above him grew larger as he approached and he made out a figure bending over the water. He broke the surface and heaved in a breath.

'Jimmy, oh Jimmy.' Amy was frantic. 'Jesus honey, I thought you were drowning. I thought you weren't gonna come back. Oh my God, don't you do that to me. Don't you ever do that again.'

He watched her from the water while his breathing settled, enjoying the sight of her vulnerability. Enjoying the idea that he'd scared her; affected her in some way other than sexual.

'You wanted to know how deep it was,' he said.

'Don't be a smartass.'

She was crying.

'Get in with me.'

'What?'

'Get in with me. You won't be disappointed, I promise. There's no feeling like it.'

He held his hand out to her, not believing for a moment that she'd join him.

'Come on. Please. You'll love it.'

She took her clothes off with care. He watched as she released her full breasts and bared her rounded tummy. She removed everything, revealing her heavy hips and the minuscule triangular tuft between her legs. He didn't know why he always expected her to be hairy but she wasn't; there was hardly any hair at all. She was Rubenesque in her nudity, all dimples and pinkness. He would have preferred a hard-bodied girl ten years her junior, at least that was what he told himself, but every time he saw her weight and the imposing feminine presence it exuded, he grew so stiff he thought the skin of his prick would tear open.

Daintily, almost comically, Amy dipped her toe in, shivering. She lowered herself to the edge and slipped in with a gasp before swimming out to him, blowing a little as she came.

'This is incredible,' she panted. 'It's cold but it's not cold. I can't explain it. It's like it fills you with energy.'

He was surprised how near that was to the truth. As she held him close to her, he realised it was arrogance to think that he could protect the wilderness, keep it for himself. Whether she knew it or not Amy was in a magical space, experiencing the power and rejuvenating qualities of the wellspring.

Her skin was still warm and everywhere her body touched his there was a slick sensuousness enhanced by the cool current. They kissed again, treading water. Her hand closed around his erection and it was his turn to gasp. He squeezed her to him and for a moment they sank below the water. In that cold womb they touched and turned until the need to breathe sent them upwards again.

Instinct overtook Kerrigan. They had to get out immediately. If they stayed a moment longer, they would taint the wellspring. He couldn't allow that. He could not be the cause of such sacrilege.

'Come on, Amy. We're going to drown.'

'Don't be silly. You wanted me to come in.'

'I know. But we can't do—everything in the water.'

Without another word they both slipped to the edge and climbed out. The sun was well past its hottest time but there was enough brightness to keep them warm. There was no wind at all in the shelter of the wellspring's clearing. Where the sun still lit the grass he lay down with her.

'Do it like before, Jimmy.'

He felt a deep need; something unnatural, a perversity he

couldn't explain. It was like a thirst for something tasted in a previous life, a flavour he couldn't quite recall.

'I want you,' he said.

'Have me, then. Take everything you need.'

Her words were petrol to his flame. He hauled her over him with a strength that surprised them both and positioned her above himself. He forced her to squat, disappearing into her warmth with grave satisfaction. Her breasts hung down to touch his chest; the prize he truly desired. He seized one, forcing as much of it as he could into his mouth. He did not simply lick and chew, he sucked. Kerrigan sucked as if his very existence depended on what he found there. He drew hard enough to bruise her.

'Oh yes, Jimmy.'

She moved above him and he was in the heaven of her. Then it came to him. That flavour. He tasted a liquid in his mouth. He had drawn fluid from deep inside her breast. He took it into him, feeding on her. The taste was sweet and rich. He drank Amy; drank her milk.

CHAPTER 7

The creature lived for the night.

It spread its limbs out into the darkness as though submerged in a frigid sea of pleasure. It sensed the life in all things that slumbered and it was drawn to them. Everywhere in the forest were sleeping creatures; hidden, curled, buried or roosting. The creature knew their vulnerability and was thrilled. It could take whatever it wanted.

And so it danced.

In silence between the trees it whirled and leapt, its tattered garments barely covering its ancient, emaciated frame. It crouched and crawled and pressed itself against the earth, the nourisher of all things, that abhorred the creature and could do nothing to stop it. The creature vaulted high above the tips of the pines, twisting and diving down again beneath the open sky to land, silent among the ferns.

It was monarch of the night kingdom; the usurper of all the sun could not touch.

When its dance was complete, it sank close to the ground once more and swept towards the dwellings of the town with no more noise than a shadow. Every living thing it passed drew away from it. The very air parted before its reviled lord. Where the lights were, where men had built their houses of stone and wood it held less sway. Less but enough. And there was much sport to be had there.

Kerrigan woke to find himself lying fully clothed on his bed. The manuscript he'd been correcting was beside him along with the marker he'd failed to recap before falling asleep. Now there was a deep red stain on the coverlet and some of the pages were mashed where he'd rolled onto them. The bedside light was still on.

His conscious mind, rapidly returning, wondered what had woken him. His subconscious, still strong in those first few moments of waking, knew the answer. He wanted to sit up. The longer he lay still, the less likely it was he would be able to move. He wrestled with himself; told himself it was only indecision keeping him from moving, but his increasing heartbeat told another story. He couldn't move for fear he'd make a sound. Someone was in the house.

If he didn't make his move now, he'd lose the ability. Paralysis would take him over. Blood rushing faster in his ears, he reached for his chest and felt for the binder.

It wasn't there.

Suddenly, he needed to piss like he'd held it in all day.

Christ, where had he put his binder? Why had he taken it off? Now he would have to reach for the bedside drawer and open it. They'd surely hear him then. Feeling like his joints were rusted beyond use, he stretched his left arm out towards the drawer.

Before his fingers made contact with the bare pine of the bedside table, the lights went off. All of them. He froze, mid stretch. Any noise he made would be louder in that darkness. His hand grew stiff. He was losing control; no longer able to make his body move the way he wanted it to.

Something was stopping him. Something close by.

'I am here, James. Right here with you now.'

The voice was everywhere. Wasn't it? Or was it only in his head?

'I'm so near, I could touch you if I desired. I could touch you *anywhere* I wanted and then what would you do?'

He felt the weight then, same as always. It started on his

stomach, a medicine ball rolling towards his chest, crushing the air out of him, constricting everything. Below it, he could not move. Not now, not ever. The weight rolled higher until it crushed his sternum. The breath went out of him and that was his last movement.

Limbs frozen. Air gone. Lungs crumpled.

He felt the initial contact against the ribs on his left side, not far below his armpit. It was warm and wet to begin with. A blunt, insistent pressure against his flesh, nuzzling his inter-costal muscles but pressing inward, pressing hard, search-ing for an entry point. The skin of his chest went numb but Kerrigan knew what was happening to him; it was forcing its tube-like proboscis through a tear in his stretched epider-mis, parting his muscles, widening the space between two ribs and burrowing deep.

He was screaming, sitting up in his bed and screaming with every molecule of air inside him. When he stopped he breathed in and screamed again.

'Jesus, Jimmy. Jesus Christ, baby, what is it? What's wrong?'

The light clicked on, and squinting into the sudden glare he saw Amy, naked, but holding the sheet to her chest. She hadn't taken off her make up and her eyes were dark-ringed and wide, staring. Kerrigan clutched the side of his chest, squeezed his eyes shut, crushing the phantom sensations away. Soon he was rocking back and forth, crying.

'Jimmy, talk to me, Goddamnit. Are you having a heart attack? Do you need me to call the doctor?'

He shook his head, still breathing hard.

'Jimmy? What's that?'

He looked where she was pointing at a large dark stain on the coverlet.

'Jimmy, honey, I think you peed yourself. God.' She swung her legs out of the bed. 'Shit,' she said, realising that she'd been lying in his piss. Grabbing her discarded clothes she ran for the bathroom and closed the door.

Kerrigan lay back against the headboard, too exhausted to move. The heat of his urine quickly faded and became cold. Goose bumps lifted on his arms and legs. Still, he couldn't move. The urine gave off a sweet smell like honey flavoured puffed wheat. It smelled like the piss of a child.

Amy came back into the bedroom fully dressed.

'You gonna be okay?'

He nodded.

'Good because I gotta go now. I can't sleep here — you know, like this. Sorry.'

She turned away. He heard her turn the key to unlock the door, heard the door slam behind her.

Knowing the door was still unlocked; that was what got Kerrigan out of bed. He ran naked to relock it. He knew she'd hear that clicking behind her as she walked to her car. The Honda's engine started, screeching as she pulled away. As the noise of the engine faded, the silent howl of loneliness returned.

Back in the bedroom Kerrigan pulled the sheets and blankets from the bed. He took them to the washing machine and started a cycle straight away. In the kitchen he filled a bucket with hot water and took it and a cloth and some detergent spray back to the bed to wipe down the plastic mattress cover. He dried it and put fresh sheets on.

He couldn't turn the lights off. Not now he was alone. He lay there touching the binder that always hung around his neck. From time to time he was sure he heard footsteps outside. But he prayed the laughter, the whispered manic laughter, was only his imagination.

When dawn came, Kerrigan was still awake. He had no recollection of the dream or what had woken him but when he saw light outside his window, he wept. Only then did he let go of his binder to find its shape imprinted into the flesh of his palm.

CHAPTER 8

Kerrigan groaned and looked up from the article he was writing.

He gazed out of the window, grasping for the perfect word. Nothing came. A cloud darkened the view. Kerrigan shivered and reached across to the bookshelf for his thesaurus. When he sat upright again, someone was outside. The sky darkened further. Frowning, Kerrigan checked his watch, before leaning towards the window. Beyond the front gate, in the middle of the dirt road that led to The Clearing, stood a dark-skinned, well-built teenager. The boy stared at the cabin, his eyes vacant. A breeze blew the boy's hair across his eyes but he didn't attempt to adjust it.

The inert kid looked familiar. Kerrigan couldn't place him at first; just another young face, like so many that passed his cabin before entering the woods below Bear Mountain. His attention slipped from the article. Tutting, he saved the document and stood up. Buster raised his head for a moment and then went back to sleep, still curled tightly on his favourite chair. Kerrigan stroked him as he passed and Buster let out a growly purr, half pleased to be remembered, half grumbling at being disturbed.

'You don't know how good you've got it, cat.'

As Kerrigan neared the front door he recalled the kid was one of those who often walked or drove past in groups to

55

party in the forest. He liked to see them enjoying themselves in the outdoors. As long as they didn't litter or start fires, Kerrigan didn't care what they did. Youngsters needed to get wild and where better than the woods to do it.

He opened the door.

'You looking to buy the place or what?'

The boy's eyes disengaged from whatever they'd been fixed on and settled on him.

'Is your name Kerrigan?' he asked.

'Jimmy Kerrigan, yes.'

'Someone said you could help me.'

'Oh yeah? Who was that?'

'The old lady. I mow her lawn sometimes.'

It all came together. He hadn't only seen this kid before, he'd arranged over the phone for him to work in Burt and Kath's garden on several occasions.

'You're David Slater, right?'

'That's me, so they say.'

Kerrigan walked down off his porch and to the gate where he held out his hand to the boy.

'Well, it's good to finally meet you, David.'

As though moving through treacle, David put his hand out and as he shook it, Kerrigan dwelt in him for a split second, seeing himself and the world through the boy's eyes.

There was something wrong.

'You want to come in for a second? You don't look so good. I could make you a coffee. There's soda. I've got beer too. What do you say?'

'I've lost something. That old lady said maybe you could help me find it.'

'Kath said that to you?'

'Yeah.'

'What is it you've lost?'

'I—I don't know.'

'Do you know where you lost it?'

The boy looked up the road into the woods once again.

'Back in there.'

'I guess you want to go take a look.'

The boy nodded. His head stayed turned, his eyes stared once again, defocusing as he gazed along the road into the shadows cast by the trees. Kerrigan looked up at the overcast sky. The clouds were in for the duration by the look of it but it was only midday. If they were quick there'd be enough time.

'Wait here a second, David. I'll be right back and then we'll go take a look together.'

David didn't move or speak.

Kerrigan threw what he needed into his backpack and took his carved walking staff from the pantry. Back outside, David hadn't shifted. Kerrigan opened the gate and gestured up the road.

'Let's go.'

It was different in the woods that day. No sun broke through the pines to warm them as they walked. Kerrigan couldn't tell if it was the chill or the silence in the trees that brought the hairs up on his arms and neck. Any joy he would usually have experienced to be walking in the woods was absent. His shoulders knotted and he clenched his teeth, glancing often into the obscured depths of forest to either side.

David, despite his trancelike condition, put on a decent pace. Whatever it was he'd lost, he wanted it back badly. He wanted it back quick. Kerrigan matched the boy's speed easily.

The road here was much broader than the trails but they kept to the edge in case someone did come driving by. It wasn't unheard of for kids to race their cars along the road to The Clearing. There was no one today, though. The road was quiet; the trees on both sides statuesque in the unmoving air. There was only the sound of their breathing in time with their steps.

The boy didn't speak to him and it didn't seem odd that he expected Kerrigan to help him search for something even though they hardly knew each other. When people passed Kerrigan's way or fetched up at the cabin, he helped them.

He helped them all.

There was a mustiness in the air as they walked, reminiscent of the fungi that grew on rotting fallen branches. It was a damp smell with a sweet note to it. The odour lingered throughout the walk and it wasn't until they were almost in The Clearing that Kerrigan realised the smell was coming from David.

When the two of them arrived at the border posts of the picnic area Kerrigan turned and spoke to the boy in gentle tones.

'So, what are we looking for, David?'

'We stopped there.' David said and pointed. 'We passed a joint around. Good shit, you know, from Acapulco or somewhere.'

'Uh huh.'

'Then she got out and I followed her. I think we must have gone this way.'

He began to walk, retracing his steps. He didn't stop at the border but walked through it and into the pine trees.

'Who was she?'

'Gina Priestly.'

'I don't know her.'

'Everyone knows Gina. She pulled me through these trees. Something hit me here.'

David put a hand to his face but Kerrigan saw no signs of a cut or bruise. He looked the way the boy was pointing and he could see some evidence of disturbance but they looked days or weeks old. It was still possible to see where people might have rolled on the ground, flattening some of the debris from the trees and making bare patches where the black dirt of the forest showed through.

David moved a little closer to the site of the disturbance.

'Here. This was where she did it. She . . .'

He knelt down and placed his palm on the ground. His

other hand went to his forehead as he tried to concentrate. Kerrigan felt he'd seen all these things before. Many times. It seemed both strange and perfectly normal.

'That bitch. That dirty—I don't know what she did. She took it from me. Right here. She took it and she . . .'

Kerrigan watched the boy struggle, grasping at memories that were just out of reach. David turned towards him, his eyes those of a wounded animal, pleading and feral at the same time. When he spoke his voice was lost among a host of others. The sound that came from his mouth was that of twenty people whispering a prayer in unison. None of the voices belonged to him. Kerrigan took a reflexive couple of steps backwards, careful not to back himself up to a tree.

'I remember now.' David's voices said. 'I remember how she entered me; a violation it was, Mr. Kerrigan. Yes, she tricked me. Took what it was she needed and left me.' The boy spread his arms wide. ' Left me like this.'

It was strange to watch the boy alter even though Kerrigan suddenly knew he'd seen it happen more times than he could count. He didn't really see the change, not on the surface; he just knew it had occurred. Would anyone else be able to notice that inner shift? That *ripple*? Would anyone else know what it signified? Kerrigan doubted it. Even if they could; afterwards, they would forget. The way David forgot.

The way Kerrigan, too, forgot so much.

He kept his voice low and calm.

'I can help you, David. You have to trust me.'

'No more trust.'

'You let me bring you here. You asked for my help. Don't you remember?'

David appeared to try and recollect but it was clear he couldn't.

'Maybe I do. But no one can help me now. I've changed. Forever.'

'No, David. Not forever. There's still time to undo this. Will you let me help you?'

Kerrigan watched the savagery rise within the boy like a sudden fever. David's conscious mind lost its supremacy; his humanity was subsumed. From nowhere, Kerrigan had a name for what was happening to David: Fugue. And he knew things; things he hadn't known only moments before. The girl could have fed without infecting David. Why had Gina turned him? She could have stayed hidden but she had not. Was it just inexperience?

David's agitation increased. Kerrigan watched him scanning their surroundings for a way to escape. He looked past Kerrigan, back into The Clearing, but it was obvious the boy had no idea what to do or even where he could safely go. David knew nothing about himself.

'That's right, David. In this state, you need to stay in the shadows or you'll die. You're fine here in the comfort of the trees but you can't stay here forever. People will wonder what happened to you. They'll come looking.'

'If I disappear no one will care. It happens all the time.'

'It happens occasionally, that's true, but it doesn't happen often. The last one was two years ago. Is that what you want? To go on the run and leave your family and your life behind?

David launched himself towards Kerrigan with pure instinct and Kerrigan responded in kind. The boy was quick, one of the fastest he'd seen. They attacked because they wanted him to save them; that was what Kerrigan believed. Because they trusted that he was equal to the task. He was.

He flicked a binder at the boy from where it had nestled in his palm ever since they left his cabin. It stopped David mid air and sent him back with twice the force he'd engaged in his attack. A ratcheted crunch came from the boy; dozens of the joints in his body popping and relocating in response to the tremendous concussion. The sound was that of knuckles against ribs and teeth, the sound of splitting skin. A pall of vapour escaped his body in the moment of impact, as if an old carpet had been thumped with a tennis racket to release a cloud of dust. The vapour was purple. It twisted into eddies and melted away. David hit the ground slack-bodied.

Kerrigan approached and knelt to check him. The boy had been knocked senseless by the force of the binder. It was the one Kerrigan had dug through the compost pile to retrieve. He'd been right too; it was a good one. Not wanting anyone to see him carrying a body along the trails, he slung David over his shoulder and carried him through the tightly spaced trees, creating his own trail to the wellspring.

Half an hour later, they reached the wellspring glade. Kerrigan laid David down, carefully undressed him and placed a binder around his neck to keep him from re-entering Fugue while he worked on him. The boy might continue to look and behave human, but until Kerrigan's work was complete the disease would be locked deep within him, woven into the double helix of every single cell.

Kerrigan undressed David first and bound his hands and feet tightly with leather braids that had been blessed and dipped in wellspring water when he made them. He smudged them both before he began the purification. It was instinct that guided him—he had no manual for what he was doing, no memory of ever learning the techniques. Yet he watched his hands perform gestures and listened to his own voice utter words in a language he neither recognised nor understood.

Using a handful of spongy moss he took water from the wellspring and bathed the boy's body entirely from head to toe. This baptism would help to drive the Fugue from his body. He would not be immune in the future but he would at least be healed. While he mopped David's dark skin, Kerrigan searched for signs of entry and found what he was looking for in the clefts of the boy's groin. The flesh was withered and dry around the penetration marks. He knew what Gina must have done to distract the boy while she fed. It was always done with trickery and seduction. Every feed was a kind of rape.

David was lucky to know he'd 'lost something'. Most

people never realised. Kerrigan doubted if Gina Priestly was aware of the Fugue in her own blood. There was a good chance she'd never find out. Whilst the Fugue was dormant, as it was most of the time, a human was perfectly safe from sunlight and binders or any other kind of control mechanism. But eventually the infection would surface like a malarial rigor and when that time came the human would recede and let the Fugue rule. For some it happened once every month. For others only one day in the year. But it always came. There was no denying the Fugue or the need it engendered.

Kerrigan himself had always shown Fugue tendencies. It was only when he was hunting that he remembered. When he hunted he remembered it all; every Fugue he had healed, every one he had destroyed, every human life saved. But even when he was awake to the hunter within him, he never recalled where it had all begun or how he had learned the things he knew. His fear of the dark amused him in these moments, but the very next night he would be close to paralysis when the dusk faded into night.

The boy moaned as he finished the anointing.

'Almost done now.'

Kerrigan placed a binder against the boy's forehead and stood up. He took hold of the staff and placed its tip against the binder, pressing it hard into David's skin. He whispered into the top of the staff and felt the vibration move downwards. His voice awoke the blood that generations of Fugue Hunters had drained from themselves and worked into the carved ancient pine. The staff hummed, its resonance passing into the bones of David's skull. The boy began to shake.

David opened his eyes and screamed. A cry of loss, a cry of triumph. That of the dying and of the reborn. The boy's tears flowed freely. Kerrigan removed the staff and untied him. David curled into a foetal ball, wracked with sobs.

'You can cry on the way back,' said Kerrigan. 'Put your clothes on. We need to get moving.'

A few seconds earlier the moment of chill that he hated so

much when he was human had arrived. As a hunter, the drop in temperature and the failing of the light made his heart beat faster and his senses sharpen. Now that the valley was in shadow, Fugues could walk free. David dressed quickly and without speaking while Kerrigan stashed his equipment and pulled his backpack on. When David was ready he looked pale and weak, like someone recovering from a month of illness.

'Can you walk or do I have to carry you again?'

'I'll be okay. Thanks, Mr. Kerrigan.'

'It's Jimmy.'

He started to hand Kerrigan the binder that had been around his neck.

'HEY!' Kerrigan shouted.

David stared back at him, wide-eyed.

'Never take that off. Ever. Understand?'

The boy nodded and slipped the binder back over his head.

'Come on.'

With the staff in one hand and a binder ready in the other Kerrigan led the boy home through the gradually deepening gloom.

CHAPTER 9

Reminders: August 19th

Don't forget Buster's worm medicine. He's spending way too much time with his tongue up his ass.

Jimenez family have been gone for four days. With that cheap gear and their city-folk legs, they ought to have given up after forty-eight hours. If they're not back by tomorrow morning: GO AND GET THEM.

Important: Find out what's up with Burt. Kath says he's been acting up all week. Keeps telling her he can see an old man outside the window. If he's mistaking his own reflection for someone else, he must really be losing it.

Not that I'm likely to forget this but it's over with Amy. Really freaked her when I pissed the bed, I guess. How's a weirdo like me going to get laid now, huh? Shop at Randall's until the dust settles.

CRUCIAL: Take a flashlight for the walk home after dinner tonight

Kerrigan timed his walk down to Burt and Kath's place so he'd arrive while it was still light. Walking home would be different. If there'd been a cab, he'd have taken it, but there wasn't any kind of taxi service for seventy miles in any direction.

The nebulous purple twilight was already heavy on the

64

air as he walked up the creaking wooden steps and knocked hard on the doorframe. He took a step back to wait for Burt and turned to gaze out at the street. He looked from side to side along the porch too. Every second drew more life from the sky. In some of the houses on the Terrace, people were already turning on their lights.

He slung off his backpack and reached inside, casual at first then frantic. No flashlight.

'Jesus Christ. You fucking space-case.'

The darkness rose like a flood around him. Burt was taking too long to answer. He banged again, louder, and peered through glass in the door trying to see beyond the fine mesh curtain that obscured the view. There were no lights on inside. If Burt couldn't get to the door, then why hadn't Kath come instead? Kerrigan stepped back from the door and looked around again. Gooseflesh rippled under his clothes. Someone was watching him, he was certain; waiting for him to look away before . . .

Unable to endure another moment of the swelling darkness, he tried the handle and was surprised to discover the door pulled easily open. These days, Burt and Kath never left the door unlocked.

He closed the door behind him and stood a moment in the hallway, listening. There was nothing but the ticks and creaks of an old house breathing. The same noises it had made when he was growing up there. Remembering the nights he'd spent terrified in his upstairs bedroom when Kath turned the lights out didn't help to steady him. This was the place where it had all started.

He reached out for the light switch and flicked it on. Nothing happened.

It had to be a bulb. Surely the power wasn't out. Maybe a fuse had blown. If anything, the darkness was worse inside the house: more intimate. He knew his folks weren't there. It was plain enough, but he called out anyway.

'Hey, Burt. It's Jimmy. Kath? I'm here.'

There was no answer. He didn't call again. His voice was hollow and pathetic in all that gloom. It sounded weak, fearful.

He went to the kitchen first, the old boards of the house complaining beneath his soles. When he flicked the kitchen light he found that it was out too. Oddly, there *was* a smell of cooking, maybe a pot roast or something. He stood for a while smelling the food and feeling no hunger at all. Surely they would come back at any moment. Maybe they were out buying a new fuse. That had to be it.

He walked out to their bedroom. In the old days they'd slept upstairs just as he had, but when Burt's legs began to let him down, they made a new bedroom in the old living room and converted part of the hallway into a downstairs bathroom. They didn't alter the room much. The only major change was moving their bed in there. It looked strange and out of place with a sofa stuck at the end of it and an ancient TV beyond that. Everywhere the shelves were stacked with old books and papers and the walls were decorated with paintings by unknown artists from who knew when.

There was no one in there.

The darkness was almost total by then. Kerrigan began to panic, his heart so loud in his ears he was afraid he wouldn't hear an intruder until it was too late to act. He had to find some light.

He prayed the fuse for the upstairs circuit hadn't blown too. The staircase was wooden just like everything else inside the house and it creaked worse than the floorboards. Every step he took telegraphed that he was on his way up and he cursed the place for giving him away so easily.

The stairs bent back on themselves at a small square landing and there was a set of switches there. When they worked, flooding the upstairs with an unhealthy yellow light from low wattage bulbs covered by thick light shades, Kerrigan was delighted. He sighed and felt his heart rate settle down a little. He could wait upstairs until they got back. Or he could probably see well enough to call Maggie on the hallway phone downstairs to see if she knew where they were.

It was as he placed his foot on the final step that he heard the rumbling growl. It was up there with him. He froze, his right hand gripping the stair rail. His left hand instinctively went to his chest and held onto the binder. He waited, unable to move.

Eventually, he edged forward. The sound was coming from his old bedroom. It was dark in there and the door was half open. He had no weapon on him and even if he had he wouldn't have entered the bedroom. He was stuck there listening to that sound; the last sound Burt and Kath would have heard. The idea made him want to weep.

The growling stopped and he heard movement; a scratching, sliding sound. Something dragging itself across the floor. Whining. He saw a black nose poke out from the darkness and into the upstairs hallway.

'Dingbat?'

The crazy mongrel scampered out of the bedroom when he heard Kerrigan's voice and started to jump up at him, whining with fear and relief all the same time.

'Shit, Dingbat, you had me scared half to death, you stupid mutt.'

He ruffled the shaggy fur on Dingbat's head.

'Is anyone up here, you hairy son of a bitch?'

They checked the rest of the rooms, Dingbat sticking with him until he was satisfied the place was completely uninhabited.

'Where'd they go, boy? Where's Burt, huh? Where's Kath?'

At the mention of their names Dingbat tilted his head to one side.

'Come on, let's make a phone call.'

Down in the hallway not much light penetrated from upstairs but he could make out the buttons on the phone well enough and was able to read Kath's neat schoolmarm handwriting. Maggie's phone rang for a long time but she didn't answer.

As he replaced the phone onto its base, the snarling began again. Dingbat was backed away from the front door, the hair along his spine rising into spikes. His lips drew back from his teeth and he shrunk into a tight crouch, ready to launch himself. Kerrigan could see the outline of the door only faintly but he had a feeling there was someone there.

In the semi darkness he watched the door swing open and saw a vague silhouette framed there.

'Is that you, Jimmy?' It was the voice of Maggie Fredericks. 'They took Burt to the hospital. Kath's with him. I think he had a heart attack.'

After twenty-five miles of winding mountain roads Kerrigan was close to vomiting. He kept quiet about it though. Maggie's kindness was the only thing that would reunite him with Burt and Kath, assuming Burt hadn't already passed on. Maggie asked him questions from time to time but he didn't feel much like talking; he knew whatever he told her would be common knowledge to all in Hobson's Valley by the next morning. He kept his replies as short and unspecific as he could without coming over as unfriendly.

The sense of emptiness that always stalked him pressed close as they drove down the far side of the mountains and finally onto a straight road in the next valley. His nausea eased but his dread increased.

By the time they arrived at Maiden County hospital, Kerrigan felt weak and old. He walked to the coronary unit as if his legs had forgotten how and asked for Burt. The nurses shared a few hushed words and asked him to wait for a moment.

It was Kath who returned, red eyed and shrunken with shock and grief. He could still see the love in her eyes, but there was anger there too. She hugged Kerrigan with the fierceness of chains, as if she'd never let go.

Maggie hung back while they embraced.

After a long time, Kath released him.

'Burt's not going to make it.'

Kerrigan shook his head.

'They said that?'

'No. But I know him. He's had enough. He's been giving up for quite a while.'

Kerrigan pushed his hand back through his hair.

'Jesus, Kath. What happened?'

'Oh, he was helping me in the kitchen. He never does that, you know. But he was excited. I haven't known him to act that way for a long time. It made me happy just to see it.'

She smiled at the memory of it.

'He went out to call you and tell you to come a little earlier. He wanted to have a beer with you on the porch. When you didn't answer, he figured you were already on your way. He went to get changed and he was laughing. 'That boy sure is a sissy' he said. He knew you were trying to make it down to us before it got dark. And then—'

—Burt pushed his walker ahead of him, grinning and shaking his head. His boy had finally bitten the bullet. Tonight Jimmy would walk home alone, in the dark, and conquer his fear once and for all.

Burt reached for the light switch in the bedroom, flicking it on and off a couple of times.

'Darn it,' he muttered. 'Need a goddamned electrician now.'

There was just about enough light from the hallway for him to see his clean shirt laid out on the counterpane. He shuffled into the bedroom and parked his walker beside the bed. The scent of the pot roast wafted in from the kitchen and Burt's stomach growled. He slipped off his old shirt and reached for the clean one. There was a tap at the bedroom window and Burt froze, mid-stretch.

'Lord above,' he whispered.

His eyes swivelled towards the sound. Framed like a living portrait was the face he'd seen twice in the last few days. The

face of an impossibly old man. Except the face was worse tonight,
swimming forward from a sea of blackness and melting. The
ancient eyes widened, livid purple veins rising in the whites. The
mouth tore open and the tongue spilled free, splitting into three
snakelike fronds, each of which now licked the dirty window-
pane—

—he called out to me. He sounded frightened, Jimmy, like
you used to when you were a kid and woke up in the night.
His voice was tiny. I heard his knees crack against the floorboards and I ran to him. He was holding his chest and staring
at the window. I held him before I called for help. He was so
cold and so tiny, Jimmy. My man for all these years. Cold
and broken.'

She collapsed against Kerrigan. This time there was no
iron in her embrace. She was barely able to support herself.
He looked over at the nurse.

'Can we go in and sit with him together?'

'Of course.'

He held Kath and she guided him back to the room where
Burt was. The old man looked frail but he looked peaceful
too. There was no tension in his face, no anger. A monitor
tracked his heart, betraying its erratic rhythm and hesitant
beats. They took a seat on either side of him and each held
one of his hands.

It wasn't a long vigil. Sometime in that next hour Burt's
heart stopped. They'd already resuscitated him once and the
doctor on duty and Kath had quietly agreed that he should
not be resuscitated again, considering how destructive the
first infarction had been. They held his hands as the monitor
sounded an alarm signalling no heartbeat. A nurse came in,
switched the monitor off and left them alone. Kerrigan whispered goodbye and kissed Burt's cooling hand but for a long
time he couldn't let go of it.

CHAPTER 10

Kerrigan spent the night in his old room with Dingbat sleeping at the end of the bed.

He rose early but Kath was already up and dressed, busying herself in the kitchen. When he hugged her she pulled away. He reached for the cereal cupboard but she steered him to a chair at the kitchen table. Despite his protests, she made pancakes and fried eggs with vegetarian sausages for him. He wasn't hungry, but he ate as much as he could.

That time in the kitchen was hard to bear. He watched Kath begin several little routines that were meant for Burt before stopping and tidying away whatever it was she'd started on. He saw how little of what she did was for herself. After a while she stood at the kitchen sink, lowered her head and wept, shaking silently. This time she let him hug her.

When the tears had passed, a squall that signalled a whole season of storms, Kath sat down at the table and withdrew an envelope from her apron pouch. The envelope was ivory with age and fat, as if it was stuffed with money. She laid it on the table in front of her.

'Oh, Jimmy. We shouldn't have waited so long to do this.' She sniffed and blew her nose. 'We just never wanted to face up to it, I guess.'

Was she talking about his adoption? They'd been through all this when he was a little boy. He understood perfectly well that they weren't his real parents. It had never spoiled anything for him. He'd always been certain that if his own parents had kept him, he'd have had a worse life; a life with less love, one in which all opportunity was closed to him. Burt and Kath had been the best thing that ever happened to Kerrigan. They pointed the way, let him make his mistakes and respected his aspirations. Even when he left for New York they didn't complain or make him feel he was making the wrong decision.

Kerrigan stared at the envelope.

'What more is there to know, Kath?'

She pressed a tissue to her mouth to stifle a sob and pushed the envelope towards him.

He reached out, froze for a moment, and then picked up the envelope with care, not wanting to damage its pristine smoothness and perfect lines. 'For James Kerrigan' was all that was written on it. Its touch filled his mind with images—a hundred stills passing in an instant—he tried to hold on to them and couldn't, except for one. It was a vision of a tall figure dressed in fraying clothes. The figure was gaunt like a starving hermit and he—Kerrigan felt it was a man, an old man—stood beside a huge tree. The trunk was so thick, its branches so vast; Kerrigan could only imagine its size. The image stayed with him.

'You have to open it,' said Kath.

He took his knife, cleaned it on his napkin and placed the blade in the space between the flap and the body of the envelope. He hesitated for a moment longer then slit it open in one sharp movement.

He took out the carefully folded, handwritten sheaves and began to read.

The first page was written in Burt's chunky hand—the neatest thing he'd ever written, Kerrigan realised—and probably the only letter he'd ever written with an ink pen. The date was August 1975, just after Kerrigan's birthday.

Dear James,

You have come to us like a blessing or an answered prayer. You will know by the time you read this that we are not your real parents, I plan to tell you that as soon as you're old enough to understand, but I hope that by the time you do read this you'll see us as your true family.

The circumstances of your birth are unusual, a real mystery to all of us. I think this letter will explain some of it — you'll understand it in a way that we can't.

The truth of the matter is that we did not seek you out from the orphanage as we said we did. We found you in the forest. You were wrapped in an animal skin, laying in a basket of reeds. Whoever left you, placed you in the middle of the Eastern Path that runs across the lower part of Bear Mountain. They left this letter too.

We took you into Hobson's Valley to the doctor who talked to the sheriff. They both knew us and our situation. We've always made our own law in this part of the country and once they were sure the parents weren't coming back, they let us keep you. Of course, we never showed them the letter.

You have a purpose in this world, James. Something many of us never find. You may not be aware of your purpose until you read this. You may find it is not what you had planned for yourself. Either way, we know you can live up to it. Remember that no matter where you go, we'll always be with you. We're here to give you strength, whatever you decide to do.

With all our love always,

Albert and Kathleen Kerrigan

He looked up at Kath and saw that she was crying. He put the letter back on the table and cried with her.

He was never going to see his father again.

When he could continue he picked up the letter and removed Burt's top sheet. What followed didn't make any sense to him at all. He flipped over one sheet after another and saw nothing but neatly spaced characters and symbols. On the last page was a map similar to the one the Jimenez family had shown him.

'I don't get it, Kath. I can't read this.'

'Yes. You can.'

'It's in another language. I don't even recognise the letters or punctuation.'

'You can read that letter, James. I know you can because I've heard you speak the language it's written in.'

Kerrigan stared.

'I never learned another language, Kath. How could I speak anything other than English?'

'I'm telling you, James, I've heard you speak it. In the right moment you'll be able to read it. I guess it doesn't have to be now.'

'When did I speak it?'

'All your life.'

'But when exactly? Was I watching TV? Throwing a baseball? What?'

'You did it in your sleep.'

He had to laugh then.

'I mumbled gobbledygook in my sleep a few times and you think I can read this? Come on, Kath.'

Her eyes were wide and defiant.

'You spoke that language every night of your life. Me and Burt would listen sometimes. It was beautiful, but it was scary too. If we hadn't had the letter as a sign of how special you were, we probably would have taken you to see some kind of doctor.'

He knew what kind of doctor she meant.

'And I can prove that it was this language you were speaking too.'

74

'You can?'

'Sure.'

She pushed her chair back and walked to their bedroom. When she came back she had a folder in her hands. She passed it to him.

Opening it, he saw drawings and language in the hand of a growing child. The first few sheets were just scribble and meaningless shapes but later in the file the scribble became the language he had just seen in the letter and the shapes became maps and drawings of people and symbols. The one symbol that repeated itself from the very beginning was that of the binder—an equal-armed cross within a circle.

There were other familiar things, a drawing of a staff like the one he used for long hikes. There was also a drawing of a primitive axe and, though he thought he recognised it, he didn't know from where. He'd drawn pictures of himself in what appeared to be mortal combat with other people. Sometimes they surrounded him. In other drawings, he seemed to be battling mythical creatures. It was all a little too much like the fantasy of a gifted child.

'It's no good sitting there and shaking your head, James. Burt's gone now and you have to face all this stuff. You've been ignoring it all your life. It's like your fear of the dark. You have to grow up and get over it. You're meant to be doing something special, something important. You better get on and do it.'

He'd rarely seen Kath so stern or determined. He felt like he was sixteen again, getting a lecture over his behaviour at school.

'You take all this stuff with you and study it. Don't you give up until you know what it means.'

'All right, Kath,' he said. 'I hear you.'

He folded the letter away and replaced the drawings in their file.

After speaking to the undertaker and making Kath promise to

call him if she needed anything at all, Kerrigan hurried back to the cabin. Buster greeted him with a barrage of affronted meows and tangled himself around Kerrigan's ankles until he got fed.

Kerrigan glanced at the Reminders stuck on the fridge and slammed his fist against the door.

'Jesus fuck.'

Bottles and cartons tumbled and fell inside. He made no attempt to right them. He tore up the pointless list. Too late to help Burt and no worm pills for Buster. He couldn't even remember to bring a flashlight to counteract his worst fear. And Amy was gone. Was it too late for the Jimenez family too? Trying to calm himself, he stepped outside and sat in his rocker but ended up pacing the porch and staring into the trees.

He couldn't have left Kath alone at a worse time but what choice was there? The Jimenez family were somewhere out on the trails. He was certain they were in danger, even though he couldn't say why. It was Carla he feared for the most. The letter, his childhood drawings, whatever Burt had seen at the window; it was all connected somehow. There was only one course of action to take but travelling into the woods meant he'd be out after nightfall.

Can I really do this?

He stopped pacing, faced the trees and closed his eyes. He let his breathing settle. Something drew on him, on his *blood*. The lure of nature, promising something: resolution, perhaps. He could feel the pull now. The call of the wilderness, a siren song of duty and desire. And his urgency to find the Jimenez's was akin to panic.

Resolved, he went indoors to pack.

On the bed, Kerrigan laid out a first aid kit, dried food rations, a bivvy bag and sleeping bag. Beside these he placed a tarpaulin for additional shelter, a lightweight camping stove, energy bars and a single change of clothes for himself. He counted out four foil exposure bags. Alongside all this he laid several binders and his walking staff. From a drawer in the kitchen he took a large, sheathed hunting knife, rope and paracord. Standing back to assess his equipment, he felt something was missing. He searched in all the usual places but couldn't find anything else that seemed useful.

Something drew him back to the pantry. He checked it several times but didn't discover anything. On his fourth trip, he noticed a dusty wooden crate on the floor that he couldn't remember putting there or ever opening. He slid it out, starting back a little when his hands first touched it; he could feel a slight hum or vibration coming from it, as though a current were passing through it.

He brushed the dust away with his fingers and coughed. It was not a crate, but a chest made of dark, ancient pine. Someone had put a good deal of effort and care into its creation. It was about three feet long, six inches high and less than a foot wide. There were markings carved into the wood like the ones he carved into the binders.

The lid of the chest was not hinged; it fitted down inside the walls with no discernible join. He saw a tab of leather poking out on the right hands side and pulled it. The lid lifted enough for him to remove it. He placed it to one side and leaned forward.

Inside was a stone-headed tomahawk, laid to rest like a corpse in a black fur lining. The fur was the smoothest, softest thing Kerrigan had ever touched. He had no idea what kind of animal might have been sacrificed to create such a comfortable resting place. Neither what kind, nor how many.

The tomahawk was simple. A heavy pine shaft, carved with similar designs to those on his staff. A thick leather thong looped through its haft. Finer strips of hide had been woven around the haft to create a non-slip grip.

The shaft passed through the centre of the head, broadening there to prevent it from detaching when swung. Crisscrossed leather strips further secured the head to the shaft.

The head itself was fashioned from a Singing River stone, similar to those Kerrigan used to hold his maps open. The stone had been knapped into a blade on one side, much like an ancient flint tool. The edge didn't look that sharp but with so much weight behind it, it would inflict devastating damage. The opposite end of the head tapered to a vicious hook, its flattened point similar to the claw of a mountain lion but far larger. The claw's inner edge had also been honed into a blade. The surface of the tomahawk head was profoundly darker than Kerrigan's map stones. Polished until it was reflective, it was almost black. Mica glinted in its surface like stars in a clear night sky.

Beneath the tomahawk, moulded into the fur, were two conical leather sleeves. It took him almost a minute to understand that they were forearm guards, each with several apertures perfectly designed to hold binders. The guards had leather lattices to adjust their tightness. Kerrigan stared at the contents of the chest and lost himself. A sense of urgency brought him back to moment.

He reached out and grasped the tomahawk's handle.

Carla Jimenez woke suddenly.

A dream? A kick from Luis?

She raised her head and blinked a few times. Eyes open or closed; it made no difference to the depth of the dark. She let her head rest back on the folded sweater she was using for a pillow and sighed.

The tent smelled of sweaty feet and her brother's farts and the ground beneath her camping mat was lumpy. Why, in a country famous for convenience and comfort, were they punishing themselves like this? She felt a brief, hot hatred for her father, swiftly followed by guilt; if she genuinely hadn't wanted to come, he probably would have let her stay with her grandmother in San Sebastian, but she'd been curious about America. She'd believed a camping trip would be fun.

A noise outside interrupted her thoughts.

Carla strained her hearing into the night. There was nothing, not even the hiss of a breeze through the pines. Then, over the sighs and snores around her in the cramped tent, she heard it again: whispered laughter. Suddenly very alert, she came up with an explanation. It was possible there were other campers and hikers out on the trails; perhaps not far away, perhaps partying. Except this hadn't sounded like merriment—to know they weren't travelling these trails alone would have been a comfort.

No. She'd heard the laughter of a single person. A man. And not the laughter that follows jokes or the laughter of friends sharing memories and swapping stories. There in the interminable dark, the laughter sounded insane. The mirth of someone witnessing a suicide on closed circuit TV or running over a dog. She'd never heard such a demented sound.

The laughter came again, closer. Moments later, from impossibly far away.

Carla lay, tense and still, trying not to breathe audibly, listening for any sound in the forest. The forest was silent. She stayed that way, rigid and immobile, until she drifted into sleep then jerked back to consciousness, her heart galloping. Time slowed and it became impossible to discern wakefulness from sleep. Still she listened, praying to Mother Mary not to hear such laughter again.

Not ever.

The phone rang for a long time before she answered.

'Hey, Kath. It's me.'

'Hello, Jimmy.'

Her voice sounded distant even though the line was clear and loud. He didn't ask her how she was doing.

'I just was phoning to say I'll be away for a day or two.'

There was a short silence.

'You're heading out onto the trails, aren't you?'

There was no point in lying.

'Yeah.'

'Well, you be careful out there.'

'I will be. You going to be okay, Kath? You know, if there was any way I could do this thing later I would but I've left it too long already. People could get hurt, or worse, if I don't do something.'

'I'll be just fine.'

Kerrigan thought he could hear her swallowing tears.

CHAPTER 11

Sixteen, and full of hot, adolescent rage, the two boys faced off in the car park behind Olsen's.

Daniel Stringer and Alfred Lindh had been best friends ever since the first fight they'd had in the playground, aged seven. They'd bloodied each other's noses that day but neither could claim victory. When all the anger and strength had gone out of them they'd started laughing. They'd laughed every day since. Sometimes they still fought over their disagreements but the status quo had been in place so long that neither boy ever came out on top.

In the matter of Gina Priestly however, things were different.

'I love her.'

'Bullshit. *I* love her.'

Without further discussion their fists flew like missiles in a private war. Everyone knew Alfie and Danny, and their fights attracted few crowds because they always ended inconclusively.

Something about this contest was different.

Alfie used his knee in Danny's stomach and Danny used his elbow to strike Alfie's jaw: both moves they'd learned watching endless martial arts movies together. Equally stunned by these more damaging blows, the boys backed away from each other for a few seconds to reappraise the situation.

'You sure you want to do this?' asked Alfie. ''Cause I'm gonna kill you if you touch me again.'

'Fuck you,' said Danny. 'I'm not kidding around. Come at me again and you're going to hospital.'

They stood tense and panting, ready for the next engagement. Gina Priestly watched it all from the corner of the grocery store, smiling.

Even when she approached, they didn't see her.

'Hi, Guys. What's up?'

Looking from each other to her they straightened their postures and tried to tidy their ruffled hair. They both mumbled a greeting.

'I know you boys were fighting over me.'

Neither of them spoke.

'You can both have me if you want. Would you like that?'

Alfie looked at Danny and they both looked back at Gina.

'I don't understand,' said Alfie.

'Well let me make it perfectly simple for you. You do everything together, right?'

They laughed, looking embarrassed.

'Well, what I'm saying is, I want you and you both want me, so . . .'

'So . . . ?' they said together.

'So we should all be together. At the same time.'

A silence enveloped the threesome.

'Uh, we're gonna need to discuss this,' said Alfie.

'Yeah, I mean—you know, talk and like that,' said Danny.

'Fine.'

The boys looked at each other and shrugged.

'We talked it over and we'd like to do it,' said Alfie.

'It was a tough decision,' said Danny.

Gina smiled.

'There's one condition. I don't want anyone to know and I don't want to get caught.'

'We won't tell anyone,' said Alfie.

'Right,' said Danny, 'And we can use his house. His parents almost never come in his room.'

'Huh uh. No way. We're gonna go up to the woods.'

'You want to do it outside?'

'No. There's this place I know. It's a hunter's cabin. It's old and run down but there's a bed up there and no one will ever find us.'

They took everything they thought they might need and Gina came for them after nightfall so they wouldn't be seen. Between them, Danny and Alfie carried the sleeping bags, blankets, beer, whisky, snacks and weed. Gina didn't carry anything, not even a jacket.

'Aren't you going to be cold?' Alfie asked

'We'll keep each other warm.'

She stopped them before they made their way past Jimmy Kerrigan's cabin and up the dirt road to The Clearing.

'Keep quiet, guys. We don't want anyone to hear us. Don't make a sound until we're well into the trees, okay?'

Beyond Kerrigan's place, the darkness closed in around them and Gina led the way. Danny couldn't stand walking blind and turned on his flashlight.

'Don't wave that around.' she whispered. 'If you really need it just point it at the ground.'

Out there in the darkness, the temperature dropping, it suddenly seemed impossible that Gina really wanted to have sex with them. The farther they walked the less he believed it.

'Alfie?' he whispered.

'What?'

'You got a smoke with you?'

'Sure.'

Alfie pulled a soft pack of camels from his shirt pocket, tapping one out for Danny and one for himself. They stopped to light up and Gina kept walking.

'You think this is for real?' Danny asked.

'Only one way to find out.' Alfie said.

'What if we're being set up or something?'

A hissed whisper came back at them through the night.

'Guys! You coming or what?'

'Yeah, yeah. Just a second,' called Alfie. And he continued under his breath: 'So you think it's a joke or something, Dan?'

'I don't know. I just find it hard to believe we're about to bone Gina Priestly. I mean, I know she puts out and all, but this is *us* we're talking about.'

'Yeah, I hear you,' said Alfie. 'We should test her.' Turning towards The Clearing, he shouted: 'Uh, hey! Gina!'

She ran back to them.

'Shit, Alfie, keep your voice down,' she said. 'What is it?'

'Danny's afraid of the dark,' he said.

'I am not!' said Danny.

'Sure you are. And I have a project I need to finish before school starts. So we're just gonna head back and catch you later.' He turned to go.

'You don't think I'm serious do you?'

'No,' Alfie said. 'We don't'

'I'll prove it to you. I'll show you I'm serious.'

'How're you going to do that, Gina? A little kiss in the woods isn't enough to prove you want to do it with us. I don't want to walk up to some cabin and discover all your friends there with video cameras and God knows what kind of unfunny gags.'

'There's no one but us.'

She knelt down in front of Danny and unzipped his jeans. She did the same to Alfie. With one hand in each opening she tugged their penises into the night air. She closed her mouth around Danny's and began to stroke and milk Alfie's with her fingers. Danny gasped at the fierceness with which she sucked on him. Within seconds, both of them were iron stiff. She changed then, taking Alfie in her mouth and using her hands on Danny's now slick erection. It wasn't long before both of them were nearing ejaculation.

She stopped.

'I want to spend the night with you,' she said. 'Somewhere warm and comfortable where no one will find us. Once we're there you can do anything you want with me.' She stood up. 'Are you in or not?'

'We're in,' said Alfie as he tried to push his dick back into his jeans.

'Fuckin' A,' said Danny attempting to do the same.

From then on they kept pace with Gina all the way to the cabin.

Far beyond The Clearing and off one of the trails, they stumbled through the pine trees for what felt like an hour before they found the cabin. Alfie shone his flashlight at the ivy cloaked, tumbledown exterior.

'Cool. How do we get in?'

'This way.'

Gina walked around the back and they followed. There was a broken door hanging from one hinge and she pushed it open gently making sure it didn't fall off. Once they were all inside she pushed it closed again as firmly as she could and struggled with the rusty bolt until it was locked.

'Don't want anyone surprising us, do we?' She grinned at them in the darkness.

'No, indeed,' said Alfie.

Danny shone his flashlight around the inside of the place, illuminating cobwebs in the corners where the walls met the ceiling. The cabin was a single large room and at one end there was a stone fireplace and chimney. There were some rickety looking wooden chairs and a table. Against the wall near the back door was an iron-framed double bed. Towards the front door, the one they'd avoided, there was a large hole in the rotten floorboards.

'We're gonna need a little more light in here,' Danny said.

'Let's make a fire,' said Alfie.

'Go to it, guys.'

Alfie took the flashlight and walked to the fireplace. Inside it was a fallen bird's nest of dried grass, twigs, and tufts of down. He broke it up and arranged it into a stack.

'Think we can use some of the furniture?' he asked.

'Why not?' said Danny. 'I don't think anyone's been in here in twenty years.'

'Help me out, then.'

Between them they kicked their way through the table, breaking off its legs and smashing through the top. The noise of splintering timber and grunts of effort were loud after the silence of the walk.

'Hey keep it down, guys. And leave us a chair each to sit on, why don't you?'

Gina stood with her arms folded as the boys demolished the worm-eaten furniture. The fire started easily and, though a good deal of smoke came into the cabin to start with, once the flames grew the fire settled down and the chimney drew the smoke up and into the night. They were putting a lot of effort into making the place cosy. She smiled as she watched them and ran her finger through the dust on the windowsill, leaving a tiny canyon. The air smelled of pine, musty cloth and decay.

Danny and Alfie opened three beers and lit a joint. Gina spread the blankets and sleeping bags over the bed's old mattress. She downed her beer in one long pull to applause and cheers from the boys.

'Let's get that whisky open,' she said.

Danny fumbled the screw cap off and passed it her way. She shook her head.

'You first.'

He drank, swallowed and grimaced. Alfie did the same.

'Again,' she said.

They looked at each other, a little uncertain.

'Come on, guys. I want to get wild tonight. Don't want you two holding back. We're gonna do it *all*.'

They drank again and passed her the bottle. She put their

little sips to shame and they took larger swallows the next time. They passed the joint around. The fire cast mocking images of them onto the far wall; the shadows shrank and grew in pulses with its flickering. The air grew warm and heavy with the cloying smell of grass and the bitter smoke from the burning furniture.

Gina danced; slowly at first, seeking a rhythm in silence. She raised her hands above her head, reaching for inspiration from the black sky beyond the roof. The darkness poured into her and she found its sinuous pace; a movement like the twisting of a vast river nearing the ocean. The boys watched, dazed by her.

Gina's explored her body as if it was another's. Hands on her face, hands behind her neck. Two chopsticks arranged in a cross held her hair up. She withdrew them and tossed them onto the bed, shaking down her dark coils.

A piece at a time she removed her clothes, throwing them away until she moved naked before them but for her black motorcycle boots. She caressed her breasts and squeezed her nipples until she cried out. Turning away from them and with her legs spread wide she bent forward, fully exposing herself. She let them watch her fingers agitate and pinch the glistening folds of her cleft. Reaching behind with her free hand she circled and penetrated her anus.

The boys looked on, erect and enraptured until Gina moved to the bed and sat down on its edge, beckoning them with a slick, shiny finger.

She made good on her promises. Each time they came she made them hard again in any way she could. Their fluids excited her, increased her thirst. The boys were inexperienced and Gina had to make herself come with her fingers as they stabbed at her with their young, strong erections. She didn't care. She milked them and forced whisky down their necks until they were close to passing out. Then she let them sleep.

As the fire burned down to red embers she fetched the old

tin wash tub she'd hidden under a dustsheet. The metal of the tub had been scrubbed clean and all the rust removed. It shone with a dull gleam when she positioned it in front of the fire. She placed two wooden chairs, one on either side of the tub, facing towards it.

She woke Danny with difficulty.

'Come on. Up you get.' she said

'I can't do it anymore,' he mumbled.

'You don't have to do anything, just sit in this chair.'

'No. I'm tired.'

'Get up, Danny.'

Finding himself impelled by something in her voice, Danny sat up with his head hanging towards his chest.

'Go sit in the chair.'

Reeling and stumbling, he did as she'd asked him. She roused Alfie in a similar way. The boys sat facing one another in their chairs with the tub between them. Danny lost consciousness and began to slump to one side.

'Up straight!'

As if hoisted, he sat up, his head still lolling.

Gina retrieved her chopsticks and approached the inebriated pair. She touched each of their foreheads and spoke a word in a snarled unrecognisable tongue. They became rigid and immobile. Leaning over Danny she licked the skin a couple of inches below his sternum numbing it with the secretions from her tongue. She placed the thicker end of one of the chopsticks against him. Though it would have looked solid to a casual observer, it was hollow; a tapering steel tube painted black. Its tip was cut at an angle like a quill or a hypodermic needle but it was broad; the width of an index finger at the end that touched him, slimming to the width of a straw at the other.

Using her thumbnail as a scalpel, she incised a tiny opening in Danny's skin and through this she pressed the tube deeply into him. Once past the superficial tissues, the nerves were less reactive. She knew Danny wouldn't feel much. She pushed until she felt a firm resistance with a strong pulse. The broad end of the tube was now touching Danny's aorta. She put a hand over her mouth to suppress a giggle and then performed the same operation on Alfie. She stood back, hands on hips, impressed with her work.

'You can wake up now, guys.'

Their eyes snapped open, but they were bloodshot and glazed from the booze and pot, ringed and tired from their exertions.

'What is this thing?' asked Danny.

'Fuck, man. Is this . . . ?' Alfie struggled to make sense of what he was looking at. 'Is this thing inside me?'

'Hey, Alfie, I can't move, man. I'm stuck.'

'What the fuck are you doing, Gina?'

They saw themselves naked and immobile in their chairs. They saw each other. They saw a steel tube protruding from their stomachs, pointing down towards the tin washtub. They saw the tubes bouncing in time with their pulses like thin steel erections.

'You've had your fun. Now I'm going to have mine.' Still naked but for her boots, Gina sat down in the tub between the boys. 'I'll give you some advice. The louder you scream and the more frightened you become, the higher your blood pressure will rise and the quicker you'll bleed. So, seeing as you *are* both going to die, freaking the fuck out is probably the best policy.'

She placed a palm against each tube. Alfie and Danny were already screaming but neither of them was able to move anything but their mouths.

'I feel dirty, guys,' said Gina Priestly. 'It must be time for my bath.'

With a swift punching action, she rammed her palms outward and drove the tubes simultaneously through the walls of their aortas, provoking a half-screamed 'hunh' from both boys.

Taking her palms away from the ends of the tubes, her

bath began to fill immediately, though much of the blood that jetted from the tubes splashed over her shoulders and hair first. She opened her mouth, catching some and swallowing it. The warmth of it washed down over her and began to collect in the base of the tub. She slithered her behind in its slick stickiness and was once again aroused. With wet red fingers she rubbed her swollen sex and laughed.

For such young, fit men, Alfie and Danny had very high blood pressure.

CHAPTER 12

The backpack slipped and slapped against him as Kerrigan jogged away from the cabin. He adjusted the straps and glanced constantly to his left and right, tense and skittish.

The crisp morning air chilled his face but he knew he'd soon be sweating. An undernourished pre-dawn light illuminated the dirt road between the trees, making every object monochrome grey. The usual tinges of twilight purple were nowhere to be seen. He relaxed a little.

Still, it was dark enough that a careless step could topple him or cause him a nasty sprain. He focused a few feet ahead of himself, watching for uneven patches in the trail. Running became the only sensation. His body rubbing against the material of his clothes, the backpack moving against his spine, the sound of his breathing and the crunching thump, thump, thump of his footfalls on the rough ground. Somewhere in that percussion, he found a rhythm and stuck to it.

At the Clearing he turned right onto the Eastern Path where the trail was closer on both sides but still wide. The trees enveloped him and for a while it became almost dark again. An ache began in his legs. He ran through a stitch and rasping lungs. Once those discomforts had passed, Kerrigan felt like he'd never done anything in his life except run and he knew that he could run all day. His nostrils filled with the waxy scent of pine needles. His body loosened, the day brightened, his strength grew.

He picked up the pace.

An hour after leaving the cabin Kerrigan reached the fork that gave him the choice between Trapper's Trail and the continuation of the Eastern Path. On any other day, he'd have taken Trapper's Trail, broken through the tree line and headed for the steep paths and open skies of Bear Mountain. That would remain a luxury for another day.

He broke to the right and the forest closed in on him.

Branches had grown across the trail causing him to side-step and dodge as he ran. From time to time dead pines leaned into his path making him duck. Twice he came across trunks that had fallen across the trail like gates. He jumped the first near its root without testing his leg muscles but the second was an impasse. It spanned the trail like a wall and at its lowest point the branches reached ten feet into the air. Some kind of madness made Kerrigan keep running when he saw it.

Part of him balked, refusing, but another part, suddenly much stronger than all his fears, willed his body onward. As he approached, the tree loomed vast in front of him. He accelerated to a speed that seemed impossible. At the last moment, he leapt and soared high over the huge fallen pine. His boots didn't even scrape the branches. It was like flying. He whooped a call of triumph into the woods and landed without breaking his stride.

The sun was overhead by then and Kerrigan smiled as he ran. Ecstasy overtook him as he sprinted onwards, dodging or vaulting every obstacle.

Kerrigan felt the imprints of the Jimenez family, each of them, on the ground and in the air long before he saw any signs of them. They were alive—at least, they'd been alive at this point in their journey. Kerrigan could feel their fear too, especially that of Carla.

Why? What has she seen?

A couple of miles beyond where he first sensed the family's passing, he found a break in the trees to his right. Beyond was a tunnel through low branches, ferns and thorny undergrowth. He could see they'd used a machete to gain access to the choked trail. No more than a few paces within, cocooned by thick plant life, the path was almost totally dark.

Kerrigan placed his backpack on the ground outside the newly broken trail and removed a bottle of water and a sandwich. He was immediately ravenous. As he unwrapped the sandwich, he remembered the envelope and pulled it out of his pack. Once more, he removed the folded sheets and found it was the first page — Burt's letter — that was impossible to decipher.

All the other pages were now clear to him.

He sat down; his heart still hammering from exertion, his breathing laboured, and began to read while the sensation of intensity still electrified his body. The words he saw written there were enough to make him forget his hunger. He had a strong sense of the man who had written those words; he felt an intimacy in them that he didn't feel for anyone, not even Burt and Kath.

Little one, you do not even have a name and I have left you to the whims of the forest. If you survive you will read this, perhaps in anger. Please believe that I had no choices left.

I have sent strong images to the minds of the childless in Hobson's Valley in the hope that they will come walking this way and find you before the animals or the frost end your tender new life.

But, if you are found and adopted I know you will return to this valley and take up your rightful place as its protector.

It is not a happy task nor is it an easy one. It is, however, in your blood and, above all else, it is your duty.

I am an old man now. I have guarded the people of this valley for many decades though they do not know it and, most of the time, neither do I. There is a disease here that has existed for generations immemorial. It is called Fugue and it causes its hosts to hunger for the liquids, and particularly the blood, of living creatures. You and I are infected with a similar disease, Lethe, a counterpart illness that equips us with the means to destroy or heal Fugues.

Fugue is a sickness. This is true of your uniqueness too, child. I introduced Lethe to your blood and you must learn to live with it and manage it. Fugues will not do this. You must do it for them.

A Fugue hunter should pass his responsibilities on, before he becomes vulnerable, and allow his successor to release him. I was proud and I waited too long. Now I face not death as my end but something far darker. The very Fugue I have been destroying all my life now infects my blood and, though I can save others from such contamination, I can do nothing to prevent myself from developing the disease.

I have therefore used my knowledge to pass the Lethe into your blood so that there is someone to succeed me. It is a bad decision to choose you this way; ordinarily, each Fugue Hunter takes a pupil and trains them. But the Lethe will show itself in your blood, nonetheless, and you will heed its call. You are nature's ally, the living antidote to a parasite that threatens all life. This power you carry comes at a cost. It will make an outsider of you and you will live much of your life in fear — of the dark, of things you are unable to name. And you will forget your gift when it is not awake in your blood.

The pattern is similar for Fugues. No one knows they feed on living fluids, least of all themselves. Many of them only feed once in several weeks or months, but they must drink eventually and the longer they leave it the fiercer their ultimate attack will be. When threatened or unfed for too long, Fugues develop a higher phase of illness known as Rage. Rage feeders will be your greatest challenge.

Your own mother was killed, drained white by a Raging Fugue, before I could prevent it. I brought you to the forest and passed my power to you before leaving you here to be discovered. By now you will have powers and abilities that most men would sell their souls for. Lethe is entwined with your blood, with your soul. You can but answer its call. Like Fugue it is too powerful to resist.

Through instinct alone, you will use ritual and diet to keep yourself purified for battle. You will understand how to craft fetishes to stun Fugues into unconsciousness so that you can release them from the disease. These fetishes are called binders and are similar to the dream catchers made by the people who lived here long before we came. They were the first to fight Fugue and we have inherited that duty from them. In difficult situations you will have the use of more powerful weapons; a staff for controlling and subduing Fugues and a tomahawk for when your only alternative is to destroy them. The understanding of all of this exists within you already. When your life is threatened or the odds against you are great, you will enter your own higher phase of Lethe. It is called Fury.

As Kerrigan read he noticed a change in the light of the day and looked up but it was only a cloud passing across the sun. A few seconds later it was gone, the brightness returning. The words of the language in front of him made sense. Total sense. He began to make connections between the letter and almost every inexplicable or difficult aspect of his life.

Fugue is particular to this valley. You must keep it that way. If a carrier ever escapes Hobson's Valley you will be responsible for the spread of the disease to other places. Were that to happen, Fugue would become uncontrollable. Life everywhere would be threatened.

When I turn, as I inevitably will, you will be the one to come and deal with me. I only pray that I can control my sickness until you are old enough to do the job. I will be here waiting in the forest and I will not welcome you. The longer I prevent myself from feeding the worse my hunger will become and the greater my desire to kill and spread Fugue.

Each time a Fugue feeds they become more powerful and versatile. Each time you cleanse or destroy a Fugue you too will become more powerful but ultimately you will become old and frail like any human being and the Lethe will change; it will become Fugue. Before this happens you must do what I did not; you must take a pupil, a willing one if possible, and you must introduce Lethe into their body so that they can take your place. As long as there is Fugue, there must be a Fugue Hunter

Your duty is to release me, destroy me if you must. But, I beg you, end the sickness that already threatens to steal my mind and my desires.

End it well, child.

Kerrigan's heart rate slowed and the endorphin rush from running abated. Fatigue and weakness settled over him and the words on the page became indistinct.

As the skill of understanding disappeared so did his memory of what he'd known only moments before. All Kerrigan could remember was leaving the cabin in the darkness before dawn and being full of fear.

PART II: INFECTION

'There is no disease for which God did not also provide a cure.'
10th century Persian proverb.

CHAPTER 13

Stale cigarette smoke and the taint of spilled beer choked the air conditioning. Hard rock, soft rock and the occasional fifties tune sprang like genies from the jukebox. The barman was lecherous, the drinks cheap and familiar, but there were compensations. Mulligan's was the only bar in Hobson's Valley dedicated to hardnosed drinking and that was what Amy Cantrell was in the mood for.

Sure, she could get a drink at Segar's cabin but she didn't want to sit alone in there and get approached by the same old losers or partially available men. She didn't want to see Jimmy Kerrigan either. Although it was rare, he did sometimes eat in Segar's on his own and they'd made a couple of trips there in their time together.

During the course of our relationship.

That wasn't accurate enough. *Association* was better, but she preferred to think of the connection as having existed over a period of time.

Eighteen months.

Not that it was an eighteen-month relationship. If she added up the time they'd actually spent together, she figured it was about four weeks.

She laughed out loud.

'Want to share the gag?'

The barman smiled as he wiped a glass clean and replaced

it next to a hundred others. Amy watched him for a moment and picked up everything she needed to know. He was a man who took advantage of drunks and lonely women, ready to say a supportive word or two if it spread someone's legs or opened their wallet one more time.

'I would if I thought there was anyone in here that might get it,' she said. 'I'll take another draft instead.'

Neon signs for Miller and Bud lit the bar and behind it glass-fronted coolers presented ranks of icy bottles. Above them liquor brands gleamed their pale and golden colours and the TV mounted over the countertop flashed silent images into the smoky room.

Amy liked the song and she swayed to it on her barstool. Brash, powerful drums and grinding guitars vibrated in her chest. She drank. Closing her eyes she absorbed the gravelly voice of the singer. The buzz from the beer took hold and she felt lighter, more alive than she had since she'd finished it with Jimmy. The passion of the song grew and she gave in to it a little more.

God, Jimmy, why did you have to be so weird with me, honey?

It had been hard to let him go. Jimmy didn't love her and she knew she only *wanted* to love him, but there'd been *something* between them. Was it the sex? Maybe that really was all it added up to. But good sex added up to a lot. Jimmy had made her feel things she'd never felt with any other man. He'd made her do things she'd never done before too, and it was all good. But he couldn't handle the day after in any meaningful kind of way. She'd given him so many chances.

'God damn.'

The barman glanced her way and left it at that when he saw the look on her face. She was remembering how he'd pissed himself. Like a little boy.

She looked around and sighed. Sitting alone in a bar going backwards wasn't going to help. She drained the glass and reached down for the purse at her feet.

'You're not leaving now, are you?'

A girl with untamed dark hair and moon pale skin stood beside her at the bar. Amy was drawn to the girl's eyes; irises of forest green fractured by shards of sunlight orange. The girl was young but her eyes were ancient. All Amy could do was stare.

'I've been meaning to come over for a while, but I was too afraid,' said the girl.

'Afraid?' Amy frowned. 'Of what?'

'I wanted to buy you another beer but I thought it would seem a little odd, you know?'

'Are you old enough to be in here?' asked Amy.

The girl looked at the barman and he turned away.

'I guess so,' she answered.

'Well, I think I've had enough for tonight,' Amy said.

The girl wasn't put off.

'Only if you're drinking alone,' she said.

Amy glanced around Mulligan's. It was almost deserted — one old timer with his hat still on occupied a small round table. A young couple in jeans and plaid shirts played pool. A drunk watched the silent TV through half-closed eyes. She looked back at the girl.

'You been watching me?' she asked.

'No,' said the girl. 'Not watching. But I couldn't help noticing you.'

Amy was half amused, half disbelieving. Was this girl coming onto her?

'Well, like I said, the evening's over for me.'

She said the words but she didn't move; still held in the cool gaze of the girl with the woodlands in her eyes.

'Have one beer with me. Coming over here to ask you was one of the hardest things I ever did. I don't want you to leave thinking I'm weird or a lesbian or something—

or something

—I wanted to talk to you. Is that such a bad thing?'

Amy felt her will collapse. She wanted to talk and drink long into the night. She wanted to connect. She wanted what

Jimmy had never given her—care. Something other than orgasms that made her weep with loneliness afterwards.

She released an exasperated laugh.

'Okay, whatever. One more beer.'

The girl faced the bar to order and Amy watched her. She wore motorcycle boots and dark stockings, a purple mini skirt and a leather jacket with buckles and straps and zips. She looked both lost and wild.

The girl turned, pushing a beer towards her.

'Listen,' said Amy, 'any other night I'd have said yes straight away, so don't feel bad. You caught me on a bad day.'

'It's okay. I get those too.' The girl smiled for the first time and Amy was charmed. 'You want to stay up here or shall we find somewhere else?'

'Where were you sitting?'

The girl gestured into the gloom

'In that booth right there.'

Amy noticed the bar creep taking an interest in them. Anywhere far from him would be fine.

'Looks great.'

She followed the girl, watching her slender behind sway in its thin coating of fashion and wishing she wasn't so heavy these days. She'd look like a moose sitting next to the kid. Yeah. A dark corner was the best place.

She set her beer down and slid in but the girl remained standing.

'I'm gonna punch in some more tunes. Any requests?'

'I don't know what they've got on this machine,' said Amy. 'Let me give you some quarters though.'

'No way. I got it.'

The girl clomped off to the jukebox and leaned over to inspect the selection. The guy playing pool checked out her ass and Amy didn't blame him one bit. The guy's girlfriend snatched the cue from his hand and took her shot, missing badly. The bar was desolate with so few people in it. The music that roared from the jukebox boosted the limp vibe.

The girl returned and slipped into the seat opposite, raising her glass.

'To fulfilment.'

Amy couldn't hide her surprise.

'Amen,' she said.

They clinked their glasses and drank, the girl downing half of hers in a swallow. Amy didn't try to keep up.

'I guess you work out, right?' she asked the girl after a while.

'Yeah, I do. When I was sixteen I started to get real fat. I always said I'd never be fat. Mom says when I was a kid I used to cry when I met fat people. I wouldn't watch them on TV or anything.'

Amy felt herself reddening.

'Oh hey, listen,' the girl said, 'you are not fat. I would never have said that in front of you if I thought *you* were fat, I swear. You're beautiful. You're how I imagine a real woman to be.'

'A real woman?'

'Shit, I'm just going to stop digging this hole right now. When I said I was getting fat, I mean I was huge. I looked sick. That kind of fat. I decided I'd die before I let myself stay that way. Now I work out five times a week at home. I don't drink soda—beer is fine, by the way—and I run three times a week too.'

'Where do you get the energy?' asked Amy.

'Doing it gives you energy.'

'Really?'

'Sure. It's like being high but you feel clear-headed and full of life.'

Amy shrugged.

'It's a while since I felt anything like that,' she said

'Come for a run with me sometime, then.'

'Oh, God. I couldn't. It'd be like a whale and a dolphin going swimming together.'

'You should come. You'd like it.'

'Where do you run?'

'All through the Bear Mountain trails. It's beautiful out there.'

'Cold in the winter.'

'You don't feel it,' said the girl. 'You're warm by the time you reach the woods. Anyway, the offer stands if you change your mind.'

The girl was really trying hard to be nice. Amy decided she ought to loosen up and have a little fun instead of worrying about the difference in their ages and appearances. She put her hand out across the table.

'My name's Amy Cantrell.'

The girl shook it.

'Gina Priestly.'

'Well, it's a pleasure to meet you, Gina. You've saved me from a lonesome night.'

'You got guy trouble?'

Suddenly, Amy was able to smile.

'Not any more,' she said.

CHAPTER 14

In daylight the creature hid itself within the darkest places of the forest, safe where no brightness could penetrate. During those hours it entered a resting state, in which it tried to escape its own hunger. But when the sun fell beyond the peak of Bear Mountain, it could hide from its purpose no longer.

As the twilight came it rose from its bower and wandered in the woods or ran along the trails or sat among the rocks of the high passes. Sometimes it pranced in time with the silent pulse of the night. The deeper the darkness, the more restless it became. By midnight, it was demonic with mischief and hunger and lust. It came then to the town to answer the bidding of the master in its blood.

It revelled in its power. It didn't matter that the creature was an abomination, that it did not belong among these trees and mountains, that it was a stranger to the very earth beneath its feet. It only mattered that it was free, abroad upon the night and able to prepare for an even greater liberty.

In the meantime, there were playthings in the valley and in the woods, trinkets for the creature to toy with. Nectars to be sampled. Agonies to be appreciated

José disappeared into the trees at the side of the trail to look for a secluded spot where they could pitch camp. Better to get away from the path and find a place where their tent wouldn't cause trouble for others.

He didn't find a space. There was barely enough distance between the pines to peg out their ground sheet. The 'clearing' had to be made by cutting back the branches of the trees until they had enough room to set up the tent without ripping it.

Carla watched him work with her arms folded.

'Papa, can't we sleep in the open?' she asked.

'Have you found somewhere better?' he replied.

'What is wrong with the trail?'

'We will be in the way there.'

'In the way of who?' she protested. 'No one comes this way.'

'Perhaps not often, but the trail is officially open and we can't block it.'

When the tent was erected, José set up the gas stove for Maria, placing it a safe distance from the porch guy ropes.

'I'm starving,' said Luis. 'What's for dinner?'

Carla smirked.

'All you think about is your stomach, cochino.'

'All you think about is which colour nail varnish to use to impress which one of your boyfriends.'

José glanced at Maria. She ignored him.

'We're having boil in the bag chilli con carne with rice,' she said.

'You have a boyfriend now, Carlita?' José asked.

'Boyfriends,' said Luis. 'Dozens of them,'

'Don't cause trouble, Luis,' said Maria. 'There's tinned fruit, too, if you want it.'

'It is true then?' José was unsmiling. 'Why do I not know of this?'

Maria said: 'She's almost seventeen, José. She's old enough to have a boyfriend.'

'Perhaps. But more than one?' Finally he grinned. 'Is that legal?'

'Why do you always pick on me, Papa? What about Luis and his cigarettes?'

Luis looked up, wide-eyed.

'Shut up, Carla,' he whispered.

José turned to his son.

'If I catch you smoking there will be serious trouble, Luis.'

'She's making it up to get herself out of trouble.'

'I am not,' Carla shouted. 'Why do you do this to me?' She glanced at each of them and José noticed something more in her expression than simple annoyance. 'I didn't want to come here,' she said. 'I don't like these woods.'

'Carlita,' said José. 'This is a special journey for us. It is like a pilgrimage that we are making in the name of family. It is hard but it is our duty and we must do it.'

Maria dropped the plastic bags into the boiling water and Luis looked on with impatience. The blue glow from the gas burner became steadily brighter as the woods darkened. It was still early but the night advanced swiftly, lending everything a hint of violet.

Carla crept a good distance away to relieve herself amid the pines. That way she wouldn't have to go later in total darkness. Even in the half-light she was jumpy and snapped her head around at the slightest sound. She wanted so badly to make them all understand that they needed to get out of this place. She unzipped, pulled down her pants and squatted in the undergrowth. It was too late to turn back tonight but if she could get Papa to realise they were in danger, they could begin the long journey home in the morning.

In the few moments she'd been away, the forest twilight deepened. It was as though the light had been sucked away. She dried with a tissue, dropped it, zipped up and fumbled through the grasping branches towards the sound of her family. Before she reached them she heard a branch snap behind her. She spun round to look but it was difficult to see more than a few yards through the pines.

For a while she crouched, staring in the direction she thought the noise had come from, but the darkness soon made the forest indistinct, transforming every shape into a threat. The woods were silent. Nothing moved. Before it got too dark to see, she crept back to their tiny camp, crouching to avoid low branches.

'What's the matter?' Maria asked her.

'Nothing, Mama. I'm fine.'

'You look scared.'

Carla sat down on a tiny fold-out camping stool, completing the family circle. She glanced at each of their faces before dropping her gaze to avoid their searching eyes.

'There's someone else out here,' said Carla. 'Someone watching us.'

CHAPTER 15

'Sheesh. Fucking guys,' said Gina. 'I had a couple who just wouldn't leave me alone.'

Amy snorted.

'I wish I still got that kind of attention.'

'No, you don't. Even ten guys chasing you still adds up to nothing if they're all jerks.'

'I guess. So what happened with your two?'

'Didn't have what it took to satisfy me.'

Amy suppressed a laugh of surprise.

'I didn't mean it that way,' the girl said. 'I'm just saying they didn't measure up.'

Amy put her hand over her mouth but even the couple playing pool heard her howls over the jukebox.

'Come on, Amy. It wasn't like that.'

Soon Gina was laughing too.

'I'm sorry,' giggled Amy, 'you sounded like such a porno queen for a second there. You seem so young to me that it was, I don't know—incongruous.'

Amy took a tissue from her handbag, blew her nose and wiped her eyes.

'So how old *are* you, Gina?'

The girl looked out of the corner of her eye towards the bar and whispered:

'I'm twenty.'

The kid was lying but what did it matter? Gina reminded Amy of herself fifteen years younger. She wasn't going to give her a hard time over it.

'How about you?' asked the girl.

Well, I should have seen that coming.

'I'm thirty-three.'

Amy watched Gina's face for signs of shock, the typical teenage disbelief that anyone could be *that* old, but she saw nothing there; no flicker of boredom or disappointment. She smiled. One more drink with her new friend and then home.

She stood up.

'Same again, Gina?'

'Oh, you don't have to do that.'

'I want to.'

'Well . . . okay. Sure.'

Amy was a little unsteady on her feet. She hoped it wasn't too obvious. The barman poured two beers then leaned towards her.

'That girl old enough to be drinking?'

'What are you asking me for?'

'You could get into a lot of trouble for buying her alcohol.'

'I didn't let her in here, Brains. If anyone gets into trouble it'll be you. You want to kick her out, go ahead. Otherwise, shut up.'

He turned away, put the bills into the register and handed her the change.

'I could kick you both out if I wanted to.'

'Do it. You can give me my money back first, though. Right now, it looks like we're paying your wages.'

Amy walked back to the booth triumphant.

'What was that all about?'

'Not much. Just giving that asshole the facts.'

Gina raised her glass.

'Right on.'

They drank the beers and talked. The more they talked the

less Amy wanted the evening to finish. When the songs ran out on the jukebox, Amy made her own choices and sat back down as the tune she'd been listening to earlier played again.

'Excellent choice,' said Gina.

'You think?'

'Yeah, I love this one. Sometimes I can't get it out of my head. Hey, we should dance.'

'What? You can't dance to this kind of thing.'

'Why not?'

'It doesn't have that kind of beat.'

'Sure it does. Come on, let's dance.'

Amy looked around and saw that they were the last people there except for the barman. She didn't give a fuck what *he* thought.

'Okay.'

There was a tiny dance-floor on the other side of the pool table but there were no lights. It was even darker than where they'd been sitting. She looked at Gina for some input on the matter and their eyes met for longer than they should have.

'Yeah,' said Gina. 'That's where we should do it.'

She took Amy's hand and led her into the shadows. In Gina's smooth, cool grip, Amy felt real companionship. The closeness between them made her stomach flutter. Gina, eyes closed, one arm above her head, let the music bend her. She twisted at the waist, shifted her weight from one leg to the other, ground her hips. Amy watched, unable to move at first and hypnotised by the sinuous movements. Soon, she too closed her eyes and let the music have her body. She squeezed Gina's fingers and Gina squeezed back.

When the song ended, the dead silence swamped them. Amy let go of Gina's hand. When a new track started she didn't know what to do. Two hands reached for hers, closing the distance between them a little further. They danced again, this time becoming part of each other's movements. When Gina placed Amy's hands on her hips and put her own hands behind Amy's neck, Amy stopped thinking about the future and the past. She slipped deep into the exquisite moment. Their foreheads touched. They turned and turned.

When the songs finished they continued to move until Amy broke the contact.

'I need to go to the bathroom,' she said.

Returning from the too-bright ladies room, she found Gina standing by the door of the bar with both their handbags.

'Ready to go?' asked Gina.

'I could stay all night but I've got to work tomorrow. I ought to get home. Can I walk you somewhere?'

'How about your place?'

Amy hesitated. Could she really invite this girl home for—for what? Her confidence fled.

Gina made it easy for her:

'Hey, I understand if you don't want to. I mean: we hardly know each other, so—'

'It isn't that. It all just seems kind of strange and sudden. And now isn't the . . . best time. I want you to come back. I really do. It just feels weird.'

'Does it feel nice?'

'Yeah. It does.'

'That makes it okay, then,' said Gina. 'So, maybe I could meet you another night?'

Amy saw the disappointment in the girl's face but that wasn't what made her mind up.

'No. Come back now. I want you to. Just tell me one thing.'

'Anything.' said Gina.

'Will anyone miss you tonight? Come looking or whatever?'

'No, my folks are away for a while. They wouldn't care anyway, they're too busy to notice me most of the time.'

Amy held out her hand.

'Come on.'

Hobson's Valley was silent but for the thump of Gina's boots and the click of Amy's heels as they strolled arm in arm along the street-lit sidewalks.

'We'll go round the back way,' said Amy. 'It's quieter.'

She led the way from the street along the unlit passage beside the house and let them both in through the kitchen door. 'We can do whatever we want now,' she said, as she closed it and switched on the light. 'Make yourself at home. Want a coffee or anything?'

'Got any tequila?'

Amy rooted through the bottles in one of the kitchen cupboards until she found an old half-empty bottle of Sauza. She poured a golden shot for each of them.

'I don't have any lime.'

'Straight is fine,' said Gina. 'Let's drink to friendship.'

'To friendship.'

They slammed the drinks. Gina reached for Amy the moment they put their glasses down. She held Amy's head in tender hands and kissed her. Amy tasted lipstick and tequila, surprised by how similar it felt to kissing a man. As the kiss lengthened and deepened Amy stopped thinking and gave into it. She took hold of Gina's waist and pulled her closer. When she felt the soft pressure of their breasts meeting and flattening, she sighed in surprise and delight.

Gina pulled away and looked into her eyes.

'I want to spend the night with you,' she whispered.

Amy led her to the bedroom. They kissed again and Gina slipped off her leather jacket. She unbuttoned Amy's blouse and slipped it from her shoulders. Reaching behind Amy's back she unhooked her bra, drawing the straps away from her shoulders and releasing Amy's breasts. Gina touched the full rounded flesh with her fingertips before removing her own tee shirt. She wore no bra beneath it and Amy felt her heart flutter as she gazed at Gina's breasts. They were also full, but a little firmer than hers, the nipples pointing slightly upward. Gina's nipples were pink and tiny whereas her own were large and brown with broad aureoles. She held her own breasts in her hands and pushed them towards Gina's until their nipples touched. Her breath caught high in her chest, she moved her breasts over Gina's in tiny circles.

They embraced again, their kisses becoming hungrier, their hold on each other tightening. By the time they lay down they were naked, both moaning. Gina slipped down the bed and positioned herself between Amy's legs where she saw the crumpled string that protruded from her glistening sex.

'Wait,' said Amy. 'You can't do what I think you're going to do.'

'You can't let the moon interfere with your pleasure, Amy.'

'No, but you just can't—'

'Shhh. Just relax and enjoy.'

Gina sucked Amy's clitoris between her lips and into her mouth, tonguing it softly. Amy didn't protest. Not even when Gina pulled on the damp string leaving Amy unprotected. The explorations of her tongue were shallow to begin with but soon they went deep.

Very deep.

CHAPTER 16

Much to Maria Jimenez's surprise, it was Carla who discovered the old trail on the third morning of hiking along the deteriorated Eastern Path. José had come down hard on the girl for scaring Luis with her nonsense and Carla had hardly spoken since.

The trail became rougher that morning. José and the children had coped well but Maria, though she said nothing, had struggled to keep up. Her blisters had popped but she did her best not to let anyone see her limping. Twice today they'd been forced to remove their backpacks and clamber over fallen evergreens and Maria was beginning to believe, like her daughter, that they should turn back.

An hour and a half of trudging later, Maria noticed a change in the trees around them, particularly on the right hand side of the trail. The pines became less frequent giving way to many more broad-leafed trees, particularly oaks.

José paused often to study his old map beside the one Mr Kerrigan had given him. It prevented everyone from settling into a good walking rhythm but Maria didn't mind at all. Her feet were chafed and sore and it had been her who slept badly the previous night. Every break in their forced march was a chance for her to rest.

The night before, after they'd all crawled into their sleeping bags, Maria had mulled over what her daughter had said.

Instead of dropping into an exhausted sleep, as she should have, she became anxious. America was a land of guns and serial killers. There were huge wild spaces where the law held no sway, of which these mountains were a perfect example. Maria knew better than to entertain the same thoughts that had so upset Carla, but in the cramped space of the tent, there was suddenly nothing else to think about. Everyone around her had already fallen asleep. Something in her, a protective instinct perhaps, had kept her on the razor's edge between sleep and wakefulness throughout the whole night.

Maria heard a voice in those fitful hours. At least, she dreamed a voice. In the smothering darkness, she had become aware of the sound very far away and lay there uncertain if she was asleep or awake. Eyes open or closed, it made no difference to the blackness that surrounded her. The voice came again. It didn't sound like it was laughing. To Maria, it seemed that someone far away in the night was crying insane, desolate tears. The wind had breathed through the trees and the voice dissolved to become a part of that sighing.

As they halted yet again, Maria leaned her backpack against a tree trunk to ease the weight and wondered about this trip they were making. She knew José would not hear any opposition and that they would keep going until thwarted or successful but now, very suddenly and unquestionably, she wanted to go home. She watched the intense expression on her husband's face as he scrutinised his maps, looking up at the trail over and over again. It was for him that they were doing this. It was his grandfather who had lived in these hills, his bones they needed to return home. It was nothing to do with her.

'I want you all to keep your eyes to the right of this path.' said José. 'Look for anything that strikes you as unusual. We are trying to find an entrance that may have been obscured by many years of growth.'

He held both maps in his hands and walked more slowly

as he kept his attention on the trees. Over the next hour they covered no more than a quarter of a mile.

'Maria, what do you see?' he asked.

'I see trees and trees and trees. That is all.'

'Keep trying,' he said.

It wasn't until noon that they found it. José had begun to lose patience.

'I don't care if we have to stay out in these woods for two or three more days,' he said. 'We are not returning to the car until we find this trail.'

Carla called out.

'Hey, Papa, look at this.'

'What? What is it?'

'Look there.'

He followed the way her finger was pointing and stared for several moments.

'I don't see it. What are you showing me?'

'Look at those two trees,' Carla said, 'They are very similar, no?'

'Yes, but—'

'So, they are like a gateway. Maybe the start of the trail was marked like that. And look, there is a little more space between them than between the other trees.'

José shook his head, irritated at her foolishness.

'There is no space at all Carla,' he said. 'It is thick with vines and bushes. You cannot go through that.'

'Papa, you were the one who said it would be overgrown,' insisted Carla. 'Can't we chop away some of the growth?'

He considered it.

'You're right. We should try.'

Using the machete, José made an opening wide enough to stand in and peered into the green gloom.

'Yes, it could be . . .'

For a few minutes he hacked further into the thorns and brush until he was out of the sunshine and surrounded by older growth, dead now for lack of light. Slashing at these was easy, they snapped or shattered and he began to see that the trees were indeed spaced widely enough for a trail to have been there. He returned to find them all staring in after him.

'Well done, Carlita. You are now officially smarter than your father. You can lead the next expedition.'

After twenty minutes more he gave the blade to Luis who hacked hard but made little progress. He was followed by Carla and then Maria, both of whom tired quickly, before José took over again, providing the longest and most productive stint each time. They were creating not so much a trail but a tunnel of sorts, for the vegetation pressed close above and all around them.

'I feel like a mole,' Carla whispered.

José, too intent on making way, kept chopping. It was slow going.

After a couple of hours the mesh of creepers and brambles thinned and the trail opened up. José took the machete, wiped it clean and replaced it in its sheath in the webbing of his pack. Even though it was early afternoon, down here it was cool and shadowy. The trail was still covered by the lower branches of trees, still imprisoning them in a 'pipeline of vegetation'. It was broader and wider, though, and they were able to walk upright without thorns catching at their hair. Back in the other direction, the path they'd cut looked like a black shaft with no light at its end.

Trees crowded close on both sides, the spaces between them impenetrable and overgrown. The ground was littered with decaying fallen leaves many layers deep. The undisturbed air was silent and dusty with mould and spores. José was able to set a decent pace again and they followed him in single file. From time to time a solitary needle of sunshine would pierce the leafy strata above them and make contact with the ground.

The path curved gently, first to the right and then to

the left, making it impossible to see too far ahead. The one advantage was that they now seemed to be walking down a very slight slope that made the walking easy for a change.

Then the trail ended. José approached the blockage of twisting thorns and vines. The tangle of undergrowth began at ankle height and reached up to cling to the lower branches of the trees.

'Mierda.' He said.

Luis and Carla giggled.

'José, if we want to find a place to pitch camp we ought to go back now,' said Maria. 'There's no space to set the tent up here.'

'We'll find space on the other side of this.'

José swung his machete again and again, its blade some-times ringing out a clean steely note as it struck through the stems and tendrils, other times thumping dully as it con-nected with solid wood or the ground.

No one spoke.

Amy woke to the sound of her own heartbeat rushing in her ears. The ache in her head coincided with every pulse. Her mouth and throat were dried closed and there was a fat worm of nausea in her stomach. The hangover was far worse than she'd expected it to be.

As she lay twisted into the sheets, she went back over the evening in her mind. She remembered the sadness, the need to go out and escape it, the slimy barman. Then she remembered the girl, Gina, and the drinks and laughter. The dancing. Then the walk home, the last drink.

And the loving.

She tried to swallow. There was no moisture in her mouth at all. Her tongue seemed to rustle in its drying cavern, with-ered like a slug in the midday sun. She could hear the soft breathing of the girl and the weight of her body affecting the shape of the bed.

As quietly as she could, Amy swung her legs over the side

and crept to the bathroom closing the door behind her. In the mirror she caught sight of herself and gasped in shock. Her mascara had spread, ringing her eyes with black. She was pale beneath what little make up remained and the bruised crescents below her eyes made her look fifty. She filled a glass with water from the tap and drank it straight down. She took another and another until her mouth felt like it was rehydrating. She brushed her teeth and gargled mouthwash silently. Then she removed her make up and moisturised her face.

The urge to pee was last in order of importance. As she sat with her head in her hands, she remembered what Gina had done to her.

God, I'll be such a mess down there by now.

She wiped herself, expecting dried and fresh blood on the toilet tissue. There was nothing. Standing up she bent over and checked her thighs for the caked menstrual flow she knew would be there. She was clean. Her period had stopped the same day it started.

Gina scared it back into me.

She put her hand over her mouth to suppress a giggle and then crept out to the phone in the front room. All the curtains in the house were closed but she could tell from the blaze around their edges that the sun was bright that day and she didn't want to face it. She called in sick. Mr. Olsen was peeved at first but when she mentioned female problems he became flustered and hung up. Amy smiled to herself. Her head was clearing already.

In the bedroom, Gina hadn't moved. She slipped in beside her and snuggled in close. She felt Gina jump at the touch. Her body tensed. For a few seconds there was no movement from her at all then, in a determined flurry, Gina leapt from the bed and ran to the wall. Turning back with the sheets clutched to cover herself, she stared around the room, a look of incomprehension on her face.

Amy watched in shock from where she lay, still naked and now uncovered.

'Where the hell am I?' demanded the girl.

Amy had difficulty speaking.

'You're in my house, Gina. You wanted to come back with me.'

'Who are you? How do you know my name?'

Amy was incredulous.

'What?'

'Please,' said Gina, 'Just tell me what's going on.'

The girl was on the edge of tears. Amy's nausea returned as she realised that she'd done something unforgivable with a girl young enough to be her daughter. But it hadn't been like that. Amy remembered it all. Gina had made the first moves throughout the entire evening; she'd seduced Amy like a professional. So what was this turning into now? Blackmail? Amy turned an angry knife of regret against herself as she thought about how pathetic her relationships had become.

'Don't you remember anything at all?' she asked.

'No. I want to know why you were in that bed with me. I want to know why we're both naked.' Gina's voice was gaining in volume and escalating in pitch. 'I want to know what the fuck is happening here.'

CHAPTER 17

'Take it easy, Gina. You want me to tell you what happened? Fine. But calm down, okay? We can discuss this without the help of the neighbours.'

'No one's going to calm down. No one is going to take it easy until you explain what the fuck you've done to me.'

Gina's eyes were wide, the whites showing. Her body was shaking and her face was pale. Amy's stomach tightened and her pulse quickened in response. She began to ease herself back out of the bed. She wanted to stand, to bring herself to the same height as Gina and put some distance between them.

'Don't you move,' Gina said. 'What are trying to do?'

'I'm not trying to do anything. You're scaring me and I'm backing off.'

'I'm the one who's scared here. I'm the one whose been fucking kidnapped. You tell me what happened.'

'You picked me up in Mulligan's last night. You bought me a drink. We talked and I bought you a drink. Any of this sound familiar?'

'No it doesn't. Keep going.'

'We had a few beers and you asked to come home with me. You said you wanted to spend the night here and . . .'

'And what?'

'Please, Gina. You're making this so hard. We had a great

time right up until we fell asleep. I don't understand why you're being like this.'

'I'm making it hard? I am? You know what I think? I think you drugged me. God knows what you did to me after that, you fat fucking dyke.'

'How can you talk like this, Gina? You picked me up. You made passes at *me*.'

Gina was shaking her head so hard in denial that her hair whipped across her face. Her voice dropped an octave and became a strangled snarl.

'You raped me and you're going to pay.'

Through the curtains the sun glowed orange but the room remained in shadow. Even that dim light hurt Amy's eyes. There was a coldness spreading through her now, something separate from her fear and anger. With it came a resolve to fight her corner. How dare the crazy bitch call her fat? After all the things they'd said and done the night before, it was too hurtful to be tolerated.

And now the girl was threatening violence.

Amy's mix of emotions was hard to keep track of. She felt anger at the insults and dismissals of the night's importance. She felt shame at being alone in her enjoyment of it. Something else was building inside her too: that coldness. An ice calm rage and the urge to silence the girl who had made her feel all of it. But Gina was changing. In the orange dimness of Amy's room something was happening to her.

Her head began to stretch. Her oval face, so beautiful the night before, elongated; the chin protruding further and further forward until it hooked back on itself like the jaw of a barracuda. Her skin became glassy and luminescent. Beneath it, Amy saw veins of purple pulsating with diseased light. The top of Gina's head extended upwards and backwards and her long dark hair fell away in wet strands. When her hair hit the floor it shrank and decomposed to a puff of vapour that shone pale lilac in the evanescence from her skin.

Gina dropped the sheet and Amy saw her legs and arms lengthening, making her taller until she had to crouch to prevent her head from touching the ceiling. The changes looked and sounded agonising. Gina was screaming and howling in a strange language. From her mouth, with its vicious lower mandible, spilled a writhing purple tongue that stretched down to her veined belly and flicked at the air. A second snakelike appendage uncoiled wetly from her vagina.

Similar, smaller tongues burst from many other patches of skin and waved in the air like roots seeking water. Bony purple spikes tore outward from her breasts and shoulders, from her buttocks and hips, all of them curving forward like some combination of armour and weaponry. Amy stood, pressed against the sliding doors of her wardrobe

I'm out of time.

Amy dived for the doorway.

The moment she moved Gina lashed out with her tongues. Amy surprised herself with her own speed and made it to the hall. She caught the door and slammed it shut behind her as she passed through. There was no way to stop Gina from following but it would slow her down. All Amy could do was run for the nearest way out which was the door in the kitchen.

The kitchen curtains were flimsy. The glare from the sun almost blinded her. As Amy neared the door an effervescent glow awoke in her bones. She paused. The heat and buzz swelled, becoming a discomfort. When she reached for the security chain, she screamed in protest and withdrew. The light brought agony to every cell of her body, a scorching current she was unable to bear.

She collapsed to her knees. The sound of thumping and slithering came from the bedroom. Amy turned away from the light and withdrew a long-bladed carving knife from its wooden block. She crawled from the kitchen towards the hallway again, hardly able to support her own weight. Her eyes watered and her nostrils stung.

Something was burning.

She reached up to her hair and pulled away a handful of scorched fibres. Some of it had only melted: the rest had roasted away. With what strength she had left she stood and dived, more with her weight than her muscles, past the closed bedroom door.

It opened at the same moment and two tongues wormed out, grasping at her like tentacles. Claws appeared on the doorframe followed by a stretched, swollen head. The Gina creature winced when she sensed the light from the kitchen and Amy, her strength returning now that she was out of the glare, swung her knife at the lower of the two tongues as she staggered away down the hall. Turning back, she saw the tongue hanging by a flap of tissue. Gina was clutching its root, back near her groin and moaning in her unreal dialect.

Still backing away, Amy saw the damaged section of lingual flesh reattach itself to the rest of its length. The wound sealed over.

Amy had one place left to hide. She lunged for the other door that led off the hallway into the small storage room that should have been a second bedroom. She banged the door closed and locked it, wedging the back of a chair underneath the handle. She stared at the handle, panting.

In this room there was one small window. Not much light came through the curtains. Not satisfied, Amy placed a huge, ugly oil painting she'd bought in a garage sale against the curtains. Instead of finding it harder to see, her eyesight improved. She stuffed old clothes and blouses around the edges of the painting until the room was as almost dark. The iciness within her deepened and, though it frightened her at first, it was accompanied by such a vibrant pleasure that she felt something close to sexual arousal despite her fear.

She sat on the carpet with her back to the wall and faced the door. Outside, Gina was silent.

Amy waited for a long time. She found herself thinking of the forest. She thought of the shadowy trails and paths and the thickness of the trees bearing in against her and to begin with it was good. Then she remembered Jimmy and the well-spring he'd taken her to and she was filled with repulsion at the thought of that water and the memory of his touch. She never wanted to see him again. The bed-pissing baby was too much of a coward to know how to make her happy

After hours of drifting in silence, Amy returned suddenly to wakefulness. The doorknob was turning. She gripped the handle of the kitchen knife and stood up. Still naked and undisturbed by the fact, she waited for the creature to burst through the cheap wood of the door. The creature was all she could remember of the past day. How it had come to be in her house she no longer knew.

'Miss Cantrell? Amy? You in there?'

She jumped at the voice and then relaxed when she realised who it was. She reached for an old bathrobe from the cupboard, one she hadn't worn for years. It smelled dusty, as if it belonged to someone much older or someone who had passed away. She caught sight of herself in the mirrored door as she closed the cupboard and reached up to her head. Her hair was undamaged. She drew the robe tightly around herself as she answered.

'Is that you, Mrs Fredericks?'

'Why, yes. Are you okay in there? I can't open the door. You're not stuck are you?'

'No, I'm not. Hold on a second.'

She removed the chair, unlocked the door and then stood with the knife behind her back as she twisted the handle and opened the door very slowly.

'It's okay, Amy, it's only me.'

For the first time in her life Amy felt glad to see Maggie Fredericks, her curtain-twitching next-door neighbour. She peeked out into the hall to be sure, but they were alone.

'I saw your door was open and you didn't seem to be around. I've never seen you leave it that way before, so I thought I'd better check.'

'You did right, Mrs Fredericks. I appreciate it.'

'What happened to you, dear? You look kind of spacey.'

'I wasn't feeling well. After I called in sick today, I must have left a door open. Thought I heard someone in the house, that's why I locked myself in here.'

Maggie turned pale at the suggestion.

'An intruder? My stars, child, should we call the police?'

Amy looked down at the floor behind her neighbour's feet and saw a scrawny old black tomcat that must have followed her in.

'Oh no, don't do that,' she said. 'I wouldn't want to waste their time.' She pointed at the cat. 'There's my intruder. I guess he must have knocked some stuff over in the kitchen. Sounded like a burglar.'

Maggie looked down and tutted in an embarrassed tone. She stamped her foot and the cat tore out of the house.

'I owe you an apology, Amy. That's a wild cat I've been hoping to tame. Probably the only reason he came in here is because I've been encouraging him. I'm a sucker for cats but that doesn't hold true for everyone. You see him again, you just shake a broom at him.'

'Well, I'll remember to be more forceful next time,' said Amy, suddenly feeling embarrassed. 'I can't imagine how dumb all this must look to you.'

'Don't you worry about it, dear.' said Maggie, patting Amy's arm, 'I get scared every night when I turn those lights out. I imagine there are creatures out there in the dark waiting to come for me. I can't stop myself. It's my imagination and I just can't control it. Us single ladies have got it rough with no man to cling to at night.'

Amy didn't reply. She didn't hold men in quite the regard that Maggie Fredericks obviously did and there was no point saying so.

'You want me to stay with you a while?' asked her elderly neighbour. 'We could watch The Wheel together and eat some popcorn.'

'Thanks, but I'll be okay now. You've already done enough.'

'It'd be no trouble at all.'

'I'll be fine.'

Amy smiled at the older woman and realised with a rush of satisfaction that something had changed for the better in her life. She was never going to be a lonely, overweight woman with nothing to do but snoop. She showed Maggie to the door and out into the twilight. Amy could sense that Gina was gone. She would be safe from now on. It was early dusk and a violet haze had settled over the street along with a pleasant chill.

As Maggie retreated reluctantly back to her own house, Amy felt drawn towards the woods. There was a hunger within her. She smiled into the strengthening gloom.

To her it felt like dawn.

CHAPTER 18

Maria watched José hack and slash through the wild overgrowth choking the path and wondered where his determination came from. It took less than half an hour but to her it seemed much longer.

'Papa, I can see something on the other side,' said Carla.

'Yes, I see it too,' he said.

'Do you think it is more of the trail?'

'No. I think we have found what we came here for. Stay out of the way until I finish this. I don't want you to lose an ear.'

As José cleared the last few branches and vines obscuring the path, an unusual clearing came into view. He stepped forward into the space they'd discovered. Maria hesitated before walking in after him, followed by the children.

They stood at the edge of a grassless expanse of ground that was roughly circular and about the size of a cathedral. At the centre of the space was a huge tree, the largest tree Maria had ever seen. Its canopy formed the 'ceiling' of the cathedral. The edges of the clearing marked the distance to which its branches and leaves extended. The tree's foliage kept the entire space in deep shadow. It looked like some sort of oak, but Maria was no expert.

'Dios mio,' José murmured.

He crossed himself and Maria followed his lead.

The ground beneath the enormous branches was covered

in many layers of leaves; they must have fallen from this single tree for hundreds of years.

'I have never seen anything like this. It's miraculous,' said José.

Maria shook her head.

'It is monstrous.'

'Mama,' said Carla, mock scolding her, 'it is beautiful. We have found the most magnificent tree in creation.'

'We could make a rope swing,' said Luis.

Carla nudged her brother in the ribs and they laughed.

'Last one around the tree and back is a gimp,' said Carla. She dropped her backpack and tore away before Luis could grab her. He slung his pack to the ground and sprinted after her.

'Where do they learn such words?' asked Maria.

'I cannot say but I suspect it is this country. I will be glad when we are sitting in front of our fire eating your potage and drinking decent wine again.'

'You will? Truly?'

'Of course, why?'

Maria sighed.

'I thought you might be thinking of moving here. You seem to like it so much.'

'I could never live here, Maria. I have been excited to find my grandfather's resting place, but it has not been an easy trip for any of us.'

'Why couldn't you at least have let me know your feelings?'

'I'm telling you now. It is only now that I realise how ready I am to head for home. And I could not let any of you think that it was hard for me, otherwise there would have been no leadership, no head for the body to follow.'

'I could kick you, José. But I am so glad to know you are still a human being that I will kiss you instead.'

The kids reached the tree's trunk and disappeared behind it. Maria used the moment to give her husband the kind of kiss that had become a rarity during the course of the holiday.

The kids reappeared and raced back towards them covering the distance very quickly. Carla won the race.

'Gimp! You're a gimp, Luis! How does it feel?' she taunted, breathless and happy.

'You cheated. No more head starts.'

Luis was flushed and panting.

'Listen, everyone,' said José, 'we need to get this tent up and the dinner ready before it gets too dark. If we work together there may be time to take a closer look at this incredible tree and make a preliminary search for your great grandfather before bedtime. Otherwise we'll have to leave our fun until tomorrow.'

The kids were still intrigued by the prospect of finding the bones of their ancestor—or even just a gravestone marking his last resting place. The tent was ready quickly, positioned right at the edge of the arbour, and Maria was able to prepare hot water and food on the camping stove.

'Can we go look at the tree?' asked Luis.

'Five minutes only and don't wander off,' said José.

'Aren't you coming?' asked Carla.

'No, I want to see it in its full glory. I'll wait until the morning. Be quick now.'

They ran to the tree and Maria stared after them. They remained just visible in the twilight as they inspected the enormous trunk. She watched with her arms folded.

'I don't like it when they go off alone like that.'

'Don't be silly, Maria. They're right in front of us.'

'Still. I'm not comfortable in this place.'

'I thought it was Carla who had a problem.' said José. Maria silenced him with a look.

'Keep your eye on them while I do this,' she said.

José didn't argue. Unsheathing the machete, he played a whetstone along its blade, honing it back to the razor edge it possessed before the trail breaking had begun.

Maria laid out the plastic plates for the meal and checked the temperature of the beans and hot dogs they would be eating. Each day the packs got lighter as they used up the supply of tinned, bagged and dried foods. She sniffed the steam from the meal she'd made with distaste.

'If we walk quickly on the way back, maybe we could reach Hobson's Valley the day after tomorrow,' she said. 'Then we can all eat some fresh fruit and vegetables. Segar's Cabin looked better than a lot of the other places we've seen. We could spend the night there and try their restaurant before we drive back to Nampa.'

She doled out piles of food onto each of the plates, making sure the portions were perfectly equal.

'You can call them back now.'

It was only as she poured the water for coffee that she realised the sound of José scraping the machete blade had stopped. She glanced up. He was no longer sitting there. Rising to her feet, she saw him racing across to the tree, the long knife still clutched in his hand. It gave off dull flashes and a whooshing sound with each sprinted step. The noise and flashing diminished as he ran. The darkness was descending swiftly by then but Maria could still see that only two members of her family were standing. The other was lying unmoving on the leaf-covered ground.

Then Maria was running too.

Kath had taken to sitting for hours at a time on her front porch overlooking the Terrace.

As she watched the kids play in the street in the afternoons she thought of her own childhood right there in the valley. Once she'd been just as full of energy and innocence as any of the children that lived there now. Some of them might die young but most would likely live to an age at which they'd sit on porches wondering where their lives had gone.

The sheer plainness and inevitability of it all weighed her down. Nothing anyone could do would change a single thing. There was a matter-of-factness about the rules of life that had always made her a little blue. Now that Burt was gone, it made her unhappier than ever.

At the hospital, a nurse had passed her some leaflets about bereavement and the grieving process. Kath had wanted to rip them up and throw them in the girl's face. What could a nurse know about losing someone she'd spent most of her life with? And who had written those leaflets, some young pup with a crisp new degree? She'd held the rage back but had crushed the leaflets in her hand as Maggie had driven them home.

Without Burt around, Kath had taken to spending almost the entire day outside. Partly because being indoors reminded her of him. Every room she entered had his smell or his imprint upon it somewhere. She needed to be free of that. It was bad enough lying all night in the double bed without him wheezing away beside her. The silence stopped her sleeping.

So Kath watched The Terrace for hours at a time.

It was strange to watch the street drain of activity and become deserted but that was what happened each day when the sun dipped beyond the mountain. She'd never noticed it until these last few days. But then, when she thought harder about it, she realised that one way or another, people in the valley had always escaped the twilight by heading indoors. She'd spent so many of these last few years inside she'd forgotten how it was. Now she wanted to see the twilight again, to experience it the way she never had.

With her hands folded into her lap, she watched the day dying out of the valley. The silence of the Terrace deepened with the ebbing of the light but in the green spaces between the houses, other sounds were starting. Crickets rasped out coded communications and turtledoves called their simple love songs to each other. Far away she heard the skittering squall of a quail.

The only life in the town now was behind its doors. Outside, the valley haze stretched invasive fingers across the forest and into the town, giving Kath a sense of greater beings than humans, spirits that lived in stone or stood in trees, and the giant mind of the mist that laid itself like sleep across the land.

The temperature dropped making Kath shiver. They'd been lucky with the weather this year but it couldn't last. Summer would turn to winter without pause for fall when the time came. Kath could feel the ice in the air. Perhaps it would snow soon. It seemed odd to think of snow when the valley had been so warm. Kath was aware she was readying herself for longer nights and the gloom that would grip the town for so many months. She'd made this mental preparation all her life but this was the first time she'd caught herself and understood why.

On the other side of the street, in the half-light she thought she saw movement. The Terrace had become so deserted that the idea of a person being outdoors at this time of the day almost frightened her. It was a woman. She walked as if she had no intention of arriving anywhere. In the dimming light that was about all Kath could make out. She couldn't see the woman's face but she seemed to be wearing unusual clothes.

The woman came to one of the trees that lined the Terrace and stopped. Although Kath hadn't moved, the woman seemed aware she was being watched. She scanned Kath's side of the street. Had they been near enough to each other, Kath would have said their eyes locked but at this distance, she felt the connection more than she could see it. She thought about waving to dispel any suspicion and to break the moment but couldn't quite bring herself to move. She was within her rights to watch the street, after all. If the woman didn't like it, well, tough.

The woman stepped away from the tree, letting her hand linger as though she didn't want to let go of anything while the rest of her body moved on. She walked out onto the street at that same meandering pace, like she'd never even heard of cars. As she came closer, Kath saw her blonde hair and realised she looked so strange because she was wearing a bathrobe. She wore nothing on her feet. She scuffed her feet over the rough surface of the road and looked like she might change her mind and go somewhere else. Everything she touched or saw distracted her.

When she reached the side of the Terrace on which Kath sat, the woman paused and looked back from where she'd come. She turned towards Kath before casting her gaze up and down the street. Kath became aware of just how deserted Hobson's Valley was at this time of day. Then, when it seemed like they were the only two people in the world, she heard an engine coming their way from out of town. The woman heard it too and stared along the road. The car slowed, its revs decreasing as it entered the residential area and a few moments later it passed them. It was a red Ford Explorer. Kath didn't recognise the driver. The engine sound faded further into town, turning off the main street somewhere in the distance. Then the silence returned.

The woman turned towards Kath.

She was close enough that she could have said 'hi' and been heard easily. Kath wondered if she should get herself indoors. She'd left it too late, though. First she'd have to struggle up from the rocker and it would take her a few moments before she could walk comfortably. Then she'd have to make it to the front door and get inside before the woman ran the few steps from the kerbside to the porch. Why she hadn't moved earlier she didn't know. Now, she was stuck.

'Hi there,' she said after too long. 'You okay?'

The woman didn't answer for almost a minute.

'Yeah. I wanted to feel the twilight. Can you feel it?'

It was strange talk; crazy talk perhaps, but Kath felt better now that they weren't just staring at each other.

'I guess I can. You need any help, ma'am? You look a little lost.'

'No, I'm not lost. I know where I am. I know where I'm going.'

'Where *are* you going?' asked Kath.

'To the forest.'

'Uh huh. Well, the forest is the other way. You're heading out of town.' Was having this conversation the right way to go? Maybe she ought to get herself inside and call the law instead.

'The forest is all around us. Out of town *is* the forest.'

Kath didn't want to argue with the woman's peculiar logic. Now that she'd had a chance to see her a little closer, she thought she recognised her. She'd seen her working at Olsen's in the days when she could still be bothered to shop there.

'Sure it is,' she agreed and then, as if it was urgent added, 'I've got to be getting some supper ready. Guess I'll see you.'

Kath took the opportunity to stand. It wasn't easy. She'd been sitting there for so long that her ass was numb and her legs were cold and stiff. Still, she pushed herself upright and began to walk towards her front door. In those long moments she didn't look back towards the street but she felt the woman watching her. She didn't like the way it felt to be watched like that and didn't think she was imagining the dynamic between them; stalker and prey.

She fumbled at the door handle, her fingers failing to gain the necessary purchase. All the time she felt the insistent eyes on her back, waited for the hand to fall upon her shoulder and spin her around. She managed to grip the handle and turn it. Leaning her weight against the door, it opened and she turned to close it before the woman could make her play. Through the glass panes in the door she saw the woman still standing on the sidewalk staring. She hadn't moved. Kath drew a small drape across the door and backed away.

CHAPTER 19

Was the woman dangerous?

Or am I just scaring easier now I'm on my own?

Maybe the woman was drunk or high or something. Maybe she meant no harm at all. Hell, for all Kath knew, the woman could be depressed or confused. She was probably more in need of help than she was of a ride in a police car. But Kath had closed her door and that was that. She turned the lock over.

The feeling was slowly returning to her backside, making her realise how much it ached from sitting so long. She kneaded her soft loose flesh and felt the bones beneath. They seemed more prominent than ever and she sighed at her advancing frailty. What a thing it was to be young and what a terrible thing it was to lose that youth. None of her musings out on the porch made any of it easier. Maybe thinking about things too much would always lay a person low.

A cup of hot chocolate and a crossword puzzle was the only remedy she could think of for the blues. She went to the kitchen, still dragging her feet a little, to put on a pan of milk. Dingbat was nowhere around; he tended to spend most of every day out back, prowling through their overgrown acre of ground. It had featured a lawn and vegetable patch until a few years previously, but now it was a jungle; Dingbat's kingdom.

She took a pan down from a hook above the stove and brought out a carton of milk from the fridge. Closing the fridge she turned back to the stove and dropped the milk. It hit the floor and split, spraying a brief white explosion across the tiles and then bleeding the rest of its contents more sedately into a spreading creamy pool.

The woman was looking in at her through the back door.

Kath's hands went to her heart as it lurched and fluttered in her chest before finding a rapid rhythm and beating it out hard enough that she felt a small stab with each thump. She prayed that she'd remembered to lock the back door but didn't dare try and cover the distance. The woman would beat her so easily there was no point trying. They stared at each other for what felt like minutes and, as each one passed, the daylight faded further, draining all colour from the kitchen as it went.

Because she was so still, Kath began to think once more that the woman just needed help. That notion gave her courage. Her heart settled down a little and she found her voice.

'I thought you were headed for the forest.'

'I am.'

'You won't find it in here, sweetheart.'

But the woman's reply was more crazy logic.

'The forest is in everything. It's inside me. Wherever I go, the forest is there.'

Kath had to find a way of getting rid of this woman.

'Is there something I can help you with?'

'Yes. You can help me.'

The woman reached out and twisted the doorknob. Kath watched as the door swung inwards and the woman stepped into the kitchen. The door slammed shut behind her. Kath felt the milk soaking through her house slippers. The woman looked at her. She seemed normal in every way but there was something wrong with her that Kath couldn't define. It wasn't just the trance she was in; her body seemed wrong but in the gloom Kath couldn't see why. The woman stepped towards her and Kath backed away. She had nothing to protect herself with. The knives were out of reach in the drawer and the broom was in the cupboard.

Dingbat barrelled through the dog flap and took hold of the woman's calf. She whirled and tried to lash out at the dog, but every time she moved Dingbat backed up, pulling her with him.

The voice that came from her then wasn't human. Kath recognised the language from a hundred interrupted nights when Jimmy was a child. She shivered to hear the language spoken in such cruel tones. Even though the words were unintelligible, the woman spat curses of pure hatred. Kath had her opportunity now; she could reach for the knives if she wanted to, but she knew the woman would be too strong for her. She'd die by her own blade. All Kath could think of was the necklace Jimmy had given her. She reached between the buttons of her blouse and held it out.

Something was happening to the woman. It was difficult to discern exactly what in the near darkness. Her fingers lengthened, her head changed shape. She sprayed Kath with spittle as she poured forth her incomprehensible abuse and laughed when she saw the necklace. But Kath approached and the woman pulled away. Whatever changes she was going through stopped. Dingbat continued to shake the leg he held in his jaws but ended up shaking himself because the woman was now too strong for him. His teeth were doing damage though, and the woman slashed at him with her newly grown claws as Kath approached.

They reached the back door and the woman seemed not to know how to open it. Instead she pressed back against it and held her hands up to protect herself. In the gloom, her skin appeared to take on a hint of purple. Kath took the necklace off and brought it towards the cowering woman as she sank down towards the floor with her hands over her head. She looked like she expected to be beaten to death with clubs.

Kath touched the charm to an exposed part of the woman's head. There was a thump and an amethyst flash that blinded Kath. She flew back from the woman as if she'd stood on a land mine and fell in the spilled milk, lying still in the dusk's deep shadows.

Kath couldn't tell how much time passed before she could move again, but when she did she was in a lot of pain. Dingbat must have been whining and nuzzling at her for a while because the kitchen was in darkness.

Once she'd managed to stand, she turned on the kitchen light to find the woman still unconscious beside the back door. She looked peaceful and Kath prayed she hadn't killed her.

'You think she's okay, Dingbat?'

The dog whined and crept forward to sniff the unmoving body. He licked the woman's face. She stirred and was soon trying to escape Dingbat's resuscitation technique. He only wagged his tail and tried harder to revive her.

'That's enough, boy,' said Kath. 'You come to me now.'

The woman looked around her, and pulled her bathrobe tighter.

'Where am I?' she asked.

'You're in the Kerrigan residence.'

'You're Kath Kerrigan?'

Kath was surprised.

'Yes I am. Do you know me?'

'I know—I knew your son, Jimmy.'

'I see.'

The woman looked confused, embarrassed.

'What happened to me?' she asked.

'Don't you remember anything at all?'

'No. Not really. I remember thinking what a beautiful afternoon it was.'

'Do you remember going for a walk?'

'Maybe. I don't know.'

142

Kath walked over and helped the woman up. There was no sign of Dingbat's bite wounds on her leg.

'Sit down over here,' said Kath pointing to a kitchen chair.

'I don't want to sit. Can you just tell me what happened?'

Kath didn't hesitate.

'Sure, sweetheart. I heard a knock on the back door and saw you standing on the back porch. I opened the door and you just fainted right where you are.'

'That's it? What about all this mess on the floor?'

'Well, I was making myself some hot chocolate. I don't get many visitors and your knock just about finished my heart off forever. I dropped the milk.'

'Oh. God, I'm so sorry. Are you okay?'

'When I've cleaned up and get that pan boiling, I'll be just fine.'

The woman took a half step forward.

'Can I help you with it?'

'Oh no,' said Kath, backing away. 'Won't take me but a minute. You better get home before you catch cold.'

The woman looked down at her bathrobe and bare feet and blushed. Kath gestured towards the back door and the woman moved to leave. She looked small and lost as she stepped into the back yard.

'Listen, do you want me to call one of your friends or something? Maybe the doctor?' Kath asked.

The woman turned back.

'No, I feel fine now. I'll be okay. My name's Amy by the way.' She offered her hand and they shook. 'Jimmy always talked about you and Burt. Said how great you were. Is your husband here?'

Kath thought she saw a hint of purple return to the woman's eyes.

'I think you'd better be going,' She said.

She didn't watch Amy walk away.

When she'd locked all the doors and checked all the

windows, she mopped up the kitchen. There wasn't too much to do; Dingbat had licked up most of the milk by then.

'You've been a brave, brave boy. I think you may have saved my life.'

CHAPTER 20

Nicholas and Isobel Priestly sat opposite their daughter in the living room of the home they'd built themselves after years of overtime and saving every dollar they could. The silence continued. Nicholas plucked at the hairs of his goatee until Isobel shot him a tight-lipped stare. As soon as she looked away he started again.

'What is it, Geen?' asked her mother. 'We want you to know that you can tell us anything. All we want is to help and to see you happy again.'

'I can't ever be happy.'

'Come on, honey,' said Nicholas. 'Whatever you're going through is bound to seem bad when you're in the middle of it. But in a few hours or days you'll feel better, I promise.'

'Oh, you promise, Dad?'

'Sure I do.'

Gina shook her head and began to cry. Nicholas glanced to Isobel for support.

'Your daddy's right, Geen. Nothing's ever as bad as it seems at first. You're going to start feeling better the moment you get some of this worry off your chest. We support you, we're on your side and anything you need to say will stay between us only. Within these walls. Okay?'

Gina nodded. Nicholas held out a box of tissues to her. She took one, blew her nose and let her hands fall into her lap. He waited for her to look up, a little brighter, but she couldn't meet his gaze.

'I think there's something wrong with me.'

'What kind of thing?' asked Isobel.

'It's so difficult to explain. It's like I'm sick or something.'

Nicholas was already adding things up in his mind—the mood swings, the change in diet; it was all familiar. He sat forward.

'It's not the weight thing again, is it?'

Gina's sobs, having been under control for only a few moments became worse and she shook her head, her hair hiding her face.

'For God's sake, Nick, shut up and let her tell us in her own way.'

'Sure.' He sank back into the sofa. 'Okay.'

Gina looked up at them, her eyes raw and red, her makeup smeared and running.

'I have these. . .gaps. . .in my memory. They're getting worse, I think.'

She blew her nose again. As Nicholas watched her he could see that his daughter had grown up, perhaps in some moment when he hadn't been paying attention. She looked mature.

'How long has this been going on for?' He asked.

Isobel took hold of his arm.

'Nick, please.'

He shook her hand off.

'We need to know. Well, Gina?'

'Not long. Two, maybe three weeks. But I'm getting real scared now.'

Silence again. Nicholas wiped his palm over his mouth, pinched his lower lips in his fingers. He pointed a finger at his daughter and waded in.

'What drugs have you taken? '

Gina snorted; a sad half laugh as if she knew the question would come.

'I've smoked pot since I was fourteen. Not every day but definitely every weekend. It's never done anything more than make me giggle a little and think a lot about the meaning of life. I don't do any other drugs. I never have and I don't plan to.'

Nicholas was shocked by the directness of the admission, but this was not a time for recrimination.

'Okay. What else?'

'There is nothing else. Nothing wrong with my friends or anything like that.'

'What about this meat fetish you've suddenly developed?' asked Isobel, 'Is that anything to do with this?'

'What are you talking about?'

'Come on, Gina, you've been asking for and eating nothing but beef and pork for the last three weeks.'

Gina looked at them, her eyes owlish with fear.

'I didn't realise. I do that at every meal?'

'Yes.'

Gina's head sank down until she was bent double into her own lap with her hands over her face.

'Oh God, oh God, oh God,' she whispered, 'What is fucking wrong with me?'

Nicholas stood up and took a place beside Gina on the sofa. Isobel followed, sitting on Gina's other side. They both placed their hands on her back. All Nicholas felt for several minutes was Gina's body shaking with spasmodic bursts of crying. When it had subsided a little, he spoke to her.

'We can talk about this some more later, honey. You don't have to do it all now.'

Gina sat up again and looked at her father.

'We have to talk about it now. Before I forget again.'

'Well, what else is there?' he asked.

She sighed.

'I've been waking up in strange places.'

'What places?'

'In the woods. Other people's houses. I have no idea how I

147

get there or why I went. I just have this sense that something terrible has happened. That I'm responsible.'

There was a pause. When Isobel spoke, Nicholas could tell she was trying to keep all emotion from her voice. But all he heard was dread.

'What terrible things do you mean?'

'I don't know, mom. I just don't know.'

'Think back to when it started. What were you doing? Where were you? Do you remember the first time it happened?'

'Jesus, mom, I already told you I don't . . .'

Gina stopped shaking her head in denial and looked up.

'What is it?' asked Isobel.

'Have I trained in the last three weeks?'

Nicholas didn't need to think long. It was on of the first things they'd noticed.

'No. Not for almost exactly three weeks. Why?'

'It's something to do with that.'

'I don't understand, Gina,' said Nicholas.

'I was running in the forest. Something happened. That's where this started, I know it.'

Nicholas thought it over for a few moments.

'Maybe you fell and knocked yourself out. That would explain a lot of this. You could be suffering the after effects of a serious concussion.'

'Did you have a headache or a lump on your head anywhere?' asked Isobel.

'No. It's something else. I feel like I lost something. Something real important.'

Nicolas frowned.

'Lost something? What the hell does that mean, Gina?' He stood up and paced to the window before turning back. 'Can you tell us anything more about who else might have been out there that day? What time it was? Who saw you running? Anything at all?'

Gina thought about it for a while.

'I left here around four in the afternoon, I guess. I remember thinking it was a little later than I usually go. That kind of purple haze was already out and I ran a little faster than usual because it gave me the creeps.'

'Which trail did you take?'

'The Eastern Path, I think. That's the one I like best.'

'Do you run past that guy's place out on the edge of the forest there?' asked Nicholas. 'What's his name?'

'Jimmy Kerrigan,' said Isobel. 'God damn, I'm sure he's got something to do with this.'

'Take it easy, Izzy. We don't know enough about this yet. He may not even have been there.'

'He's always there. Typing away in front of that window. And when he's not there he spends way too much time in those woods.'

'That's enough, Isobel. We're going to do this the right way if we do it at all. You can't accuse a man of something when you have no evidence. That's how people in small towns get hurt.' He turned back to his daughter. 'What else happened, Gina?'

'Daddy, I swear I don't remember anything much after I reached the Clearing and turned onto the Eastern Path. I still wasn't warmed up by the time I got there but—

—feeling cold was no reason to stop running or turn back. It was a reason to increase the pace. The willingness to respond to a challenge in that way was what had turned her life around eighteen months earlier. Gina could have given into the bulge the way so many other kids seemed to but that wasn't how she saw her future.

I will be beautiful. I will be desirable. I will be happy.

She said the words to herself over and over. In the morning when she woke up and again at night before she fell asleep, changing the ocean of her subconscious a droplet at a time from negative to positive. When she ran, the affirmations became her mantra. And there she was, curvaceous but strong;

flat stomached, full breasted and with no sign of fat in her face.

It was easy to run faster when she thought of all the good things that had happened since she began to change her thoughts. It was so simple, and yet she seemed to be the only one who knew the secret.

Boys asked her for dates all the time now and she agreed often. Usually she only went once, sampled a little of what popularity and beauty tasted like and left it at that. But her desires were flowering and she wanted more of everything.

Her ponytail bounced from side to side behind her head. She wore black leggings and a sleeveless black spandex top that showed the strength of her shoulders. A support bra, essential because of her build, kept her breasts from moving too much.

Her rhythm settled and she repeated the words in time with her steps and her breaths. The mantra had changed, of course

I am beautiful, I am desirable, I am happy

The buzz it created was sublime. The physical effort of running began to recede from her awareness the way the sensation of clothing against the skin disappears seconds after dressing

She was about ten minutes along the Eastern path, reflecting as she often did on what a shame it was that there were no circular trails, when she noticed a figure coming towards her far ahead on the broad track. It looked like an old man. She thought she could make out his white hair and gaunt frame but that was all.

Her speed meant she approached him quickly. He wasn't merely skinny; he was painfully thin, something she never wanted to be, and his clothes were ancient and tattered. She figured he must be some kind of hobo living wild, but how he could survive out there with so little protection she couldn't imagine. She saw his bare feet and her curiosity grew. Should she stop and lose the rhythm of her run for that day? Getting back into it would be hard. As she approached she saw his eyes, bright, intelligent, furtive. She slowed and stopped a few feet ahead of him on the path.

He backed away from her.

'Hi.' she said. 'You from around here?' She gestured into the

forest. The man followed the movement of her hand. She thought he nodded but she couldn't be sure if she'd imagined it or not.

'Uh, you look like you could use a decent meal and some clothes. I could maybe get some stuff for you. Would you want me to do that?'

For a long moment they stared at each other. Gina looked away first, noticing that the light really was beginning to leave the valley

'Okay, well . . . I gotta go now.'

She didn't wait for a response this time. She turned away and she ran.

She was three or four miles from home and the twilight was taking hold. Mist seeped from between the trees like violet-tinged dry ice. Everything was cast in shadow. She risked a look back. The old man was where she'd left him, but as she watched, running backwards for a few steps, she saw the man fall to his hands and knees. She thought he was sick until he pursued her on all fours. He covered the ground between them like a cheetah. Disgust and fear rose in her, adrenaline flooded her bloodstream and she broke into a sprint. Behind her there was laughter; too soon the sound of hands and feet against the earth and the panted breaths of a predator. She wanted to scream but she knew it would be better to conserve her breath.

The laughter came again, right at her heels. She pumped her arms and legs in a furious attempt to shake him but as she did so, he drew alongside, loping in huge, easy bounds, his ragged trousers and soiled shirt flapping. His elbows and knees were visible, their boniness made her think of whippets. He turned his head towards her and she saw the purple in his irises, the mania in his wrinkled face. He shook his head like a lunatic, spraying spittle into the trees and cackling.

Her legs started to hurt badly, filling with extra weight as though her blood were wet sand. Her head wobbled from side to side like an athlete trying to claw back the finish from a better competitor. She grunted in frustration. Her legs were no longer springing over the ground. Now they were thumping it, her feet landing heavily, her arms still grasping for momentum.

She allowed herself to glance at the old man for a moment, hoping the fear it caused her would squeeze a little extra speed from her protesting muscles. It didn't. She turned back to the track ahead of her and saw how far she was from home. She still believed she could save herself right up until the moment she tripped. It felt like she'd snagged her foot on a root, but it could just as easily have been the old man reaching out a limb to bring her down.

She did scream then but not loudly. It was more a screech of thwarted fury. How could she have been so stupid as to think she could outrun him?

When she hit the dirt, what little breath she had left went out of her in a bruising rush. She tried to stand and couldn't. But there were no cold hands around her throat in the next instant. No blade tip pressed between her ribs. When she could move again she rolled onto her side and saw him standing over her. He was neither sweating nor breathless.

'What do you want?' she asked him.

The old man's eyes defocused as he looked into the trees. His voice was low, almost a growl.

'It is impossible to say.'

'Who are you?'

'I am a sallow man who once was dark.'

Gina sat up and backed away, paddling with her hands and feet. Everything in her body felt leaden and uncoordinated. She backed into a pine trunk. The sallow man approached her.

'Why are you doing this to me?' she said, breathless.

'I want to taste you.' he said. 'Your sweat. Your saliva. Your milk. Your vitreous humour. The juice within your marrow. The fluid in your spine and joints. The wetness of your sex. The fecund jelly within your ova. Your blood, my dear. I want it. All of it. I wish to enter you and draw you into me. It has been so long and I am STARVING!'

He screamed the last word and her eardrums overloaded,

continuing to ring long afterwards. As the cry receded she saw his face pulsate and a lucence pass across his ancient skin. A silvery thread of saliva leaked from one corner of his open mouth lengthening impossibly and touching the ground before breaking away.

'Come now. For my mind is verminous with hungers and I do not wish to hurt you.'

He held out his elongated hand. Tears spilled from her.

CHAPTER 21

The sallow man watched as the girl reached her hand towards him. Her whole body shook and she appeared crushed by the effort of running. Seeing him, she withdrew her hand and turned her face away.

'Look at me,' he said.

She resisted.

He drew her, pressurising the fluid in her eyes. Her orbs swivelled towards him, the tiny muscles that controlled them no match for his gravity. Her head followed her eyes. The sallow man grinned and pulled harder. He was a desert seeking the rain in her. The girl's eyes bulged forward in their sockets and she squeezed them closed. He watched in delight as her eyelids parted, the swollen whites, marbled with broken capillaries peeping out.

'No!' she screamed.

'Then look at me.'

She opened her eyes and looked. He let her go and she sank back against the tree, touching her eyes with her fingertips, pressing them in with her palms.

'You have only one choice. Come willingly or by other means. But come you will.'

'How can I come willingly when you're going to kill me?'

'I will not kill you. I will show you true power. I will give you freedom.'

He saw how she responded to his promises. There was a flicker of true eagerness there, a desire that existed without the need for threats. He knew he'd judged her well. He took her hand and swung her onto his back like an infant, before dropping to all fours once more.

'Do not let go.'

The journey began. The girl was silent but the sallow man felt her thighs tighten against him as he increased his speed to a gallop. She rested her head against his bony back and squeezed her arms around his skeletal chest. The last of the light wasted from the sky and the trees and the darkness nuzzled them as they skimmed across the soft earth, moving away from the town and far along the Eastern Path.

The sallow man felt the girl's tears against his neck and in the purple blackness he sent back his tongue to catch her brine. His needs deepened with each day now. In the past there had sometimes been several years between feeds. Now they were becoming more frequent. The more he secluded himself, the more he concentrated on the simple life of a forest gatherer, the more the need for other nourishment grew within. No matter how he tried to avoid the pangs, the desires grew stronger and stronger, threatening to destroy his sanity. He was Fugue now and he would stay that way until satisfied. He did not know if he could keep the promise he'd made her. He wanted nothing more than to leave her skin and bones dry and desiccated; to return her to dust.

He left the trail and raced into the trees following a run he knew well. Even though they were close to his dark home, he didn't know if he could wait. A second tongue split from the skin of his belly and thrashed against him as he ran. Spikes grew from his shoulders and he could not control it. All he could do was run. The girl tightened her grip on him as she felt his pace increase to recklessness and she cried out as thin branches whipped at her flanks and legs. As they reached the broad expanse that was the tree's enclosure, he smelled blood leaking from a small cut she'd sustained.

He howled, but by then they'd reached the tree, his haven

and sanctuary. This was where he would take from her what he needed. He stood upright and she slipped to the ground, too weak to rise.

Gina looked up at the creature the sallow man was becoming. She wanted to run but she was exhausted and his transformation was the most fascinating and terrifying thing she'd ever seen. He was growing taller. He removed his clothes with hands too long and bony by then to work efficiently. When he was naked she saw it all.

The clearing was filled with the same purple half light that hung over Hobson's Valley every night, but here it was brighter. The light emanated from the enormous tree at whose roots she lay. The clearing was a vast arena, enclosed by thick forest and impenetrable brush. At its heart, the tree pulsed with an inner light that shone in veinlike pathways ascending from the roots along the trunk and out to every branch and leaf. There were blossoms on the branches of the tree and they shone brightest.

The sallow man looked down at her and she watched his jawbone extend into an under-slung hook. More spines erupted from the skin at his hips and shoulders and purple tongues unfurled and swayed towards her from his stomach and beneath his arms. The smell of decaying leaves and forest fungus was strong on him.

He reached out with one slender arm and lifted her by the waist. She put her hands to his grip, trying to prise the fingers away but it was impossible. With his other talon-tipped hand he tore at her running gear, stripping the vest and bra from her in a couple of frantic slashes and doing the same to her leggings and underwear. She tried to scream, knowing it was his will that prevented her.

He swung her towards the tree and pressed her back against it. She felt the slow rhythm of warm, luminous sap flowing beneath the skin-like bark. She kicked at the sallow man with her running shoes and tried to cover her nakedness with her arms. Many tongues extended towards her, each diverging into two or more tips. They snaked across her bare skin, seeking the cuts she sustained as they came through the forest and licking the blood away. Spikes protruded from every part of him by then and she knew that when he approached, the points would kill her. He had lied.

That lie was not the worst of it. Below the tongues in his belly, his penis jutted upward, pumping in time with the sap of the tree behind her. It was glowing slightly, lit from within like the rest of his body, but what appalled her most about the penis were the backward pointing barbs that lined it above and below.

He spoke to her but she no longer understood his language.

Though it was night the sallow man could see her perfectly.

Her skin was so smooth, so pale and delicate that he wanted to tear it open. He allowed her to struggle but let no sound escape her. Her jet-black hair was still pulled back into a tight ponytail and he released it with one hooked talon. It fell down around her shoulders like a spill of black ink. She was like fluid in every sense. Even her breasts moved with a liquid rolling motion. Her skin was tight over her frame, her blood vessels, ducts and sphincters tight around her juices. He wanted all of it for himself.

She promised a sea of tears for him alone, and he had the whole night in which to absorb them. His thirst was great, years in the making. He moved in towards her, his tongues stretching further and further from him. They twined themselves far beyond her, slithering around the gargantuan trunk of the tree and coming back around to meet each other over her now trapped body. The creature let go with his hand and she hung, pressed to the tree by four vine-like tongues. They clamped her body, wrists and ankles against the living bark.

The tips of each tongue pressed against her axillae. He smelled and tasted her saltiness. He knew everything about her from the teardrops and blood he'd already tasted. Her cells were now part of his. As soon as he penetrated her, his cells would then flow into her and she would know him; everything from his birth to this moment would be accessible. To feed was to share it all.

He did not exude the anaesthetic serum. She would know what was happening to her; she would feel it all. If she survived there was a chance that she might remember, but he doubted it. The Fugue was too efficient, too total to bypass. He forced himself through her skin with his soft flesh first and he felt her trying to scream even harder than before. He wanted to hear those sounds, to make the feed complete but he could not risk detection. He stifled every utterance by controlling the saliva in her throat and mouth and drawing it to other areas. When four of his tongues had breached the walls of her femoral and brachial arteries, the satisfaction of the first intrusion was complete. Above her skin, the thick bodies of each tongue pulsed in time with her heartbeat. He let the blood come slowly; there was no reason to rush.

The desire to crush himself against her was strong. Every spike on his body would wound her and yet more fluid would be his. She tried to look away from him but he turned her face back with one cold claw and looked deep into her eyes.

'I am within you now, girl, and you are within me.'

She stared back, uncomprehending, eyes wide with the pain of his invasions. He looked down at the thick black hair of her crotch and could restrain himself no longer. He could feel the totality of her fear and was ready when her bladder gave way; his belly tongue waited at her lower lips and wasted nothing. It retracted and he pressed the tip of his snaggled penis into her resistant warmth. She could do nothing to close herself to him, not even her eyes. As he began to thrust and retreat, her face contorted into a mask of extremity. He thought he saw the madness of acceptance in her eyes. So, finally, she was his.

He laid his body against her, puncturing her flesh in a dozen more places, and put his head against hers.

'I am sharing the forest with you, girl, and I am sharing you with the forest.'

All night he sapped her and made sure she did not lose consciousness. He drank her pain with her fluids and took nourishment from it all. Towards the end he felt her spirit beginning to slip free and he pulled himself away, tearing much skin and flesh from her as he did so. But none of her blood was spilled upon the ground of the dark clearing. Her flesh was pale and bloodless, almost dry. It was only his will that kept her alive, making sure there was enough blood concentrated in her brain and organs. Her end was near. He was at least partially satisfied by her sacrifice and he wanted to keep his promise to her. She would be another of his kind if he stopped now and gave her a chance to heal, but he could never feed from her again.

The knowledge made his heart ache with loss.

But his body was swollen with her fluids now, particularly her blood, and some of those fluids he had fed to the tree out of respect. It too had its hungers, its desires. He relaxed his tongues and her wounded, drained body fell to the leafy ground. There was no strength in her and she landed in an ungainly tangle, trapping an arm behind her back and with her legs splayed drunkenly. He saw the tearing at her thighs and crotch and yearned for more of her.

As he watched, her wounds began to close. Very slowly at first, but rapidly gaining momentum. The thinness caused by the feed also began to repair. Her shrivelled skin filled out again, her breasts inflated from lifeless bags to heavy mounds once more. Her face, narrow and gaunt, began to swell. The Fugue was deep inside her now. Swarming through the cells he had not absorbed. Soon she would feel the power and the call.

Full as he was, he felt he would not need to feed for a score of years, but in the back of his mind he knew the folly of that. The more he fed, the hungrier he became and the wider spread became the Fugue. He sank to his knees in exhaustion and the change from Rage to Fugue to human began.

He was asleep before it ended.

She awoke in the near blackness and found the clearing scattered with gently pulsating blossoms from the branches of the tree. They faded and died as she watched to be followed by more that spun down like tiny lilac lanterns. She was naked and did not know why but her body felt strong and vibrant. The tree was beautiful and she looked at it for a long time, her eyes now able to see in the low-lit gloom. Near the tree were tattered clothes she did not recognise. Strangest of all was the naked body of an ancient-looking man. His bones shone though his skin; the ribs and the shape of his skull making a cadaverous starveling of him. She wondered if he was dead. She did not know him. She did not know the place where she was but she knew that somewhere there was a home for her to go to and this home, the arbour, the dark sanctuary, would wait for her to return.

Wearing only her running shoes and enjoying the feel of the night air against her skin, she walked away from the tree and into the forest in the direction of the town.

—apart from the cold, all I remember after that is waking up here the next morning.'

'Did you feel sick or hurt in any way?'

'No. I felt better than I had in weeks.'

'Gina, I need to know if you even suspect that someone assaulted you that day.'

'Something happened out there. But I felt so good afterwards. I don't think it could be that. If someone had hurt me, I'd know, wouldn't I? I'd have scratches or bruises, right? It wasn't like that, I just felt great.'

'Maybe you were drugged and your euphoria was the result,' said Nicholas.

Gina looked at her mother and then at him. He saw the uncertainty in her eyes and the fear. They were pushing her too hard.

'Geen, honey whatever happened out there we just want to help,' he said. 'I know this must seem kind of intense but we're doing our best. We'll do anything we can to make sure you're okay.'

'It isn't really me I wanted to talk to you about.' Gina said. She disengaged from them and slouched back against the comfort of the sofa cushions. Nicholas adjusted his place on the sofa so he could see her.

'What do you mean?' He asked.

'Well, it is me but I don't think I'm the victim in all this.'

'I don't understand, Geen,' said Isobel. 'If you've been hurt in some way, we have to do something about it.'

'I think other people have been hurt worse than me.'

'What people?'

'Alfred Lindh and Daniel Stringer.'

'You know those boys?'

'Sure. Not well, but I know them. They're always fighting and making up. Everyone knows them.'

'Gina, what are you saying here?' asked Isobel. 'Did you help them run away?'

'Run away?'

'Yes, that's what they did isn't it?'

'I don't think so,' she said.

Nicholas leaned towards her.

'What do you think happened?' He asked.

'I think they may be hurt or worse. I think I may have had something to do with it.'

Nicholas's voice was quiet, shocked:

'You make it sound like you think they're dead.'

'That *is* what I think.' said Gina.

'Do you know where they are?' he asked.

'All I remember is agreeing to meet them late at night. We were going to go into the woods.'

Her father was incredulous.

'In the middle of the night, Gina? What the hell for?'

'I don't know!'

Gina's face was pale; her eyes clenched shut and her fists bunched. She looked like she was about to tear the place apart. Nicholas stood up, gestured for Isobel to follow him and walked down the hall.

'We'll be right back, baby,' Isobel said. She smoothed her skirt down when she stood and walked after Nicholas. He waited for her by the telephone table under the stairs.

'We have to make a call to the sheriff right now,' he said.

'I don't know what Gina's trying to tell us but, I'm afraid for those boys.'

'I don't believe I'm hearing you correctly, Nick. Our daughter is suffering severe memory problems, possibly due to an assault, and you're concerned over someone else's kids? You know what I think? I think those boys drugged and raped our daughter in the woods three weeks ago. I think they then tried to do it again. Maybe they didn't get away with it the second time and that's why they've run off. You'd rather believe that Gina is a killer than accept she may have been sexually assaulted. *That* would be easier for you to deal with.'

Nicholas couldn't speak for a few seconds. He spent those moments resisting the urge to break his wife's jaw.

'We're going to call the law and let them do their job. You go sit with her while I phone them.'

'Call a doctor too. I want her checked out for signs of assault.'

'Isobel—'

'Just fucking do it, Nick, okay?'

'Fine.'

While he made the calls, Nicholas was aware of Isobel running from room to room. When he hung up he walked back to the living room and came face to face with her in the hallway.

'What happened?' he asked.

'She's gone,' said Isobel.

CHAPTER 22

They knelt next to Carla beneath the spreading limbs of the tree; beside its thick, leviathan trunk. The clearing was almost in darkness but for a faint glow that had no apparent source. José was too concerned with Carla to give the phenomenon any thought.

'What happened, Luis?' José had laid his machete down and was listening to Carla's chest.

'I don't know exactly. She reached out to touch the tree and the next moment she was lying there. Her charm necklace glowed purple. It was as if the tree gave her an electric shock.'

'José, is she breathing? asked Maria. Can you hear her heart?'

'Yes. It sounds strong and fine.'

He checked her pulse next.

'Well?'

'It is a little weak. I think she has fainted.'

'Mother of God, I cannot wait to leave this forest and this country.' Maria stroked Carla's forehead and then bent over to kiss her cool cheek. 'What can we do?'

José gathered the limp body of his daughter into his arms and struggled to his feet.

'Luis, take the machete.' Slack with unconsciousness, her weight was difficult to manoeuvre. José walked back towards the glow of the fire. 'If it is a faint, she will come round very quickly.'

As if she'd heard his words, Carla began to stir in his arms.

'Oh, thank you, Lord,' said Maria.

'How are you feeling, Carlita?' asked José.

'What happened?'

'You fainted,' he said

'She was thrown, papa, I swear it.'

'Quiet, Luis. No more teasing tonight.'

'But papa, honestly—'

'Enough.' José's voice echoed around through the darkness. 'Don't make me raise my voice to you again, Luis. Clear?'

'Clear.' said the boy.

'Do you feel all right Carla?' asked her mother.

'Yes, fine. I'm just very hungry all of a sudden. Please put me down, papa. I can walk.'

José lowered her feet to the ground and she stood holding his shoulder for a moment more before walking ahead to the tent and the food. José turned to Maria and spoke quietly.

'I expect she has walked too far and not eaten enough. It is my fault for being so insistent today. I'm sorry.'

'You should be apologising to her not to me,' said Maria. 'The sooner we leave here, the better it will be for all of us.'

'Yes. We will eat and go to sleep early. Tomorrow at dawn we will make a swift check of the clearing for signs of my grandfather and then we will go.'

'You may be searching on your own, José. As soon as we are packed up, I'm going back along that trail. I no longer care whether we find your grandfather's last resting place or not.'

The dinner was served in silence. When Maria saw Carla fingering the wooden amulet that was still around her neck, she stopped eating and let her plate and cutlery settle down into her lap.

'I thought I told everyone to take those things off.'

'I wanted to keep wearing it,' said Carla. 'What harm can it do?'

'It is unchristian to wear a misshapen crucifix. It is an occult symbol that has no place next to the skin of a catholic.'

'It makes me feel safe.'

'Take it off immediately.'

Carla looked to her father for support.

'You'd better take it off, Carlita,' he said. 'Just for now.'

'No, José. Not just for now.' Maria reached out her hand to her daughter. 'Give it to me.'

Carla pulled the leather thong clear of her shirt collar and brought it over her head. She handed it her mother. Maria tossed it into the darkness. José said nothing. He looked down at his plate and continued to eat. Around them there was a brief surge of brightness as if lightning had flashed silently in the distance. The light left an afterglow in the clearing.

'Did you see that?' asked Carla.

'Yes, like a phosphorous flare,' said José.

Maria busied herself with tidying items of cookware and cutlery, ignoring the conversation.

'Do you see how the whole clearing seems to be lit from the inside?' continued José.

The children nodded. The glow was very faint, especially with the camping lantern still on to provide light to eat by, but they could see it faintly all around them like barely lit purple neon.

'Some trick of nature no doubt,' said José. 'but very beautiful, nevertheless.'

Maria ignored him.

'Children, I want you both up early, ready to pack and leave at first light. The earlier the better. Your father may stay a little longer and then follow us. It is up to him.'

When she'd tidied the plates away and rinsed them with

a little of the water they had, she was first into the tent to change and take up her position for sleep. Carla followed, then Luis.

José spent a little longer sitting alone in the strange light of the clearing with the lantern off so that he could appreciate it better. A mist came up, creeping along in a thin layer next to the ground and he felt suddenly exhausted. He took off his boots, slipped into the tent and fell asleep with his clothes on. As he slipped into unconsciousness, he thought he heard faraway laughter.

Luis was the first to wake and see that Carla was gone.

He looked over at the shapes of his parents in their sleeping bags and their slack, inanimate faces and smiled. He preferred them that way. Taking care not to wake them he unzipped the tent flap, crawled out into the early morning light and zipped the flap shut again. He assumed Carla had gone to look for her binder before mama could catch her at it and he strolled in that direction in his unlaced boots to check.

He found the charm straight away, lying in the dirt near the border of undergrowth that marked the edge of the arbour. He picked it up, his theory about his sister temporarily quashed, and put it in his pocket next to his own. Perhaps she had become tired of waiting for their parents to wake up and had gone to explore the tree again or look a little further afield for great grandfather Jimenez's resting place.

He leaned over to tighten the laces of his boots ready to go and look for her. One thing that gave him great pleasure was knowing that his parents had overslept in spite of everything they'd said the night before. Mama had especially annoyed him with her stupidity about the charm. As far as he was concerned she deserved to be the last out of bed and have to live with that fact after all her panicked crowing. He set off in the direction of the tree, still fascinated by its size.

Standing right beside the trunk was where he could see

its greatness most strikingly. Even from the edge of the space it occupied, it looked unusually large, but within touching distance its size was frightening. The four of them with arms linked wouldn't have reached halfway around it and though the trunk began to separate into branches no more than thirty feet overhead, each branch angled upward and outward further before forming the slightly domed canopy of limbs and leaves that shielded the entire clearing, apparently preventing any other plants from growing.

Its roots bulged like buttresses from its sides and tapered down towards the ground where they flattened out a little before disappearing into the earth. Luis wondered if there was a wind strong enough or lightning powerful enough to knock it over or kill it. He doubted it.

The bark of the tree was grey and there was no hint of moss or lichen on its surface. Beneath the bark, the contours of the wood were impressive and muscular. They hinted at an anatomy of unimaginably powerful strength. The bark reminded him of elephant hide and the massive and bunched shapes below were like the bulging sinews of some giant body builder. The way the roots spread into the ground and the branches into the air made him think of a huge disembodied forearm with a hand at each end. One hand gripped the earth with thick, unrelenting fingers while the other spread its digits skyward. Both ends seemed capable of clenching into a mighty fist.

After what had happened to Carla, Luis dared not touch the bark but he wanted to hurt the tree for hurting his sister. He thought of hacking into it with the machete and imagined that he would see real blood flow forth, that he would expose the vessels and living fibres that the bark hid. Somewhere inside, he mused, would be bones too, bones as thick as the trunks of ordinary trees.

Of the dimly glowing emanations they'd seen the previous night there was no sign. He ran back to the tent to collect the machete and heard hissed whispers from inside.

'How could you oversleep like this, José?'

'Don't blame me for this, woman. If you didn't wake up it's your own fault. After all you said last night, it's hardly the example to set for the children. They're both up before you.'

'Why can't you support me in this? Why must you torment me? I was exhausted. I needed to sleep.'

'You can tell that to Luis and Carla yourself when you see them. I'm going for a piss.'

While his father fumbled out of his sleeping bag and tried to open the zip door of the tent, Luis ran silently to the back of the tent and as far away as he could before his father emerged. Then he turned and pretended to be sauntering towards the camp, looking all the while into the undergrowth. It wasn't until after José had relieved himself, just a few yards from the tent, that he noticed Luis dawdling along.

'Morning, Luis.'

'Morning, papa. Sleep well?'

'Too well, apparently.'

'What time do you think mama will want to leave?'

'Very soon I expect. Why don't you help me pack some of these things up?' José glanced around. 'Where is your sister?'

'She was up before me. I haven't seen her yet.'

'Well how long have you been awake?'

'Not long. A few minutes perhaps. She's probably gone into the woods to go to the toilet. Scared we'll hear her farts or something.'

Luis laughed but only for a moment. Maria emerged from the tent and he could see she wasn't happy.

'Why didn't you wake us up, Luis?'

'You looked tired, mama. I didn't want to disturb you.'

'Well now I'm up. We're late and I'm in a hurry so start packing.'

'What about breakfast, Mama?'

'There won't be any breakfast for you if you don't show some enthusiasm. I want to leave here as soon as possible.'

Between the three of them they had most of the equipment stowed in less than half an hour. The tent was the last thing to be packed away.

'If Carla wants to change her clothes she'll have to do it in the bushes,' said José as he un-pegged the flysheet.

'Go look for your sister, Luis.' Said Maria. 'I want to leave now, tell her.'

Luis ran, knowing that his mother's mood was not going to improve. This would be a day of damage limitation. He jogged along the edge of the circular arbour calling into the brush. He glanced into the centre of the clearing from time to time to see if she was near the tree trunk but she wasn't. Soon he was completing the circuit, coming back to where his parents stood with all the rucksacks packed up. They were waiting at the opening in the trees that led into the tunnel-path they'd made the previous day.

'Is she coming, Luis?' asked José.

'She hasn't answered me yet. I don't know where she is.'

Maria's look of determined unhappiness became one of concern.

'Did you actually see her this morning, Luis?'

'No, she was up before me.'

'What time did you wake up?'

'I don't know.'

'Did you hear her get up?'

Luis shook his head, feeling the blame being put on him.

'She could have been gone for hours,' said Maria.

'Let's call for her again,' said José. 'All of us.'

They left the collection of brightly coloured canvas and Gor-Tex backpacks and walked together around the broad clearing shouting for Carla. They called loudly and their voices echoed in the wide space.

Half an hour of shouting into the surrounding woods yielded nothing. They walked back to the pile of camping gear and stood, arms folded and heads bent slightly downward, in a triangle.

'We can't leave her here,' said José, 'But, at the same time, we have to make a start for the car. If Carla really has wandered off or is lost or hurt, we need to organise help for her. Pass me the phone.'

Luis went to the pocket of the bag it was packed in and switched it on.

'It's no good, papa, look.'

José took the phone. The battery was almost dead but it hardly mattered; there was no signal. José sighed.

'Okay, turn it off and save the battery. Maybe we can get a network nearer the town.'

'José, what are we going to do?' asked Maria.

'We're going to split up.'

'What? No. Not possible.' she said.

'It's our best chance of success. Someone stays here by the tree and waits for Carla to come back and the other two begin hiking back to the car. If Carla doesn't return within some space of time that we all agree on, then that person also leaves and heads back.'

'Can't we just leave a note for her on a tree or something?' asked Luis.

'We could but there's no guarantee that it wouldn't blow away or get rained on. We could leave her a sign of some kind but she might not understand it. My plan makes sense. It's difficult, but we have to do it and the quicker we get started the better. Whoever leaves takes the phone and gets help as soon as there's a signal. Failing that, we can get help in Hobson's Valley.'

'Who has to stay?' asked Maria.

'I do. You and Luis set as quick a pace as you can and I'll catch you up, hopefully with Carla.'

'How long will you wait for her?'

'Until tomorrow morning, unless you think otherwise.'

Maria considered it.

'If she's not back by then, what will you do?'

'Chase you two as fast as I can. If she isn't coming back,

we know she has either decided to go back on her own or has run into some kind of. . .problem.'

'I don't like this plan, José. Not at all.'

'Listen to me, Maria. I think the most reasonable explanation for her disappearance is that she was upset and decided to leave early, on her own, to frighten you. She wants to pay you back for treating her like a child. She wants to prove she is not a child any more. I expect that if you hurry you'll find her an hour or two ahead of you on the Eastern Path, stomping back towards the car.'

'I hope you're right.'

'I am.' He gave Maria a kiss on the forehead and then a more tender one on the mouth before turning to Luis and taking him by the shoulders in a mock gesture of fatherly imperiousness. 'Look after your mother, okay?'

'Whatever, papa.'

'You'd better get going.'

'What about the extra back pack?'

'We'll take out everything except Carla's stuff and share it out. I'll carry it with me if she doesn't come back here.'

José watched the dark tunnel of brush swallow his wife and son and listened to their footsteps and voices recede as they hurried back towards the Eastern Path. When they'd been gone half an hour he began to call for Carla again.

CHAPTER 23

Randall Moore took the cherry-handled .38 snub from its velvet-lined box and turned it over in his hands. The weight felt good and though it hadn't been fired for a long time he could still smell the faintest hint of spent powder. The wood was warm against his palms, the black steel cold and unyielding.

He took a cloth and began to rub the gun over to remove any dirt and dust from the exterior. Then he released the chamber and spun it, eliciting a whisper of a whir that told stories of careful oiling, cleaning and maintenance. He smiled to hear the ease of the movement. Flicking the gun shut he took aim and pulled the trigger. There was an innocuous metallic snap that made him jump even though he knew the gun was empty.

In thirty-five years of retailing, no one had ever given him a single reason to use the gun. No robberies, no attempted break-ins at night, not even a case of shoplifting. That was the way it was out in the big country. But that didn't mean he wasn't in danger. Hobson's Valley was a strange place. It had its secrets. Danger could walk in at any moment and he intended to be ready.

There'd been a rumour going round that Jimmy Kerrigan might be involved somehow with the disappearance of the two boys and now the Priestly girl. It didn't surprise him one bit that the smug little city slicker was some kind of closet maniac. Randall was always glad when Kerrigan bypassed the store to shop at Olsen's. The way he walked around trying to look like some kind of wise woodsman was a real insult to Randall's intelligence. The guy was city and suit to the bone. Dressing like a hippy and living in that cabin like a hermit might fool a few folks but it didn't fool him.

The guy had always been an outsider. Randall knew more about his adoption than Jimmy Kerrigan realised. He knew it was a 'rushed job' based on 'local' approaches to law. Wherever the man came from, he didn't belong in the valley and never had.

Randall pointed the revolver at a can of beans and imagined it was Jimmy Kerrigan's head. He knew he'd have no problem pulling the trigger.

The ringing made Kath jump as usual. While her heart settled down she promised herself she'd get a new phone, with a choice of soothing tones instead of the shrill alarm clock ring of the ancient machine in the hallway. She put down her crossword and pushed up from the chair. Dingbat's ears twitched a little with each ring and he opened one eye as Kath left the kitchen.

She walked as if she needed oiling, her ankle joints popping and her knees clicking and grinding until she'd taken a few steps.

'Kerrigan's,' she said as she placed the receiver to her ear.

'Hi there, Kath. How're you doing?'

'Hey, Maggie. I'm okay, I guess. I've been passing some time thinking and being good to myself.'

'I am glad to hear that,' said Maggie and Kath could hear the sincerity. She was glad someone else was thinking about her. There was excitement in Maggie's voice too. 'Did you hear about the posse?'

'What posse?'

'Remember those two boys that went missing a few days ago? Well, Sheriff Powell had a tip-off about where they might be and he's organised a search party. A girl has disappeared too, I heard.'

'You said it was a posse. Are they armed?'

'Some of them will be, I guess.'

'My God.' Kath sat down on the stool beside the phone. 'James is out there in the woods.'

'I know. That's the other thing I thought you ought to know. There's a rumour that Jimmy had something to do with the disappearance of those boys. It looked kind of weird that he wasn't at home when Sheriff Powell wanted to talk to him.'

'God, I pray he stays out of harm's way. James is a good man, Maggie.'

Kath twisted the phone cord in her fingers as she thought about her boy on his own in the woods with a group of trigger-happy vigilantes. It was rough justice in a place like Hobson's Valley. People would shoot instead of thinking if they believed they were righting a wrong. Not only that, they'd make the most of the excitement this kind of search created. It was probably the most diverting thing they'd ever do; had to be twenty years since anything similar had happened; a time when some hikers had gotten lost in the woods.

Maggie's voice interrupted the memory.

'Kath, I was wondering if you'd like a change of scene for a few hours. I've just made a batch of oatmeal cookies and they've turned out real fine. I thought you might enjoy walking up to my place. Otherwise, I could come and pick you up.'

'Maggie, I'm going to take you up on that. If I stay here on my own I'll go crazy worrying about James.'

'That's great. Want me to come and get you?'

'No, I'm going to walk. I need the exercise. Is it okay if I bring a friend?'

'Does Dingbat like cookies?'

'I'm sure he'll develop a taste for them.'

CHAPTER 24

About fifteen cars drove past Jimmy Kerrigan's place on the way to the Clearing that morning. Isobel Priestly and the mothers of Daniel Stringer and Alfred Lindh were the only women in attendance. When the cars came to a halt in the Clearing, everyone stepped out into the pre-dawn twilight to find Sheriff Powell already there. He'd parked next to the Jimenez's white Toyota. He wore his hat tilted downward and his thumbs were hooked into his belt. The fingers of his right hand tapped on the leather holster of his pistol.

One by one the members of the search party stepped towards Powell and bid him their good mornings. The mood was tense but anticipatory. The air was fresh; the first really cold morning of the year and many in the group wore thick jackets against the chill. For a while the sounds of birds calling to each other were interrupted by the slamming of doors and trunks. The noise level in the Clearing rose. Laughter echoed as the men swapped jokes and yarns. Soon, their adrenaline pumping, they made more aggressive comments about what they'd do if they found 'some fucking psycho' roaming their beautiful woods and trails.

Sheriff Powell stepped onto one of the short wooden posts forming the boundary of the picnic area. He didn't wait for anyone to notice and he didn't shout or clap his hands to attract their attention. Instead he took a deep lungful of chilly morning air and began to shush very softly.

The people nearest to him heard it and shut up. The noise level dropped. The people they'd been talking to also stopped talking. The quiet spread like a soft breeze and before Powell had expended his air, the clearing was once more silent but for the dawn chorus.

He spoke quietly but everyone heard him.

'People, there are very few facts to guide us, but we must use them as the basis for our work here today. First, we know that Alfred Lindh and Daniel Stringer are missing. A suggestion has been made that they are somewhere in these woods, possibly on the Western Way. My information leads me to believe this and that's why we're here. Our priority is to find them as soon as possible.

'Second, Gina Priestly is also missing. There's nothing to suggest she left town so there's a strong possibility she's out here too. We don't know how prepared these kids are for spending nights in the woods. They could be holed up somewhere trying to stay warm. They may be injured or sick and that means they won't be moving around. Keep your eyes open for makeshift shelters or anything that looks like it might serve as a hiding place.

'We do not know why these kids came up here. We do not know their condition. We do not know how far they may have travelled. Keep these things in mind as you look for them. There is no proof to suggest that Mr. James Kerrigan is involved with these kids. In my opinion therefore, his unavailability is still a coincidence and he is not under any suspicion. If you see him out here, you can tell him I'd like to speak to him. You have no other power or authorisation to act further than that. If he comes willingly to me, then fine. If he doesn't, I'll consider him a suspect. Either way, you are *not* to interfere with the man.

'Over the years there have been alleged sightings and rumours of sightings of an old man said to live rough in these woods. As far as I'm concerned this is not a fact. If you see such a person, you are to treat them in exactly the manner that you will treat Mr. Kerrigan and you will pass him the same message.

'Spread out and search in pairs or threes. If you find the missing kids, stay with them and radio back to me with your position. No matter what their condition is, you will follow that instruction. Whatever happens, I want to be first to know and first on the scene.

'Now, I know some of you here are armed and that is your right. But if I get wind of any vigilantism, I will personally see to it that the culprit regrets it for the rest of their lives. If you think you're here for some kind of turkey shoot you can turn around right now and go home. You need to remember that there are likely to be visitors to our community hiking in the woods. I don't want you giving them any reason to be frightened. You can tell them what's going on and that my advice is to head out of the area unless they have information I might need. Otherwise you're to leave them be. Anyone have any questions?'

Randall Moore spoke up immediately.

'There could be a murderer loose in this forest, Sheriff. Are you saying we can't defend ourselves?'

There were a few nods and grunts of agreement.

'As I've stated, and I'll state it again for the hard of hearing, there are no facts to suggest that there is anyone dangerous in these woods. I don't want to hear you stirring people up like this Mr . . .'

He waited for several moments. As a new sheriff he wasn't familiar every face.

'Moore. Randall Moore.'

'Mr. Moore, I am noting that it was you who asked the question and if anything stupid happens out here today, I'll be wanting to talk to you. In answer to your question, if you are attacked, you have the right to defend yourself. Just don't go looking for trouble where there isn't any. Got it?'

Randall nodded, bitter and sullen.

'Anything else?' Sheriff Powell looked around at every face. He tried to gauge the personalities and thought he was close to the mark with most of them. But search parties always attracted the aggressive cases and there was nothing he could do about that. Right now, he needed all the help he could get. 'Okay. I'm going to hand out hunting vests so that we can identify other members of the search team in the woods and be safely visible. I'm also going to provide photos of the missing youths, so you all know who you're looking for. After that I'm going to give each pair or trio an area to investigate and we can get started.'

He was about to step down from his post when he saw Mrs. Stringer's hand up.

'Go ahead, ma'am.'

'Sheriff Powell, why aren't there medical units here? What if the boys are hurt?'

'I'm sorry, Mrs. Stringer, this community can't afford to have paramedics on standby when there's no perceived emergency. Some of us are trained in first aid and CPR and we'll be able to provide care should the need arise. I hope it does not. If we do have a medical emergency, that will be when we call for outside help. I'm sorry, but it's the best we can do.'

Powell checked his watch and stepped down to his car. From the trunk, he handed out orange vests and Xeroxed snapshots of the kids. He saw the defiant look in Randall Moore's eyes and chuckled to himself.

Spreading a map over the hood of his cruiser, Powell showed everyone where he wanted them to go. He kept the areas small and tight so people would be thorough. As the last pair of figures disappeared onto one of the trails, he unscrewed the lid off his thermos and poured himself a half-cup of coffee.

He thought about James Kerrigan and the missing youngsters. He thought about the Priestlys and their story. He thought about Gina and why she ran away. He thought about the guns. He went over the organisation of the whole search in his mind several times but there was something important missing in it all. He couldn't help feeling he'd forgotten one vitally important detail.

PART III: WAR

> *'Adapt or perish, now as ever, is nature's
> inexorable imperative.'*
> H. G. WELLS

CHAPTER 25

Kerrigan stepped into the mouth of the trail sore and tired from running and wanting nothing more than to lie down on the earth and sleep. Much of the daylight was shut out by the denseness of the foliage above him, turning the trail into a half-lit cave. Beneath his feet were withered cuttings that had fallen to the blows of a machete. The smell of sap and split bark lingered. The Jimenez's were certainly determined.

Having sat down for some time to recover after his run, Kerrigan had cooled off and now, out of the sun, he couldn't get warm again. His legs, hips and back ached from the strain of the pack; his feet were bruised by the extra weight. He felt far worse now than when he'd been running. The closeness of the undergrowth on both sides and the trail's low ceiling crowded him. The air was cold and still and no sounds came from the forest.

Kerrigan wondered how long it would be before he was just plain scared.

Luis and his mother walked in silence.

The trail seemed far longer on the way out than it had on the way in, even without all the machete work. Luis found his mother's mood difficult to bear. She wore an expression of nonchalance but her body gave everything away.

She was walking too quickly for the pace to be enjoyable.

As she swung her arms, Luis saw her touching each fingertip to her thumb—little finger, ring finger, middle finger, index finger, then back the other way, like she was counting. But he knew she wasn't counting anything. From time to time she would cast a glance over her shoulder as if checking how far they'd come; impossible because of the way the trail meandered. So what else did this gesture signify, he wondered? He thought he knew the answer. Occasionally, she would begin to hum a tune, something jaunty from a musical she liked, and would get only a few bars into it before stopping, the woods crushing her attempts to be breezy and unconcerned.

All of this annoyed rather than worried Luis. She was letting her thoughts get the better of her. Everything that had pissed her off about the holiday would be festering, boiling up until she could keep it in no longer. He knew who'd bear the brunt of her erupting feelings when the time came.

He allowed his pace to slow a fraction and let her take the lead. The few extra inches between them meant he didn't have to catch sight of her face telling lies as she tormented herself into a rage.

He had his own reasons for being angry. Hadn't it been his mother who had taken Carla's charm necklace away? After what he'd seen when his sister touched the tree, he was sure the charms had some purpose. Even though she'd been hurt by touching the tree, he had the feeling that it might have been worse if she hadn't been wearing the special necklace Mr Kerrigan had given her. If it had protected her and now she was out in the forest alone, then it was his mother's fault that Carla no longer had anything to keep her safe.

Luis had been excited about coming to America; the best adventure their father could have chosen. Not only would they be searching for a piece of family history, but they would also have the chance to *taste* America. Luis had loved all the junk food his mother hated: the pizzas, the burgers, the steaks and fries, the hot dogs, the tacos. It was fabulous. In Spain there was nothing like that. The only thing stopping him from sitting down for a rest right now, was knowing that back in Hobson's Valley he could get a huge bacon double cheese burger at Segar's Cabin.

Warm saliva flooded his mouth at the thought of it.

Not even the apparition of a flame-grilled stack of meat was enough to stop him from worrying about Carla, though. He could understand why she might walk off in a mood but after all she'd said about being followed, he wondered why she would go on her own. Was she really going to try and make it back to the town alone or was she just trying to give mama and papa the scare she thought they deserved? The idea that Carla might actually be in danger, even the simple notion that she might be lost and unhappy, was enough to cause him some hurt. The emotion was raw and surprising.

Only when his mother turned around did he realise he'd fallen several yards behind. She didn't stop walking to shout.

'Luis! Please try to keep up. We have a long way to go. I really think that if we keep a strong pace we might be back by tomorrow night.'

'Sorry.'

He ran to fall in with her again.

Luis heard the footsteps just before he saw the figure appear in front of them from around a sharper bend in the trail. When Maria saw the man she threw her arm across Luis's chest in a defensive gesture. When she recognised the hiker's face, she snatched her hand away in embarrassment. Despite this, her air remained one of forced politeness.

'Mr. Kerrigan.'

'Maria, Luis.' He nodded to them, the exhaustion in his face plain even through his demure smile. 'I'm pleased to see you,' he said. 'I was . . . concerned.'

'What are you doing out here?' asked Maria.

'Looking for you.' Kerrigan smiled at Luis and looked beyond him into the gloom of the rediscovered trail. 'Where are José and Carla?'

He searched their faces for the answer and seemed to find

it, at least in part, because his own expression changed from relief to fear. It shocked Luis to see it. He'd had such a sense of steadfastness from Mr Kerrigan when they'd first met. After what Luis took to be an embarrassed silence, it was his mother who answered.

'José is by the great tree at the end of this trail waiting for Carla. She . . . she was up early this morning and we haven't seen her since then.'

Kerrigan's frown deepened.

'She went for a walk alone? Why?'

'I think she was upset,' said Maria.

Luis stepped forward.

'They argued last night,' he said, careful to avoid his mother's stern stare. 'Mama threw away the necklace you gave Carla.'

Maria's eyes flashed warnings. Luis ignored them. Let her shoot him all the dark looks she wanted.

'It wasn't like that,' she explained. 'Maria fainted last night. I was worried about her—'

'Did you really throw her necklace away?' asked Kerrigan.

'Yes. I did. She should not be wearing such things.'

'I've got it in my pocket. Here.' Luis pulled the charm from his walking trousers and held it out to Kerrigan.

'You should hang on to that for her,' Kerrigan said. 'So you say there is a tree at the end of this trail? Just like on your old map?'

'I have never seen a tree like it,' said Maria. 'I think it is the biggest living thing in the world.'

Kerrigan smiled at first

'Really.'

'It is enormous, Mr. Kerrigan,' said Luis 'and it looks like . . . like it's made of flesh or something. Really strange. Carla touched it and it knocked her out.'

Maria took hold of her son's shoulder.

'Luis, for God's sake.'

'It's true. I was there right beside her and I saw it happen.

The tree shocked her and just before she touched it her charm necklace was glowing purple.'

'That is enough, young man. Not another word from you.' Maria turned to Kerrigan. 'I'm sorry, Mr. Kerrigan, he's . . . It's his imagination.'

Kerrigan wasn't listening. He was intent on the boy.

'It's not a charm necklace, Luis. It's called a binder, but you're almost right. I give them to people for protection.'

'That's not what you told us before, Mr Kerrigan.' Maria was upset now, close to losing her temper.

'No?' asked Kerrigan. 'What did I say?'

'You said they would make our time in the forest special.'

Kerrigan closed his eyes as if trying to remember.

'Yeah? Well, that's kind of the same thing. Where are you headed? Back to Hobson's Valley?'

'Yes. We're hoping Carla is going the same way. José will follow us if she doesn't return to the camp by morning. You wouldn't happen to know where she is would you?'

Luis hit his mother's thigh, disbelieving that she would be so challenging to the only person that had offered any help since they'd arrived in the town.

'No, I don't know where she is.' Kerrigan's tone was mild. 'Why do you ask?'

'Carla thought we were being followed,' said Maria. 'She said she heard voices and laughter in the night. Later, I heard them too.'

At this, Kerrigan changed. To Luis it looked as though he expanded somehow. There was something wild about the man as he reached into the two side pockets of his pack. His hands reappeared holding two broad leather straps. He whispered to Maria in harsh tones while he laced the leather tightly to his wrists.

'You need to keep to the paths in this forest. You need to hurry back to town and you need to wear the binders I gave you if you want to be safe.'

Luis was pale. When his mother didn't respond, he said:

'Will you find my sister, Mr. Kerrigan?'

The wild man looked him in the eye.

'If she's out here, I'll find her.'

As she walked along the path between the pines, Gina tried to understand what it was that had happened to her. With so many gaps in her thinking it wasn't easy. She'd heard her parents talking about calling the sheriff, heard what her father was prepared to believe about her and it had been enough to make her want to leave.

She still couldn't remember what she'd done with the boys that night, but whatever it was she was incriminated now. Everything was going to change.

Gina didn't want to face the questions and the accusations. She couldn't even recall what they'd wanted to know. She was frightened she'd developed some kind of brain disease; maybe a tumour that was eating her memory before devouring everything else. But if she could walk away and forget about that, forget about everything, then there was a chance for happiness still; a chance to live the life she'd dreamed of.

This was a trail she remembered well. At least, she remembered that she liked being here. What had she done, gone for walks?

The trail was broad, but even out here in the forest where a little peace could return she was still trapped somehow. Her clothes felt tight and unnatural. She slipped off her leather jacket and let it fall to the ground. She felt a little better then, a little lighter. Things weren't all bad. She was strong sometimes. Gina had a vague memory of using that strength to get what she wanted. There was a satisfaction in that.

She tugged her black Spandex tee shirt out of her jeans and pulled it over her head, letting it drag in the dirt for a while. As she walked she felt the air on her skin like a ghost trailing fingers over her. It felt so good she let the tee shirt go.

Her appetite had changed; her parents were right about

that, although she hadn't noticed it herself until they said something. She felt hungry

thirsty

almost all the time and nothing she could drink or eat could make the feeling go away. In many cases she'd forced herself to be sick because the food she'd eaten felt tainted

dead

and unwholesome. She'd thought it would help to talk, but it hadn't. There was something else, something far deeper within her that she did not understand. It was a desire

need

to be in the forest. A summoning. A *call*.

The touch of clothing against her skin became unbearable. She had to feel the forest. Stopping on the path, she slipped off her scuffed motorcycle boots and socks, leaving them where they fell. The jeans came next and last her underwear. Finally she felt a tiny glimmer of freedom. Naked, her black hair cascading around her shoulders, she strode proud and determined along the trail, her soles welcoming the caress of the earth.

CHAPTER 26

Kath tutted to herself as she walked through the knee-high grass almost obscuring the paving slabs and made a mental note to call David Slater in for some serious mowing and weeding. The yard was a disgrace. Maybe now that she was just buying for one, she could afford David more often; make the place look smart again. It was something to look forward to.

As they walked along The Terrace, Dingbat matched her pace, not quite to heel, but not pulling either. Kath took her time, not knowing how much her legs could take and not wanting to pay for it later.

When she came to the corner of the block she turned right into The Grove and the gradient steepened a little. She was surprised and pleased to discover that she was still able to get around so easily. Burt's frailty had really held her back.

His funeral was scheduled for the following Friday at the Baptist church where they'd attended until Burt's legs began to let him down. He was to be buried in the Hobson's Valley cemetery, where most of the residents ended up, regardless of their creed. Kath tried not to think about the service. All she knew was she wanted her boy there. They were only going to bury his father once; Jimmy had better turn up.

Maggie's house was at the far end of the Grove and her property bordered the woods. The gradient took its toll on

Kath so she stopped for a rest and Dingbat sat down to wait for her, as patient as if he'd been trained for the job. When she had her wind back they completed the stint in just a couple more minutes. With Dingbat wagging his tail in anticipation, Kath rang the bell and waited on the porch.

The smell of baking was strong even outside the house and when Maggie opened the front door the house exhaled a warm scent of oats and cinnamon. Underlying the sweetness of the smell was something savoury too, reminiscent of a joint roasting or sausages broiling. Kath was surprised when her stomach growled in response. She swallowed a rush of saliva.

'My, my, Maggie. That sure smells good.'

Maggie smiled and ushered her in, not trying to conceal her pride.

'I think they've turned out all right this time. I've been experimenting.'

'Well, I'm a willing guinea pig for you.'

'Come on through to the living room and make yourself comfortable.'

'Is it okay for him to come in too?'

'Sure it is.'

'I thought you had cats.'

'I don't think they'll be a problem. Come on and siddown.'

In the living room Dingbat lay down and rested his head on his paws as if he went out for afternoon tea every day of the week. Maggie disappeared out to the kitchen and Kath leaned over her well-mannered dog.

'I sure am proud of you, boy,' she whispered.

She took in the surroundings and decor a piece at a time, building a more thorough picture of Maggie. The profusion of quilts thrown over every piece of furniture gave a clue as to how she must have spent a good deal of her time, but there were other projects that were the result of deft fingers everywhere around. On the floor were rugs made from kits. Behind glass in picture frames were cross-stitch patterns and motifs in fine detail. Over some of the quilted throws were crocheted blankets of many colours. Displayed in the cupboards and on the pieces of furniture around the room were items of pottery, obviously home made, but which showed real talent. It all seemed kind of twee to Kath but she couldn't deny the air of wholesomeness it projected. The room was welcoming.

As Maggie rattled the coffee pot and cups in the kitchen, another smell came to Kath's nostrils, that of cat urine. No doubt the cats had gone into hiding the moment they'd got a whiff of Dingbat. Maggie must have had several cats for the aroma to be so noticeable over the smell of baking. She imagined them draped over the furniture in languid poses, completing the picture of a house where a homely older woman lived alone.

Maggie returned with a tray and on it were several types of cookies arranged on three tiers of an elaborate glass dessert display. Kath had never seen such a fancy way of serving cookies and coffee. Maggie used a triangular silver dessert slice to serve the cookies and Kath had to bite her lip to keep from laughing. When she'd been at home as a child, they had cookies with glasses of milk and when the cookies came out of the oven, the little fingers of grubby hands reached out to take them. She wasn't about to reject Maggie's hospitality, but she could see that if this kind of meeting were to become a regular occurrence, she'd have to say something and bring the formality down a notch or two. At this rate she'd be scared to drink her coffee in case she slurped it.

'Try these first.'

Maggie handed her a side plate with a single cookie on it. It smelled wonderful. She accepted the plate and took a bite straight away.

'Oh, that is delicious. What have you put in these?'

'Well, that's just the test run. Actually, I don't think I like oatmeal and raisin much any more, but I thought you should try them anyway.'

'That's it? Oatmeal and raisin?'

'Uh huh, and a little cinnamon and sugar, of course. Do they meet with your satisfaction?'

'They taste great, if that's what you mean.'

Maggie took the dessert slice and placed a different kind of cookie on Kath's not quite empty plate. Dingbat sat up and stared at the coffee table between the women, making meaningful glances to Kath who ignored him.

'Would the gentleman care for a little delicacy?' asked Maggie. 'We did promise you one, I believe.'

Kath was astounded to see that Maggie took a third china side-plate and used the dessert slice to place one of her oatmeal and raisin creations on it before placing the whole thing in front of Dingbat with a:

'I do hope that this will be to sir's liking.'

Dingbat wolfed the cookie in a couple of hasty snaps of the jaw, after which he licked his lips over and over. Kath began to think either that Maggie was having a bit of a joke with her or that she was losing a fundamental screw. Maybe it was so long since the woman had had company that she really didn't remember the appropriate way to behave.

The coffee was good and the cookies were great. Kath decided to let it all slide in favour of a little sociability. She tried the new cookie that Maggie had placed on her plate and found it to be as good, if not better, than the first.

'You're going to have to give me the recipe for these if you want to avoid me moving in here, Maggie.'

'Oh, I'm so pleased you like them. That one was oatmeal with chocolate and peanut butter chips. I'm saving the best for last, though. I'll let you have a few moments to clear you palate before I serve them.'

Kath shook her head and sat back in the armchair to relax. The company wasn't as good as the baking but hell, who cared? Dingbat sniffed the air and looked distracted. After a while he stood up and snuffled his nose into the carpet and along the furniture. Kath kept an eye on him and when it looked like he was following his nose out of the room she spoke up.

'You stay here, boy.'

He stopped and looked back at her.

'Oh, he's okay,' said Maggie. 'Nothing he can get himself into out there. You should let him wander and kind of get used to the place. He might want to come up and visit on his own sometime. He's welcome to.'

The strangeness of the suggestion only hit Kath as Maggie scooped up the third cookie and dropped it onto her plate. She frowned. Was Maggie suggesting that when she died she would take Dingbat for herself? What the hell was the woman trying to say? She was about to challenge Maggie on it but she was pre-empted.

'Now don't take it the wrong way. All I'm saying is he can have a change of scene and you don't have to come over if you don't want to. I know I'm kind of an odd bird these days, but animals never notice do they?' She smiled broadly as if it was the most natural suggestion she could make and before Kath could protest or question it, she handed back the newly laden plate. 'This is the one I was saving 'til last. My great experiment.' She flapped her hands beside her face. 'Hoo, I'm nervous. I sure hope you like them.'

Kath was tight lipped. Maggie was further gone than she'd thought. She was leaving after this cookie and taking Dingbat with her. The last cookie turned out to be the one with the savoury smell but there was still an aroma of sweet spice to it like nutmeg or cinnamon. She tried to pick the cookie up but it was so moist it fell apart and she ended up holding only a tiny piece.

'Darn it,' said Maggie. 'Haven't perfected the texture yet. Going to need more practise.'

Kath put the morsel into her moth and chewed, her tongue unable to discern the flavours. The dough was warm and chewy, more like stiff, dark porridge than a cookie. But the flavour was intriguing; she finished the cookie and took another.

Dingbat appeared in the doorway of the living room with something in his mouth. Clearly he'd been rummaging through the trash and stolen something. After all his good behaviour, now he'd let her down.

'Dingbat, you fool hound, put that down right now. You can't steal from friends.' She turned to Maggie 'Maggie, I am so sorry. I really thought he was going to behave himself. I don't know what to say.'

She looked back at Dingbat trying to make sense of what was in his mouth. It looked like a length of stiff black rope. One end was pink and shiny. Her hand flew to her mouth in the next instant as everything came together. Kath stood up to run from the room knowing she wasn't going to make it to wherever the bathroom was. Maybe it would be better to vomit outside the front door so that she could keep walking and get home to call the sheriff.

Dingbat followed her, the cat tail still in his mouth. In the hallway Kath unloaded her stomach, far from either the bathroom or the front door. The spasms stopped her from walking and though she hated herself for getting sick on someone else's carpet she felt she had every justification. As the cookies wormed back out of her mouth she made the connection between the savoury smell and the flesh of cats and the retching worsened, hurting her stomach and chest. Dingbat began to whine.

Maggie followed her out to the hallway and stood watching with her arms folded.

'Kathleen Kerrigan, no one has ever been so rude or disgusting in this house. Those were the best cookies I ever made. I've eaten twenty already this afternoon.'

Kath stopped retching and fell to her knees, her hands clutched over her chest. Maggie stepped past her and stared.

'My God, Kath, are you having a heart attack?'

Kath fell against the wall, slipping down until she came to rest in an awkward position in her own pile of sickness. She lay back in the warm dampness managing to push one leg out from under herself. Maggie put her hands on her hips and shook her head.

'Well, I shouldn't do this when you've been so ungrateful. Just think of all the favours I've already done for you, and here I am about to do another. No one could ever call me uncharitable.'

She knelt beside Kath, whose eyes were starting to close, and rolled up her sleeves.

'I know CPR,' she said.

The last thing Kath saw was Maggie's tongue, as it turned from pink to purple and split into several flailing tips. The tips squirmed into her mouth, forcing her clenched teeth apart. They flexed and twisted their way down her throat.

CHAPTER 27

It hurt to run again at first but after a few minutes the pain passed and in its place Kerrigan felt a surge of euphoria akin to intense sexual arousal. He was Lethean now: invincible. His pack seemed weightless as he sprinted along the path. Where he felt the load was on his conscience; he'd wasted too much time. If he'd left the previous morning, he might have been able to prevent Carla from wandering off alone. He'd already failed to keep the family from harm.

Something else bothered him. They seemed to have found the tree that was marked on their old map. How was it possible that he didn't know about such a tree? The closer Kerrigan came to the place where José was waiting for Carla, the greater the sense that he was being played; like he was one crucial step behind in everything he set out to do. How that could be possible, he didn't know. The only person who could be directing things was the writer of the letter; now a Fugue or something worse. The same person who was preparing for his arrival. Perhaps he'd been preparing for years.

Up ahead, the trail had been hacked through another obstruction of plant growth. On the other side of the opening Kerrigan saw a different kind of ground; leaf covered and dead. As he ran through the mouth-like opening and into what he would come to know as the arbour, several things happened at once. He tried to make sense of what he was seeing:

The tree was indeed huge and he stopped dead when he saw it. But there wasn't time for him to think about its size or wonder how it had become such a monster. The tree reacted to his arrival as if it had been stung. Even from fifty yards away he saw the trunk of the tree buckle, ripple and contract. Its grey, elastic bark shuddered and the entire giant shook. He heard the branches above him rustle and leaves, thousands of broad fleshy leaves, rained to the earth all around. Not a single one touched him.

Those drifting close on their way down blew away as though repelled. He heard a low rumbling under the ground and the forest floor shook. Where the trunk met the ground, there was a tightening; the roots thickened and shortened as they contracted, drawing the tree even more tightly into the earth.

Above Kerrigan the branches shrank away, allowing sunlight to make a pool of brightness where he stood. There was no question that the tree feared him. The rumbling in the ground receded, the soil settling around the new position of the roots.

At the same time, he saw José Jimenez, who had been approaching the tree as Kerrigan arrived. It was the man's tiny figure beside the unnatural hulk of the trunk that made the size of the tree so striking. Jimenez was thrown to the ground by the force of the tree's movements. It must have felt like an earthquake to him. The Spaniard flew back from the tree long before he was close enough to touch it. He landed on his backside and kept going. He crawled frantically, kicking and scrabbling away from the tree, trying to stand and run all at the same time. When he gained his feet, he ran until he saw Kerrigan then changed direction, the look of gratitude on his face suggesting he was happier to know someone else had witnessed what he'd seen than he was to be still alive. He reached the edge of the arbour where

Kerrigan looked on and stood panting beside him as the tree became quiescent once more.

A charged silence returned.

It was then that Kerrigan saw a woman crawl like an animal from the undergrowth far to their right. Mesmerised by the tree, she didn't notice them at first. Her clothing was torn and shredded from where she'd caught herself on thorns and branches in the dense undergrowth.

It was only when the woman stood up that he realised who she was. Her 'clothing' was a ripped bathrobe. Her knees and the palms of her hands were gritty with blood and dirt. Her blonde hair was tangled and frizzy, the dryness of it all too obvious. It stuck out in random directions, restyled by the undergrowth as she'd passed through it on all fours. Dead leaves and twigs still clung there. Cuts and scratches crisscrossed her face.

Amy rose up slowly, all the time focussed on the tree, an expression of deep awe on her face. That, at least did not strike Kerrigan as inappropriate. Immediately she was upright she began to remove the rags that had once been her robe. She walked naked and unashamed towards the tree, her motherly breasts swaying a little as she went, her thigh flesh rippling with each step.

Kerrigan withdrew a binder from each wrist strap and sprinted towards her. Immediately, the tree responded with shudders and rustlings. From high above, over the centre of the trunk he heard the tree utter a scream like gas escaping under intense pressure; neither an animal nor human sound, but one that implied intelligence.

When he was in range he flicked a binder towards Amy. It flew in a slight arc, as true as if it was guided. It sang its own song as it sped into her, a whirring whistle like a single note from a wooden flute.

The tree bent a branch down towards her, moving with liquid grace. It encircled her waist and raised her high up over Kerrigan. The binder missed. She smiled as if the tree's touch completed her. Other branches reached out to caress and stroke her naked form, exploring her the way a blind man's fingers explore a face. They moved with supple fluidity like the tentacles of an octopus.

Kerrigan aimed a second binder at her, a difficult shot because she was almost directly overhead. The tree swung her out of the binder's trajectory and it connected with a branch behind her. Where the binder touched the branch the sinuous grey wood tightened as though in pain, turning immediately black. A moment later the branch, only a small one, snapped at the point of contact and fell writhing to the earth. It twisted there for a few seconds and then lay still.

All the while the tree hooted and screamed and flailed its numberless limbs. It was a dubious victory to have severed and destroyed such a small part of it. Kerrigan knew he didn't have enough binders to kill the tree even if he threw them for a month. Meanwhile, Amy was beyond his help.

He retreated to the old trail where José crouched watching. The tree called out a low whistle of triumph and was still once more, except for the branches that had taken Amy. Those limbs still stroked her as though she was a priceless talisman. She seemed to have fallen into a peaceful trance under the tree's ministrations. When it had finished exploring and comforting her, the tree held her outwards to the forest—perhaps a shield or warning to anyone who saw her. As he looked on, Kerrigan felt a hand on his shoulder.

'Please explain to me what I have just seen,' said the Spaniard.

Kerrigan's explanation was flat, matter of fact.

'The tree is using the woman to protect itself,' he said.

'There are no trees that can do what you say.'

Kerrigan turned to see if Carla's father really meant that after what he'd seen. It was clear he was in shock. The Spaniard mashed a fist against his lips and looked away.

'I cannot leave my daughter to wander in such woods as these,' he said.

'I'll find her.'

'I will come with you.'

Kerrigan shook his head.

'You need to be with Maria and Luis. They'll have a better chance of making it back to your car if you stay together.'

Jimenez pondered the choice and Kerrigan could see it was a hard one to make.

'I'm trusting you with my daughter's life, Mr Kerrigan. You have to bring her back to us.'

To Kerrigan, it was a simple matter. He would give his life if necessary. It was his duty.

'I promise you I will do everything I can to return her safely,' he said. 'Anything.'

Jimenez nodded.

'You should hurry,' Kerrigan said. 'If you run you'll catch up to them soon. They need you.'

'Can you tell me what is happening here?'

Kerrigan didn't have to think too hard.

'War.'

'When we get back to the town, should we call for help?' asked Jimenez.

'There's no one you can call. Just wait for me to bring Carla back and then drive away. Here, take these with you.' He handed Jimenez a few binders for throwing. 'Do you still have the binder on the necklace?'

'I never took it off.'

'Make sure it's visible.' Kerrigan reached out, pulled the leather thong up from under the man's collar and dropped the binder out onto his chest. 'Did you find your grandfather's last resting place?'

'No. There is no sign.'

'I'm sorry you had a wasted journey.' Kerrigan placed his hand on Jimenez's shoulder. 'Go,' he said. 'And don't stay in the Clearing when you get there. Wait for me in my cabin.'

When Jimenez was out of sight, Kerrigan stepped back into the arbour. Amy and the tree were motionless, as though they were sleeping. He began to search for signs of Carla.

When it came time to pair up, no one wanted to partner Randall Moore. It was only then that he regretted being so outspoken with Sheriff Powell. He ended up with a bookish man called Ricky Flowers who looked seventeen but was probably thirty-five; one of those people that never seem to develop beyond adolescence. He was a lanky man with a prominent Adam's apple; looked like he'd tried to swallow a child's building block and never finished the job. Judging from his emaciated frame, the man hadn't eaten anything else since, owing to the blockage. The orange hunter's jacket swamped the man's shoulders and hung down like it was draped over a wire hanger.

Randall cursed his big mouth.

Still, he reasoned, at least he'd have no problems keeping the guy in line. They'd been given a section of the Eastern Path to search and some of the woods to the south side. Neither of them knew the terrain well. Randall hadn't been out hiking in the woods for twenty years and Flowers, a computer nerd from what Randall could make out, never went outside unless he was in a car.

Randall watched as Flowers took long gangly strides along the trail, looking up at the trees or biting his fingernails but never actually looking for anything on the ground.

'Where are you going in such a hurry?' asked Randall. 'This is meant to be a search, understand? You got to look for things.'

'It's nice out here,' said Flowers, stopping to acknowledge Randall's admonitions before walking on just as fast. 'Everything seems ... fresh.'

'Yeah, but we're trying to find some missing kids. You can't just stroll off.'

'Can you smell that? That's real pine.' Flowers stepped

over to a tree and swiped a few needles from it. He walked back and held them under Randall's nose.

'I can smell it already, Mister Flowers. Okay if I call you that? We need to concentrate on the matter in hand here, you get me?'

'You can call me Ricky or Flowers. Whatever.' Suddenly Flowers froze and then pointed, 'Hey, what's that?'

Randall turned with his hand already reaching for his pistol. All he saw was a reddish blur and a movement in the higher branches of a pine.

'That, Flowers, is a squirrel. Can we focus here, please?' Randall's heart was pounding a little. 'Do you even understand what we're doing?'

'Sure. We're looking for two boys and a girl.'

'You think we're gonna see 'em up in the trees?'

Flowers's Adam's apple bobbed up and down. It looked painful.

'I guess not,' he said.

'You got to help me out, Flowers. We're meant to be a team, okay?'

'Okay.'

'So let's be the ones to find these kids and then everyone can go home. What do you say?'

Flowers nodded.

'All right, I'm gonna lead the way and you do what I do, got it?'

'No problem.'

Randall moved forward taking slow steps, scanning the ground for signs of disturbance and casting wide glances into the woods on their right from time to time. He exaggerated the movements to try and set an example for the keyboard-tapper behind him. After a while he looked back to see how Flowers was doing and saw him staring up at the treetops again. Randall sighed and kept walking.

Randall stopped to take a leak about a half hour later and

it was while he relieved himself that his teammate made an important discovery.

'Hey, Mister Moore. I think I found something here. Look.'

He glanced over his shoulder expecting Flowers to be pointing at a bird or a rock and was shocked when he saw the guy holding up what looked like a black tee shirt.

'There's more stuff over there,' said Flowers, pointing.

Randall finished his piss and walked over to investigate. He found a bra. Further along the path he could see a pair of jeans and some black boots. He couldn't believe it was Flowers who'd spotted it. If he'd waited another minute or two to take a leak, he'd have found the clothes first.

'You think this is that girl's stuff?' asked Flowers.

Randall nodded, saying nothing. Flowers walked further along to the boots and then picked up a pair of white underwear. He held them to his face and inhaled.

'God damn it, Flowers. You put those down.'

Randall marched over and slapped the underwear from the skinny guy's hand.

'What are you? Some kind of fucking pervert? You want to explain to Sheriff Powell why you were touching the evidence?'

Flowers shook his head.

'Don't touch anything. Nothing, understand?'

'Okay, okay.'

Randall pulled out his radio.

CHAPTER 28

'Sheriff Powell, this is Randall Moore, we've got something out here.'

There were a few moments of silence and then the radio crackled and spat Powell's response.

'Copy that, Randall. Where are you?'

'About a mile and a half east of the Clearing.'

'Stay put until we get there.'

'Will do, Sheriff. Out.'

Randall stared at the strewn clothes and wondered what they might mean for the girl who'd worn them. Was she dead? Raped? Just crazy?

'You know, Flowers,' he said. 'I think we should go a little further along here and see if we can find her. Maybe she's hurt.'

'Uh, I don't think so, Mister Moore. We're meant to stay with this stuff until the sheriff gets here.'

'Shit, boy. When did you ever listen to instructions? You coming or not?'

Flowers looked down at the clothes, particularly the underwear, as if he wanted nothing more than to be left alone with them for a little while. That settled the matter for Randall.

'You're coming with me. Let's go.'

'Wait, one of us should make sure this stuff is safe.'

'It'll be safer without you, panty boy. Come on.'

Randall had to physically push Flowers away from the discarded clothing and get him started up the trail. Even then Flowers kept looking back. Randall shoved him along without pretending to be nice about it.

'Keep your eyes open, Flowers. We're looking for a naked girl.'

After that the guy started to concentrate like he was in an exam.

Randall checked his watch. It would take the sheriff at least a half-hour to arrive. He figured they'd walk for ten minutes and then turn back if they hadn't found anything. He was checking his pistol for the third time that morning when he bumped into Flower's back. He was about to give the guy another mouthful when he saw why Flowers had stopped in his tracks. In the path about fifty yards ahead of them was the girl they were looking for. He recognised her from the photos they'd been given. Even from this distance she was more striking than her picture had suggested. For a start she was as naked as he'd predicted.

The effect of this on Flowers would have been amusing if Randall hadn't been so similarly affected himself. He was standing, staring, with the pistol still in his hands, mesmerised by the naturalness of her marble-pale skin against the greens and browns of the trail and the forest beyond. She stood with her feet apart in a posture of strength and confidence, her hands on her hips and her head tilted a little as if waiting or inquiring.

She was so achingly seductive that he was developing a rare erection.

Flowers was the first to move but he lifted his feet like a diver in a weighted suit. Randall watched as the sapling of a man set off to help Gina Priestly. His orange hunting jacket flapped a little in the breeze and Randall saw the bumps under the orange day-glo where the guy's shoulder bones poked upward.

He tried to shout to Flowers to tell him to hold on a second but his throat was so dry it was stuck shut. When he tried to move his legs he had to look down to make sure he hadn't sunk into quick mud. His feet wouldn't do what he wanted them to do; it was like trying to walk through treacle. No matter how hard he tried he couldn't catch up.

The girl stretched her arms out to them. Her palms were held upward and her hands beckoned. Randall was a little closer now and with every slow pace he could see her shape more clearly, the curve at her waist, the strongly muscled legs and shoulders, her dark pubic triangle, the grave appeal of her breasts. Her black hair contrasted her skin so totally, she looked like an actress that had stepped from the reels of a silent movie.

Flowers, looking like a hopeless sinner, fell to his knees in front of her and pressed his angular cheek against the smooth curve of her abdomen. She enfolded his head in her arms and Randall imagined the guy inhaling the scent from her cool white skin. The girl stroked Flowers's hair with great tenderness whilst Randall Moore was still thirty yards away and struggling to make his muscles work. She had a look of such loving tenderness on her face as she looked down that Randall was overcome with a rush of animal jealousy.

He reached for his pistol.

Flowers's demeanour changed from that of a man who had found salvation to that of a bear that had found honey. He turned his face towards her belly and began to kiss her below the navel. Randall wanted to tear the guy away from her and smash his face with the butt of his pistol but he was too far away. The air around him had grown thick. His breathing became laboured. He could hear nothing through the cloying atmosphere except the sound of Flowers's tongue licking and rasping against Gina's black, course curls. It was impossible the sound could be so loud, but Randall could hear nothing else.

Balancing perfectly, Gina wrapped one leg behind

Flowers' head and drew him closer. The movement separated her legs, giving his tongue easier access to her crotch. She tightened her grip on his head and Randall saw him react by trying to pull away a little. Her skin shimmered giving off flashes of purple. Dark vessels pulsated beneath the surface. A tube-like tongue spilled from her mouth and snaked down towards Flowers. Everything about what was happening made Randall's erection harder.

Then he saw the tongue, as if it had its own life independent of the girl, wrap around Flowers's neck and burrow through the skin of his throat. Something about the sight shocked him so deeply that for a moment he regained some control over himself. Randall was only ten paces from them by then and had no idea how he'd covered the distance. Soon she'd be able to reach out to him.

He raised the pistol and she looked up from her prey. Too physically committed to Flowers in that moment, there was nothing she could do but snarl. Randall didn't want to kill her. He didn't even want to hurt her. He had in his mind only the memory of her pale skin and dark hair perfectly placed against the background of the woods. He didn't want to destroy that image. He didn't want to damage her in any way. But she was killing Flowers, and Randall knew that if he didn't do something it would be him next.

He aimed for her foot and pulled the trigger. The earth blew open in a small dark circle beside her foot. He'd missed, but the sound of gunfire had scared her and served to startle both Flowers and himself further out of their trances.

Flowers tried to scream but Gina yanked him harder into her crotch. The stifled screaming continued making Randall giggle at the ridiculous sound. But Gina didn't let go.

She began to plasticise in front of him. Her head stretched outwards and forwards and she grew taller. The purpleness of her skin deepened and the veins that had merely flashed beneath the surface before now bulged with diseased plasma. From her mutating skin, hollow spikes tore forth. The ones that grew from her thighs and calves entered Flowers's body, wounding him and causing his muffled screams to intensify. Other tongues sprouted like vines from her belly and under her arms and flailed towards Randall who took a step backwards. As she rose up, she unhooked her leg from around Flowers's neck and the barbs on her calf ripped open the skin of his shoulder. One punctured his ear, tearing through the soft cartilage and still another caught beneath the bone of his shoulder blade, pulling him over onto the ground while the tongue buried in his neck continued to feed on him.

Randall's second shot shattered the toes of Gina's left foot. The middle toe broke off cleanly and was forced deep into the dirt. The two on either side were pulped by the impact but no blood or fluid escaped. Gina let out a scream that emanated from her entire body like pressurised steam. She walked towards Randall dragging Flowers through the needle-strewn dirt. He'd recovered himself enough to clasp both hands around the tongue that was both asphyxiating him and draining his carotid artery. He squeezed it in attempt to block the flow of blood away from his body. When that didn't work, his hands lost their grip on the tongue and his movements began to weaken.

Randall fired a third shot, this time aiming to kill. He succeeded in blowing one of the pointed tubular horns from Gina's shoulder. Again there was no blood. She seemed able to prevent any liquid from leaving her body. He aimed again, correcting his mistake and trying to compensate for the shaking of his hands. Before he could squeeze another shot off, his firing hand and the hand attempting to steady it were bound up by one of Gina's tongues. It wrapped around and tightened until he felt his bones pressing through his skin. All sensation went from his fingers and though he tried to pull the trigger again all he managed to do was drop the gun.

Gina embraced him, piercing him against her armoured body and Randall managed the full-throated scream that

Flowers had not. It was cut short by her mouth over his as she took not only his fluids but even the damp, muted exhalations from his lungs and consumed them all.

CHAPTER 29

When the sallow man saw the girl asleep with her head lolling against the trunk of a young pine tree he felt a ripple of tension beneath his flesh. The aches receded from his ageing limbs and the strength of forgotten youth swelled his muscles and quickened his thoughts. What began as a moment of appreciation, recognising the perfection of a young woman, became a visual devouring. The sallow man was rigid with lust.

Before he could stoop to his desires the tree's words coursed through him, asserting its authority.

she is the one. she is mine. she is strong. do you not feel it?

'Yes. I feel it.'

she will withstand the process. she is the future. do you understand?

'I do.'

The voice of the tree faded and vanished but the sallow man felt its presence within him, ready to take charge if he attempted to satisfy his own hungers. He sat down without making a sound and stretched his mind into hers to wake her.

When he sensed that she was about to open her eyes he closed his own and feigned sleep. He listened to her stretch herself and recognised the moment when her movements stopped as she noticed him. There was a barely audible intake of breath. It was a crucial moment; he waited for her to run but she didn't. Instead she stood up.

From the length of time it took her, he could tell she was trying to slip away without waking him. He stirred himself, as if coming round after a deep sleep and allowed himself the theatre of a loud yawn and stretch. She turned and their eyes met.

'I was dreaming of a strange city in which every light was purple,' he said, smiling.

'What are you doing here?'

'I saw you sleeping and decided I ought to stay with you. This forest is not safe, you know.'

'I can look after myself better than a sleepy old man can.'

'Perhaps,' he said. 'But the elderly feel a natural inclination to protect the young. One day you will feel the same, I'm sure.'

'Thank you, but I don't need any help.'

She turned to walk away into the trees.

'Your family needs you.' He watched her body tense up a little at hearing his words, but she didn't stop walking. The leaves and branches closed behind her and in a moment she was out of sight.

She called back her reply:

'I don't need them.'

'Your brother is hurt. He touched the tree. Your father has gone for help while your mother attends to Luis. But they all need you now. They are scared that you are lost and possibly hurt.'

He heard the rustle and crunch of her movements cease.

'You saw this? What happened to Luis?' she called back.

He didn't answer.

'Do you hear me, old man?'

'I hear you, yes. But I see that you have already made up your mind. I'm sure they will manage as well without you as you will without them.'

She staggered back through the branches, screwing her

eyes up to protect them from stray twigs and thorns. He saw the seeds of doubt weakening her resolve.

'Just tell me what happened to Luis. How badly hurt is he?'

The sallow man stroked his beard and looked upward as if struggling to remember the details.

'All I know is that he touched the tree and it damaged him in some way. He lost a hand, I think.'

'His *hand*?' Carla's own hand covered her mouth.

'Well, perhaps it was just a couple of fingers. I suppose he'll live. What message would you like me to give him? I'll be going straight back to the arbour now that I've done what they asked.'

'They sent you to find me?'

'Of course.'

Carla was crying by then.

'You have to take me back to them.'

'What?'

'Take me back to my family. Now.'

'But, child, I thought you had made up your mind to go your own way. Let me pass a message to them for you. I'm sure they'll understand your feelings.'

'Please,' she sobbed. 'Please take me.'

It made the sallow man's penis stiffen again to see her cry and to hear her beg, but the tree's influence was too strong for him to ignore. Though he wanted nothing more than to gorge himself on the sweet milk within her flesh as he deflowered her, he had no choice but to walk in the direction of the arbour. He was pleased to be facing away from her so she couldn't see his agitation. Perhaps, after the tree had used her for its own purposes, it might permit him to make use of her in his own way.

Isobel and Nicholas Priestly thought they'd discovered something but they weren't sure what. Through the trees Isobel could make out what looked like a timber wall, so old it was grey.

'Let's get a closer look and find out,' she said.

The broken down shack was covered with vine.

'A hunting shelter,' said Nicholas. 'Wonder if there's anyone living there.'

'I doubt it,' said Isobel.

Every window was either smashed or cracked and the grass that grew around the place was hip high. Tangled briars tore at their jeans as they approached. The tin roof had rusted right through in many places and the footings had given way at one corner, the frame drooping down. It looked ready to collapse. A thin swathe of trodden-down grass led, not to the front door, but around the back. It looked recently visited.

'Someone's been here,' said Nicholas. 'How old does this trampling look to you?'

'I can't say. It doesn't look too old though.' Isobel looked up at the windows of the house. Nothing moved in the shadowed interior. 'Gina? Gina, it's only us, honey. We just want to talk to you.'

'Hey, Geen? You in there? You know the whole town is looking for you—'

Isobel took his forearm, and shook her head.

'Don't freak her out any more than she already must be, Nick,' she whispered. And then towards the shack: 'Honey, you can talk to us and then we'll leave you alone. We won't tell them you're out here. You can come home whenever you're ready. Whatever it is you want to do, we can work it out. Okay?'

There was no sound from inside. The whole valley was silent. Nicholas followed the tracks and found the back door. It was half broken from its hinges and didn't look like it would survive being opened.

'You think we should let Sheriff Powell know what we've found?' He whispered.

'No way. What if Gina's in there and she's not ready to come out? You think she'll ever trust us again if we tell

Sheriff Powell where she is before she has a chance to tell us what she's doing out here?'

'I guess not.'

'I say we go in. If she's here, we talk to her, try to persuade her to come back with us.' Isobel took a step towards the back door. 'If she's not, we'll tell Sheriff Powell we found an empty shack and some tracks. If he wants to come and check it out, he can.'

Nicholas took a deep breath and sighed as quietly as he could.

'What if she's in there and she doesn't *want* to come back?'

'I don't know, Nick. We'll have to cross that bridge when we come to it.'

He hesitated for a few moments and then stepped towards the door.

'Let me go in first,' he said.

Sheriff Powell had been close enough to hear the gunshots and he knew the Eastern path was hiding a different story to the one it told. To the inexperienced eye the trail might have looked deserted and undisturbed, but there was evidence of people walking where the dark soil showed through the dead pine needles and even in the centre of the path where no needles fell.

Powell noticed the scuff marks in the path—it looked as though someone had resisted being dragged. He saw the imprints of knees and bodies that had struggled against each other. He found the places where bullets had lodged or disappeared into the ground. There was no trace of blood.

Using a fallen branch, he did his best to erase the tracks and smooth the signs of confrontation from the earth. As he stood back to check the results, his deputy came through on the walkie-talkie.

'You find anything out there, sir?'

'Nope. Not a thing.'

'What about Moore and Flowers? Did they say who opened fire?'

'There's no sign of them where they say they were. All I can figure is that some hunters are out here. Or maybe Randall Moore took my comments a little too personally and decided to waste our time to make his point.'

'You going to look for him?'

'Hell no. We've got better things to do. I'm heading back.'

Powell scanned the scene one last time and saw nothing out of place. There was a bullet stuck in a tree off to the left of the path but he couldn't remove it without it becoming more obvious. Instead he broke a branch down to hide the entry point. Given enough time the tree would heal its wound.

He set a stiff pace back to the Clearing.

'Why did you set off alone?'

The sallow man's words hung in the air and Carla felt she'd walked through them and left them far behind before replying.

'My mother doesn't treat me like she should. I respect her, but it should go both ways.'

'That's all?'

'That and what happened with the tree. I didn't want to hang around any longer.'

She couldn't read the back of the sallow man's head nor could she detect any change in him except silence.

'The tree, the tree,' he said after a while. 'It is beautiful, no?'

'No, it is not beautiful. It scares me.'

She saw him nod to himself.

'The tree ought to be feared. It is powerful.'

'Did you see what happened to my brother?'

'No. I only saw that he was unconscious and that his arm was bandaged.'

Carla frowned.

'I don't know why he would try to touch the tree,' she said. 'He saw what happened to me.'

216

'What did your parents think when you told them the tree knocked you down?'

'They didn't believe us. They thought I'd fainted from lack of food.'

The sallow man laughed. He stopped and turned towards her. His face was sympathetic and his eyes gentle.

'If it's any consolation, I had exactly the same kinds of problems with my parents when I was a similar age to you. It was over different matters, of course, but at the time they made me so angry I sometimes fantasised about killing them in their sleep.'

He laughed again before turning away and walking on. Carla took in the bare places at his elbows where his scrawny wrinkled skin showed through and the threadbare seat of his trousers. His clothes hung like torn sails from a spindly mast, as though the slightest breeze might destroy the entire construction.

'Was there a mist last night?' he asked.

'Yes, there was. It seemed to make everyone sleepy except me.'

The sallow man was full of questions. Some were relevant to their brief acquaintance but others made no sense. It was as if the man knew nothing of life outside the forest

'Where are you from?' she asked.

'I have always lived here.'

'In the forest? That can't be.'

'In Hobson's Valley. I was born here. But the forest has become a better home for me than any town could ever be.'

Carla thought about that. Here was a man who might be old enough to know her great grandfather.

'Why did your family come out here?' The sallow man asked.

'We were looking for the final resting place of a relative.'

'What was his name?'

'Raul Jimenez. He was my papa's grandfather.'

Walking in single file, it was impossible to see the man's

expression but Carla was sure she noticed a reaction. It was as if his footing faltered slightly. Before she could even be half sure she'd seen it, the hesitance was gone.

She pushed:

'Did you know him?'

'No.'

'What is your name?'

The sallow man didn't answer for a while. When he did his voice was so low she almost did not hear him.

'I lost my name a long time ago.'

CHAPTER 30

The single room of the shack was mausoleum silent and no sounds came in from outside. It was gloomy inside, but the windows allowed enough light for Nicholas to see straight away what he'd hoped someone else would find.

Isobel's hand found Nicholas's. Both sets of fingers squeezed until they hurt the other's but the contact was all they had.

'Do you think it's them?' asked Isobel, her voice dry and cracked.

Nick nodded. It had to be the two missing boys. No attempt had been made to hide anything. Their clothes were strewn across the floor and the bed, as if removed in haste. Their backpack lay open on the other side of the bed near the fireplace. An empty liquor bottle lay on its side, the back of its label showing white through the glass. A few cigarette butts and roaches lay in a rusted skillet that had doubled as an ashtray. There was a lingering smell of burnt wood. The sleeping bags were still on the bed, rumple and twisted. Nick couldn't picture Gina on that bed but it had to be a possibility. Nauseous, he broke a prickly sweat

Two naked, shrivelled forms sat opposite each other with an antique tin washtub sitting empty between them. The skin of each boy was husky like parchment, drawn tight across their bones. Nicholas could see the dryness of their

219

bodies — as though the skin might crumble at a single touch. Even the boys' hair seemed frizzy and desiccated, their bodies small and childlike; the drying process had shrunk them. The empty tub suggested water and wetness in some perverse way. The scene was like the installation of some demented artist. In each boy's stomach there was a hole no larger than kernel of dried blue corn. An expression of helplessness remained on both faces. Neither boy was bound or gagged and their bodies showed no other signs of harm or struggle.

Gina's parent's stared in silence for moments out of time before deciding in almost the same instant to retreat into the free air and the comfort of the light.

Nicholas stood staring at the dead wood of the shack wall.

'It can't have been Gina,' he said.

'Nick, please.'

'No one could have . . . she could never do something like . . . I don't understand what happened to them. It couldn't have been her. Not our little Geen.'

His knees gave way and he sank to the ground. When his ass touched his boot heels, his knee joints crackled and he bounced a little, falling sideways. Only then did he put out a hand to stop himself from lying down. Isobel knelt beside him and held his head against her shoulder.

Finally she pulled away from him.

'We need to radio in to the sheriff. I'm going to tell him what we've found.'

'No need for that,' said a voice nearby. 'You can show me.'

Sheriff Powell smiled at them each in turn and stepped past them into the shack. The Priestlys, both standing now, waited while he made his inspection.

'Where the hell did he spring from?' whispered Nick.

Isobel never answered; the sheriff's laughter came first. It sounded like someone watching slapstick; a loud, raucous HAHAHA. It went on for a long time. When Sheriff Powell appeared in the broken doorway, he wiped the tears from his face with a checked handkerchief.

'That's the best one yet,' he said when he'd recovered enough to speak. His shoulders still bounced as he thought about it. 'That girl of yours sure is creative.'

Nicholas looked briefly at Isobel.

'You're laughing because it's a set up, right? This whole damn thing, the bodies, the personal stuff in there, it's a hoax, isn't it? Someone's been stringing us all along.'

Sheriff Powell smiled with one half of his mouth and blew a brief, unamused jet of air from his nose. Then he looked at them both and shook his head.

'It's no joke, Mr. Priestly. Gina was hungry and she sucked the juice right out of them. They're so dry they'll never even rot. Shake those boys' heads and you'll hear the rattle of a nut-sized pebble that was once a brain. She shouldn't have killed them, though. It was a waste of perfectly good muscle.'

'I don't understand what you're saying,' said Nicholas.

'You will soon enough.'

Nicholas noticed a flash beneath the sheriff's skin and the hairs rose on his neck. He squeezed Isobel's hand and mouthed a single word: 'run'.

Sheriff Powell unzipped his fly and released his tongues.

When Kerrigan saw the old man moving along the narrow run through the thickets of the forest with the grace of a wild animal, he knew who he was. Something about the way he moved

smelled

filled him with recognition: even a filial closeness. A moment later he saw Carla walking behind him and that remembered bond became a knot of venom. Kerrigan knew that here was the cause of all the harm in the valley. He sensed the power the sallow man hid behind his emaciated frame and cloud grey eyes. Kerrigan knew the man was driven. He knew he was insane.

Kerrigan slipped as quietly as he could into the depths of the brush to watch as they approached. From his seclusion he reached out with his mind and tried to ascertain whether the sallow man had fed on Carla or infected her. The answer was immediate and definite — he had not yet touched her. There was no stain upon her. As Kerrigan probed the sallow man's aura, he saw the attack on Gina Priestly. He tensed. His fear for Carla made him want to spring from cover and confront the sallow man. Instinct kept him motionless.

As they neared his hiding place in the undergrowth, Kerrigan saw the old man stiffen and stop dead. He held a hand out behind him motioning Carla to be still. The sallow man squinted into the trees and sniffed the air. His eyes rolled up into his head for a moment revealing whites shot through with diseased lavender cracks. Silently, Kerrigan removed two binders, one from each wrist sheath and readied himself to leap. His heartbeat accelerated and the iron taste of fear filled his mouth. He felt the Lethean within clawing to take over. The hunter in Kerrigan wanted nothing more than to take the tomahawk and end the old Fugue's filthy existence right there. Here was the writer of the letter, the one who had condemned him to this half-life. Kerrigan could be done with it in a swift, furious moment and then turn all his energy toward destroying the tree.

The sallow man's pupils rolled back into view and he looked right at Kerrigan. He didn't believe the sallow man could see him but it wasn't seeing that mattered; the old Fugue knew he was there. He could sense it the way Kerrigan could sense the old man's evil.

When the sallow man looked Kerrigan's way it was with love and the ache of separation. Behind that look Kerrigan smelled rather than saw his true intention; the sallow man wanted him dead. He wanted no Fugue Hunter ever to walk the earth again. Kerrigan also realised the sallow man had the power to follow through, and for the first time, he knew fear even in his Lethean state. The sallow man smiled to himself and walked on as if Kerrigan did not exist.

Kerrigan watched as they made their way back to the

arbour and waited until they were out of sight. Carla had become even more alluring than when the family had come to his cabin. Her vulnerability had a disturbingly erotic effect on him.

If he could separate Carla from the sallow man, it would be a start. He broke from cover and stood breathing heavily in the cramped run. He didn't want a battle now but he had no way of stopping them from reaching the tree without confronting them or at least causing them some kind of distraction.

Swift and light-footed, he closed the distance until he could make out Carla a few yards ahead. The sallow man had said something to amuse her and she was laughing. The connection growing between them, one the sallow man was forging and manipulating, had to be halted before he gained her trust completely.

They were a only few hundred yards from the arbour by the time he'd resolved to act. Reaching what he hoped was a safe distance, Kerrigan called out:

'Carla!'

She turned immediately she heard his voice, recognising it without even seeing him. That would go in his favour. The sallow man, on hearing him shout halted and turned very slowly, his lips pressed into a tight line, his expression sombre and dangerous.

'Mr. Kerrigan?' said Carla.

'You can call me Jimmy.' He smiled as he said it, making eye contact with her. He had some catching up to do.

'What are you doing out here?' she asked.

'I was worried about you all. I came to check how you were doing and met your mom and Luis heading back to the Eastern Path. They told me what happened. Your dad's waiting for you in the arbour.' He settled his gaze on the sallow man 'This gentleman a friend of yours?'

She glanced at the sallow man seeing him the way Kerrigan wanted her to: a broken down old man with long hair and torn clothes leading a young girl through the woods.

'Uh, I don't know. I guess so.'

The sallow man stayed quiet. He must have known there was no way his identity would survive the meeting.

'I'm escorting the child back to her parents,' he said. His voice had the dry reedy quality of the aged but behind it there was a hiss that sounded powerful and inhuman. Carla didn't seem to notice.

'Oh, that's good,' Kerrigan said, addressing her. 'They're worried about you.'

'We should hurry to the arbour,' said the sallow man.

'Wait,' said Carla. 'You saw Luis, how was he? Do you think he'll be okay?'

'They're all fine but your friend is right, we should get back as quick as we can.'

The sallow man held his hand out to Carla but she hesitated to take it and Kerrigan was glad.

'Come child, your family awaits.' His voice was commanding and she almost gave in to him.

'I should take you from here,' Kerrigan said, ignoring the sallow man. 'I kind of see it as my duty to look after hikers.'

'We're wasting time, Carla. Let us go.' Using her name was a mistake on the sallow man's part. It jarred with her and she didn't budge.

'Can you just tell me how Luis is, Jimmy? How bad is his hand?'

A spasm of undisguised rage passed over the sallow man's face and Kerrigan saw his body jerk and twitch as something within him came loose.

'We're leaving,' said Kerrigan. 'Now.'

'No,' she said. 'No way. I want to know what happened to Luis.'

'He's fine, Carla, absolutely fine. There's nothing wrong with his hand. By now he and your mom are probably well along the trail back to Hobson's Valley. We should try and catch them up.'

Carla turned to the sallow man.

'But you said—' she began and didn't finish.

'It doesn't matter what I said, child.' His voice was a wet growl. He managed to stay standing despite the convulsions rippling through his body. 'You belong to the tree now.'

'Run to me, Carla, as fast as you can.' Kerrigan saw her hesitate a moment longer, turning her eyes toward the sallow man. 'Don't look! RUN!'

She'd had a glimpse of him by then, seen the lavender fluid pulsing through his now visible blood vessels. Caught, perhaps, a hint of the changes to the shape of his limbs and head. Seen one of his tongues unravelling from his body.

Carla ran to Kerrigan.

Having her between him and his target in such a narrow space made throwing binders almost impossible. He risked bruising or cutting her in order to inflict more severe damage on the sallow man. The ancient forest vagrant slipped from Fugue to Rage in seconds, his growls becoming screams of frustration and insanity. It was the swiftest transformation Kerrigan had witnessed.

He loosed two binders in rapid succession, one from his right hand and one from his left, angling them to curve inward only after passing Carla. He didn't think she even saw them as they spun past her. She did the right thing and kept on running.

Hearing the song of the binders brought a temporary halt to the sallow man's metamorphosis. His crazed eyes fixed on Kerrigan and he leapt into the thorns and brush as if they posed not the slightest obstacle to him. Both binders missed, disappearing uselessly into the soil several yards further on. The contact snuffed their harmony in two barely spaced thuds.

Carla reached Kerrigan and fell into his arms.

'Don't let him take me, Jimmy. Please.' She sobbed hysterical tears into his neck as she clung to him. The touch of her was so fresh and trusting it hurt. He wanted to end that innocence.

'Stay behind me at all times,' he said, stepping between her and the place where the sallow man had disappeared. He pulled two more binders from their slots and placed a third around her neck on a leather thong. 'Don't lose it this time.'

He crept forward. Getting back to the arbour was the only option they had. Waiting would bring nightfall, a Fugue's ally and Kerrigan's foe.

'What are you doing?' hissed Carla. 'That's the way he went.'

'We have to bind him or destroy him. Otherwise he'll stalk us all night. Chances are he'll win if we fight him after the sun goes down. I'm sorry. We have to go forward.'

They moved down the track until they were level with the place where the sallow man had leapt into the brush.

Despite his increased size, he'd hardly disturbed the foliage at all. Kerrigan couldn't see where he'd gone and he sensed a gloom settling over the trail that he recognised all to well. He pressed on for the arbour. As they passed the place where the binders had impacted he dug his fingers deep into the soft earth and retrieved them. He knew he was going to need every one of them.

Wanting only to catch up to his wife and son as quickly as he could, José removed the tent and other non-essential items from his pack and left them in the arbour. What he still carried was heavy enough, but he did his best to set a fast pace, interspersing a forced march with jogging to make up the ground. He didn't want to exhaust himself and was conscious of his limits, but every time he thought about the tree and the woman who had become the tree's 'pet', he broke into a run.

He reached the Eastern path in better time than he'd anticipated and the going became a little easier. Still, he did not relax the pace. Thoughts of the dangers his family might face without him goaded him on and he used his fear for them as a whip to his conscience when his legs felt like giving way.

Eventually, he had to rest. He cursed his body for its weakness and his mind for lacking the toughness to continue, but there was no use in being totally spent when he caught them up; the journey would be far from over even then. He dropped his backpack and sat on the ground with his back against it. He planned to take half an hour rest; ten minutes spent drinking water and massaging his calf muscles and twenty minutes sleeping. He'd always been able to program himself to wake up from his afternoon siestas at exactly the right time.

When he snapped into wakefulness there was a chill in the air that had penetrated to his bones. When he tried to move, his muscles were stiff and slow to respond. He looked at his watch and saw that almost an hour had gone by.

'Mierda,' he said and struggled to his feet.

A veil of lilac shadow had turned the Eastern Path into a twilight corridor. Looking up he saw that the sky was overcast. There were still a couple of hours before sunset. Perhaps he could catch up to them that same night if he pushed the pace.

Now the light was failing, seeing them again was all he could think about. He considered the weight of the pack and decided to leave it behind; it was sapping too much of his strength. From it he took a flashlight and some energy bars and water, stuffing everything into the pockets of his jacket. Lighter now, he ran on, westward on the Eastern path.

Even without the pack his legs hurt but he no longer allowed himself to march. He would run until he found them.

CHAPTER 31

Luis stayed close to his mother. It was becoming too dark to see the way ahead easily. Twice Luis's mother stumbled, putting out her hand to him to steady herself.

'This is where we make camp for tonight, Luis.'

'But I can still see. Can't we go just a little farther?'

'You may be able to see, but my eyes aren't as young as yours. If one of us sprains an ankle . . .' He heard the tension in her voice. 'This is far enough.'

Luis walked to the edge of the path and slung his pack to the ground.

'You think we should make camp off the trail like before?' he asked.

'No. What if your father comes looking for us? He could walk right by.'

'We'd hear him wouldn't we?'

Maria sighed.

'I don't want to take the chance that we might sleep right through his arrival,' she said.

Luis pulled out his sleeping bag, wishing it was water-proof, and laid it alongside the trees so his feet wouldn't stick out into the trail. He knew he'd be damp all over with dew come the dawn.

'Is there anything to eat?'

'There are some cereal bars but control yourself otherwise we'll be starving by the time we reach the car.'

'I can't wait to go for a burger at that place we passed on the way in.'

'When we get there you can eat all you want.'

'Really?'

'Really.'

The darkness was complete as Luis crunched through two cereal bars, savouring them as best he could. He could hear his mother making her own arrangements with her sleeping bag and he took the opportunity to wander a little further along the track and relieve himself before he turned in for the night.

'Don't go far,' he heard her call softly after him.

As he stood aiming his pee into the trees and trying to make as quiet a splash as possible, he heard a branch snap some distance away. The stream he was making dried up. Even though he still had a good way to go before he was finished, he zipped up and listened into the darkness.

Somewhere farther up the trail in the direction they'd been heading, there was movement. Stealthy steps advanced towards him in the darkness, the caress of clothing-covered legs brushing against each other made a gentle sound like breathing. In just a few seconds his body went into overdrive. His breathing was rapid and high in his chest and he was certain the noise of it would give him away.

Attempting to make no sound, he crept back to his mother.

He felt the springy fabric of his sleeping bag beneath the sole of his boot and crouched down to be as near as he could to his mother before he spoke. In less than a whisper he said:

'Mama, someone is coming.'

'Luis, I can hear someone on this side too.'

Blind, he reached out his hand towards her and was relieved to find her reaching for him. Her grip on him was fierce and clinging. Every muscle in his body clenched as they waited; praying whoever it was would either stop and help them or pass by into the night forever.

Luis heard nothing from the direction in which they'd come and he wondered if his mother's hearing was as unreliable as her eyesight. From the place where he had started to pee he heard the noises approaching.

When the quiet footsteps were right beside them they stopped. Luis held his breath. Further away, all noise ceased. For an excruciating moment, there was utter silence in the forest. And yet the darkness around them was thick with intelligence and threat. Luis could sense it and so could his mother. Luis lost control of his bladder releasing what he'd retained only moments before. He thanked god it didn't make any noise. The warm, shameful wetness spread from his underwear into his trousers, along his thighs and downward towards his bottom. He bit his lip to stop himself from crying but he knew that in a few more seconds he would whimper and give himself away.

As his piss turned cold against his skin a male voice, so close it seemed to be in his head, said:

'That's a waste of fluid. What's wrong with you, boy?' Then the voice took on a shrill, offended tone. 'They're protected, sheriff. What do we do?'

Footsteps, no longer stealthy approached. Luis felt the chill of blunt steel against the centre of his forehead and a loud metallic click.

'Take those goddamned dream-catchers off right now or I give this kid a third eye. He'll be able to see God right through the hole.'

Luis didn't need any more encouragement. He used his free hand to remove the necklace. Maria did the same.

'Toss them into the trees behind you.'

They did as the voice said and heard the gentle release as the man with the pistol let the hammer rest gently back against the firing pin.

Luis was halfway through breathing a sigh of relief when a cold hand closed around his throat and lifted him to his feet. The hand then lifted him off the ground, the force pulling Maria upright too.

'Sure is a bonus to find some extras,' said the first voice.

'Put him down you filthy son of a diseased whore,' Maria said into the darkness.

Luis, unable to breathe, let alone speak, through his clamped windpipe was proud of his mother's fierceness and amazed at her use of English curses. Tears pricked his eyes at her bravery. Still she clung to him. He felt more bodies close in. Hands reached for her, dragging her away, and Luis held on for as long as he could.

From the blackness a beam of yellow brightness split the night, illuminating the grotesque band of stalkers. Luis had had no idea there could be so many of them. As he ran out of air he thought he counted ten or more. The light settled on the face of a man in a sheriff's uniform, appearing to blind him.

Luis assumed the sound he heard next was that of the angels singing as they came to collect him, so mellifluous was its tone. An instant later there was a flash of purple lightning beside him and the hand holding him released. He and his captor fell to the ground, Luis into a starry half-awareness.

'All of you back away,' said the holder of the flashlight, the one who had thrown the binder.

'Father?'

'Yes. Come to me. Both of you.'

José stepped forward so that he blocked them from the sheriff's line of fire. If the sheriff was the only one with a gun, he had to incapacitate him before he began firing into the light. He crouched to make a smaller target of himself and loosed another binder.

Its melody was the most heartening sound he'd ever heard, their sword and shield against the creatures of the valley.

The sheriff heard it coming and ducked. The binder's song finished in the brush between the trees. He only had two left and the one he was wearing. He aimed his flashlight right at the sheriff's body and pulled his arm back to try again. A startled cry came from behind him before he let it fly and he turned to see a man he half recognised dragging Maria away from him.

'Let her go!' he screamed at the man who had taken her. The man didn't listen. José snapped the binder at him but his aim was way off. The binder whistled briefly and connected with a tree somewhere out of sight. José watched Maria's eyes widen with terror as she tried to tear the man's grip from her. A moment later, something encircled Luis's neck and dragged him too into the darkness. José flung his last binder in the direction of the thing that had taken his son. There was no contact. Figures closed in from every side and José Jimenez collapsed to his knees with his hands reaching into the darkness.

'GIVE THEM BACK TO ME.'

The arbour was as silent as when Kerrigan had left it in search of Carla. He planned to skirt the edge of it and head out towards the Eastern path the way they'd all come in. There was no breeze there in the thick of the forest but, as he and Carla ran along the border of the arbour, a rustling began again in the leaves of the tree.

Kerrigan stopped to listen and the sound became louder. It was like a crowd of people whispering in expectation. The whispers conspired around them and the volume increased steadily. The leaves sounded excited, full of anticipation. He checked for movement in the trees behind and prepared for an attack.

It never came. At least, not then. Instead he saw two figures step from another hidden run on the other side of the arbour.

'Get down,' he said to Carla and they both crouched,

backing themselves into the thick tangle of brush and weed surrounding the arbour.

The figures stopped when they were clear of the woods and stared for a long time at the tree.

They began a relaxed promenade below the elephantine boughs and as they came a little closer, he saw that they were holding hands; two elderly ladies walking together like two schoolgirls. Above them the branches began to sway and twist and the tree reached its branches down towards the two women.

It was then that Kerrigan realised he knew them. He hadn't placed them at first because they were so removed from their usual contexts. Maggie Fredericks never went anywhere except in her car and Kath, his adopted mother—the only mother he'd ever known—could hardly walk around the block. It was impossible that they were here, so deep within the woods. But their footsteps were light and they walked without limps or stumbles or any apparent discomfort at all. They acted as if they were in the prime of their lives.

He raced forward from his position, screaming to get their attention.

'Kath,' he shouted, 'Get away from the tree.' He waved his arms at her, motioning for her to go back into the forest. 'Please, Kath. Run now.'

He saw her look at him then, such a confused and twisted expression in her eyes that it broke his heart. She recognised him, that was plain, and a smile bubbled up with that recognition. But there were new feelings inside her that surfaced too. She looked at him with a thirst and that thirst was tinged with her love for him—a love as genuine as it had always been, now polluted with Fugue. He saw that she wanted to embrace him and feed on him all at once. There was another desire behind it all too, a stronger one suggesting she could not fulfil any of those needs. There was a duty she had to perform more pressing than any of her own desires.

But the worst thing in those loving eyes of Kath's was the

thing no mother should ever feel in response to a son: fear. She knew he could hurt her, change her. She knew in some part of herself that the change he could make would save her and Kerrigan could see that she did not want to be saved.

If he could bind her, he knew there was a chance of saving her. He'd brought plenty of wellspring water with him. One shot with a binder and she could make it out of there. That very binder was already in his hand, his finger curled around it ready to launch it but, as with Amy, the tree was reaching for its children. Would it leave Kath here on the arbour floor if she was no longer in Fugue? There was no time left even to question, he had to try.

It was at that moment Kerrigan heard laughter from behind him and he was iced to his very heart. He'd left Carla unattended for seconds only but the sallow man had been waiting. Perhaps he'd even planned the diversion. Kerrigan hesitated in that last vital second and Kath was gone from the ground. He looked up in time to see her being hoisted by possessive braches into the air and held out, once again, like some kind of protection, the way he might hold out a binder to a Fugue.

Before he lost all control of the situation, Kerrigan turned and sprinted back to where the sallow man now clutched Carla with his many tongues and one of his long-boned hands.

'I've expected so much more from you all these years, foundling. I truly believed you had prepared for this meeting. Now I find you are not worthy of my concern. You are no Fugue Hunter. You are a joke.'

The words cut him, but Kerrigan let fly a binder before the sallow man had finished his taunts, snapping it from his fingers with a will and force he never achieved in casual training. It soloed like an archangel and it flew true, curving in towards the target at the final moment. Because the sallow man had advanced from Fugue into Rage, the opposition caused by the binder was even greater than usual. There was a thunderous clash as it connected with his long swollen head and a flash of lilac fire that illuminated the entire arbour, searing an imprint onto Kerrigan's retina. The sallow man collapsed backwards against a pine and let go of Carla who stumbled to Kerrigan, half blinded.

'Are you okay, Carla? Can you see well enough to run?'

He held her face in his hands. Apart from the shock of the impact she was alert and ready to act. He was about to take her hand and accelerate out of the arbour but she clasped her arms around his neck and pressed her tear-streaked face against his skin. After a couple of seconds in which she embraced him with a kind of desperation, she drew her face away a little and kissed him hard on the mouth.

'Thank you,' she said.

Behind her the sallow man lay on his back, his tongues and feeding tubes retreating back into him. He'd be unconscious for several hours, but if Kath and Maggie were already Fugues, there was no telling how many others might be wandering the woods. He had to reach the rest of Carla's family as soon as possible.

With her wrongful kiss still bruising his lips, Kerrigan took Carla's hand and they ran from the arbour out towards the Eastern Path. The look that Kath had given him weighed so heavily on Kerrigan, the mere thought of it slowed him down. A few yards into the recently cut trail that led away from the giant tree he heard another sound that laid him even lower. It was the excited barking of a dog back in the arbour. Despite the strange timbre to his woofing, he knew it was Dingbat. A moment later the noise stopped and Kerrigan chewed back on his rising emotions.

Long before they reached the Eastern path, the night laid its purple velvet blanket down over the valley and smothered it in black.

Kerrigan pushed the pace. He held Carla's hand to keep her close. He took a guilty comfort in the warmth of her skin.

Twice when she stumbled in the darkness he caught her and helped her regain her footing.

As they emerged onto the Eastern path she broke the silence.

'You can see where we're going, can't you?'

'Sure.'

'How is that possible?'

'I don't know *exactly* how but I know I've always been able to do it when I needed to.'

'I've seen you throw those—'

'Binders.'

'Right, binders. What else can you do?'

'They're not circus tricks, Carla.'

'I know that. I'm just interested. No, I'm fascinated.'

Where was the harm in telling her a little about himself now? He'd never discussed it with anyone; he wanted to let it out.

'Things just happen, it's like an instinct. I have no idea what I'm capable of most of the time. But I've been doing it all my life. Ever since I was an infant.'

'What do you call it?'

'The only word I know for it is Lethe.'

'What do you call those creatures? What do you call that old man out there?'

'They're Fugues. He was once a Lethe like me, but he's turned now. When they're threatened or hungry they go up a gear, like he did. That's called Rage.'

'Did you kill him?'

'I wish I had. But binders don't kill them. They paralyse or stun them for a while. Usually, when they're in that state, I can heal them.'

'It's a sickness, this Fugue?'

'That's right. The disease has been in this valley for centuries, maybe since before people came here.'

Carla increased her pace until she was alongside him. She held his hand a little tighter. In the darkness, Kerrigan saw her looking at him, even though she couldn't see him. There was a look of awe on her face. While he enjoyed the attention, he wasn't worthy of it. How many people had he lost to the Fugue since he'd left his cabin? Too many to deal with?

He sighed.

'What is it?' asked Carla.

'Nothing.'

There was silence between them for a while but she stayed beside him. His guilt told him he should let go of her hand, but he knew if he did she would trip or crash into something. The other part of him, the part that wanted her in spite of how wrong it was, delighted in that simple touch.

'You're like them, aren't you?' she asked.

'What?' he tried to laugh the suggestion away but she persisted.

'There's something about you that reminds me of the ones I've seen.'

He dropped the pace and turned to her.

'What are you trying to say?'

'It's in the way they move, the way they talk. It's like they've forgotten what it was they were supposed to be doing. When we met you, you had that same kind of distracted way about you. Do you know you hunt them when you're not actually doing it?'

Kerrigan drew a deep breath and shook his head in the darkness, but she didn't see the gesture.

'No,' he said eventually. 'No one remembers anything afterwards. Most of the time I'm a reclusive writer of magazine articles with a crushing fear of the dark. When I turn hunter, I have no other life. And nothing scares me. Well, almost nothing.'

Carla looked up at his face again. Somehow in all that blackness she managed to fix her gaze right on his eyes. For Kerrigan it was like looking into the eyes of a blind girl.

'I trust you, Jimmy Kerrigan,' she said.

He was about to tell her not to be so free with her trust

when he sensed a presence on the trail. He couldn't believe the sallow man had caught up with them so quickly. He put his hand over her mouth as gently as he could and moved her to the edge of the path.

'There's someone out here with us,' he whispered. 'Don't say another word and don't move.'

He stepped back into the path and stared into the night. Far along the Eastern path he saw them, a band of twenty or more Fugues coming their way at a run. Among them he saw faces of people he knew from Hobson's Valley and he covered his mouth to keep from crying out in shock. The rest of Carla's family ran with them, a look of wild hunger in their eyes.

There were more Fugues than he had binders for, more than he could deal with on his own. He had failed them all. The people of the town and the whole Jimenez family. He had let himself be distracted; ignored a worsening situation for far too long.

He crouched down beside Carla who had curled into a ball and was hugging her knees beside the path.

'There's too many of them,' he whispered. 'We have to go back.'

'No, Jimmy. What about Luis? What about mama and papa?'

There it was; the voice of the little girl, so much a part of the woman she was trying to become.

'Maybe they already got through.'

'Do you believe that?'

'Listen to me, Carla, if we don't go back, no one stands a chance. Not us, not your family, not the town.'

He didn't give her the chance to respond. He hauled her to her feet and started running back towards the trail that led to the arbour. She dragged her feet this time; all enthusiasm, all hero-worship gone. In the end he picked her up and ran with her in his arms.

A hundred yards beyond the opening of the newly broken arbour trail, Kerrigan stopped and put Carla down. Crouching, near the edge of the trail they waited for the Fugues to make up the distance. As he'd suspected they would, they turned and entered the recently re-broken trail one by one until they were gone from view.

Carla was crying beside him, her face pressed into her hands.

'They didn't make it back to the car, did they?' she sobbed.

'Carla, for God's sake keep your voice down.'

'How many of those things were there?'

'It was a large group,' he said, not able to look at her.

'They were all on this trail together. There's no way they could have made it past so many Fugues, is there?'

'They had the binders I gave them. Maybe the Fugues didn't come along this trail. Those two we saw at the arbour came right through the woods.'

Carla shook her head and looked into the darkness. He knew she couldn't see a single thing, not even his hand in front of her face if he'd wanted to put her to the test. Still the look in her eyes was a distant one.

'Don't try to make me feel better, Mr. Kerrigan. And don't lie to me either. I just want to know what will happen to them.'

There was no point hiding the truth. The chances were that neither he nor Carla would make it through the night.

'I saw them,' he said.

She looked at him in the darkness.

'What do you mean?'

'Just now in that group. They're all heading back to the tree.'

Carla's hopeful smile was pathetic to behold. He was glad she couldn't see his expression.

'So they're not dead?'

'No. Being fed upon doesn't necessarily kill you unless they drain you of so much fluid that you can't recover. They can pass the disease on to you but, until now, I've rarely known them to do that. They like their secrets. They can feed for years on a community if their numbers are small enough and their victims don't remember a thing about it. Fugue is like a fever that comes and goes.'

'What will happen to them now?'

'In normal circumstances—'

'Nothing about this is normal.'

It wasn't an easy subject to explain. He sighed.

'Usually, I find one or maybe two at any time. I hit them with a binder when they're in Fugue and then put them through a healing ritual to cleanse them of the disease. After a while they carry on with life as normal and don't ever think about it again.'

'So, you're saying you could save my family? Make them . . . normal again?'

'In theory, yes, but you have to understand, I've never seen this many of them before and I've never taken on more than two at one time. There are too many for me to handle on my own.'

'You will try, won't you?'

Kerrigan didn't need to think of an answer. His whole life was the answer.

In the silence that followed her words, though, he felt the entire forest and all its creatures, even the very valley and the mountains on either side, speak silently to him. The land wanted to be rid of the pollutant Fugue forever. He drew strength from the thought that he had the Earth itself behind him. He had taken Fugue for granted when he was in Lethe and had done all his life. Sensing the land's protest so strongly made him wonder for the first time what the origin of Fugue might be. He had a profound conviction that the disease had come a long, long way.

'Of course, I will.' he said. 'It's in my blood.'

CHAPTER 32

Some time before they reached the arbour, Carla became aware of a faint radiance illuminating the claustrophobic path. Now that she could see just a little she swung her head from side to side often, in fear of an ambush. The closer they came to the end of the trail the brighter the light became. It reminded her of the many twilights she'd witnessed since coming to Hobson's Valley, but it was different in that, instead of the light fading away and leaving a dusty purple mist, there was a source from which the light emanated. And it didn't dim: it became brighter.

Fifty yards farther along the trail and Carla could see well enough to make out the vials of wellspring water on Kerrigan's belt and the indents where the binders were embedded into the long wrist straps he wore. The straps made her think of ancient swordsmen who'd protected their forearms with decorated leather gauntlets. Even though she could see well enough not to fall over she still clung to his hand, enjoying the feel of his strength and the way his hand yielded to accommodate hers.

He stopped then.

'You okay?' he whispered.

'I'm fine. Do you see the light?'

'Yes, I see it. We can't just walk in or God knows what may happen. We'll get close enough to take a look and then we'll slip into the trees and make a plan.'

'Whatever you say.'

She watched Kerrigan turn his head from side to side, popping the tension from his neck in two ratcheted snaps. Then he eased the muscles of his shoulders, reaching over to knead each uppermost slab of muscle with the opposite hand.

'I have to tell you now, Carla, that our chances of success here are real slim.'

'We've come this far and we can't turn back. We'll just do our best. That's all we can do, right?'

'Right.'

He turned away and she followed him until they were just a few yards from the arbour.

Staying out of sight, Kerrigan lay on his stomach and tried to see into the huge vaulted space that the tree's branches had created. Carla pressed close to him and he felt her trembling.

Light emanated from the tree's trunk and branches, brightening and dimming with a slow pulse. Veins of purple beat beneath the bark of the tree. Its light changed hue in time with the pulses of its sap, mingling coronas of neon pink, purple and indigo. On the far side of the arbour Kerrigan saw a Fugue lifted into the air by a branch. To the right of it another.

There was a crunching sound right in front of them and Randall Moore stepped into view, naked and snapping fallen twigs beneath the soles of his bare feet. Kerrigan pulled Carla back against the brush. Breath locked, they waited for Randall to raise the alarm. A moment later his feet left the ground and his grizzled body sailed upward out of their line of vision.

Near the trunk of the tree, a girl was dancing, silhouetted by the phosphorescence of the tree.

'Gina Presley,' said Kerrigan.

She danced for the tree's pleasure and the rhythm built to an erotic frenzy. She squeezed her breasts cruelly with one hand and manhandled herself between the legs with the other. Gina was provoking the tree, teasing it with her lascivious gyrations. She turned away from the trunk and bent over, exposing her sex to it in the most vulnerable way. In this stance she continued to circle her hips and stimulate her labia for the tree's benefit.

Carla squeezed herself tight to Kerrigan as they hid from the creatures in the arbour; so close that he turned on his side to make their shape at the base of the pines even smaller. They watched the dance in silence and, unable to control himself, Kerrigan stiffened against her. She pressed back against him.

He reached over and clutched Carla tightly to himself. She squeezed the hand he used to hold her.

Then, she turned to kiss him, properly.

'We can't do this,' he whispered.

Kerrigan saw the disappointment in her eyes and the stronger emotion written there: a look of deep need. All he wanted to do was satisfy that need, knowing that in doing so he would satisfy himself.

In one moment he was seeing this look in her eyes and in the next she was standing over him. He didn't understand how she could have stood up so quickly. Was she that outraged? Then he saw what had made her lightning movements possible and understood the reason why her expression changed from lust to fear. She opened her mouth to scream and a pale, spidery hand closed over it.

Kerrigan leapt to his feet to see that the sallow man held her in the grip of his many tongues. The old man kept her away from the many spikes on his body, holding her at arms length so as not to hurt her. This fact froze Jimmy's heart when he realised what it implied.

The sallow man, in full Rage, clucked and snarled as he spoke:

'She's promised to another, foundling.'

In the entrance to the arbour, two silhouettes appeared with the lights from the tree throwing off auras all around their bodies. Carla immediately recognised their outlines and the sallow man uncovered her mouth.

'Mama, papa, you're okay.' She was sobbing with relief.

'Yes, Carlita,' said José Jimenez. 'We are safe and now you are too.'

The sallow man let her go and she ran to her parents, barrelling in to them so hard that she knocked them back a couple of steps into the arbour.

'Hey, take it easy.'

Her father was laughing.

'We've been worried about you,' said her mother. As she spoke she caught the sallow man's eye. He nodded to her and she nodded back.

'How is Luis? Is he safe too?'

'He's very safe. He's playing in the tree.'

They turned away as a group and began to walk towards the centre of the arbour where, even as the family watched, Gina Priestly cried out in hoarse gasps as she neared orgasm.

Kerrigan heard the panic creep back into Carla's voice as they walked away.

'But the tree is dangerous, Mama.'

'Not any more. Not to us.'

Carla took a backwards glance at him, uncertainty rising in her eyes. Then their voices were lost under the animal shouts of Gina as she worked herself towards ecstasy for the pleasure of the tree. Its light grew brighter in response and by that light Kerrigan saw the sallow man advance towards him.

He was perfect in that unholy emanation. Not diseased and freakish but tall and noble, his skin alabaster smooth and his veins defined as though he'd been cut from the finest stone. His tongues waved threateningly from his groin, belly and underarms and the tongue in his mouth darted in and out of his head testing the air, sensing Kerrigan's state of mind. The tubes that would wound and drain his victims stood in glorious rows along his abdomen and chest. They thrust, too, from his shoulders and thighs and even from his knees. He was a walking weapon. The long oval that his head had become still sprouted the grey hair he'd never cut, but in this form it looked majestic rather than ragged and his eyes showed a greater wisdom and understanding than any human eyes Kerrigan had ever seen. Gone were the scrawny sinews of the old man, the undernourished hermit. Here instead were long, supple muscles that looked iron hard and polished until they gleamed under the tree's ever-changing glow. A sneer played around the sallow man's lips and he bared his obsidian black teeth. They were tiny but numerous and set four rows deep in his mouth, both above and below. The sneer grew into a snarl and the teeth tilted forward, extending until they met and meshed and all Kerrigan could see was a shining blackness that hid hundreds of points.

'You're such a disappointment,' said the sallow man through his clenched jaws. 'You're so weak and pathetic I can't believe I ever dreaded your return. Killing you won't be any fun at all, but watching you lose your precious valley and all the people in it may be of some amusement.'

While the sallow man spoke, Kerrigan raised himself into a sitting position and when there was no response to that, he stood very slowly. Tongues quivered and muscles clenched when he reached his full height and the sallow man took a step forward.

'Nothing you can do will make a difference now, foundling.'

'I have to finish you. You're beyond saving. Then I'll take care of the rest of them. I'll recover as many as I can.'

The sallow man laughed and shook his armoured head.

'You can't destroy me, foundling. It's obvious you don't have the skill. And even if you could, everything's changed now. There's been an evolution that you can't contain. Tonight, Fugue will leave this valley for the first time. It will take a new form. You will be gone and there will be no more Fugue Hunters to contain the spread. Tomorrow there will be a purple dawn.'

Kerrigan glanced into the arbour. The Jimenez's had nearly reached the trunk of the tree but they'd slowed a little as they neared Gina. Something about her behaviour made them hesitate. Kerrigan could see that Carla too, had lost most of her joy at being reunited with her parents. She'd looked up into the branches of the tree and seen the many people suspended there. Kerrigan could make out her parents' hands, not embracing her anymore but forcibly steering her towards the tree. He looked back at the sallow man.

'Why haven't you turned her?'

'The tree needs her more than I do,' said the sallow man in guttural tones.

'What does that mean?'

The sallow man stepped closer still to Kerrigan, his tongues hovering in the air near both sides of his face. Kerrigan could smell the scent of raw human fluids on the sallow man's cellar-cool breath as he spoke.

'The tree needs a human female, young and strong, to carry its seed. It will use one of those it holds to pass its seed into her and she will be the mother of the new Fugue.'

Kerrigan tried to take it in, but all he found within himself was anger. His staff lay out of reach on the ground but he had a binder in each palm. He let them fly simultaneously and dived away from his target, rolling before standing up again and facing his foe.

The sallow man had been knocked into the trees on the other side of the narrow trail but was already pulling himself free of the tangle of brush. Before he had regained himself, Kerrigan loosed two more binders at him and sprinted to collect his staff. The sallow man was even quicker to recover after the second pair of binders made contact and Kerrigan realised that letting him rally from the first attack in the arbour had been a mistake. He should have either killed him or recovered him then and there. Now the sallow man seemed to be developing an immunity to his airborne weapons.

The sallow man advanced, stunned and damaged by the hits he'd taken. In two places on his abdomen, there were weeping burn holes. A long scorch mark smoked on the side of his head and one of his shoulder spikes had been removed completely by the fourth binder. Kerrigan smiled, holding his staff across the middle of his body ready for the sallow man's assault.

He didn't sense the tongue snaking towards him along the ground until it had seized his left ankle. It squeezed so hard he thought it would cut through his Achilles tendon. His foot lost all sensation and the sallow man yanked his tongue in, sending Kerrigan onto his back. The tongue tightened, crushing Kerrigan's ankle. He screamed. The sallow man leapt forward intending to land on Kerrigan with every available spike and puncture him mortally. Kerrigan raised his staff only when the sallow man had left the ground and could do nothing to arrest his fall. Kerrigan buried one end of the staff into the earth between his elbow and his body and aimed the other end at the sallow man's face.

The huge head was arrested by the impact and the sallow man's legs hit the ground first instead of his body. With the staff touching him the sallow man couldn't move. Kerrigan stood with the staff pressed to the creature's elongated forehead. Gas escaped from the point of contact and a scream began deep in the sallow man's belly, keening at first and then erupting in an unrestrained howl.

Using the moment, Kerrigan retracted his weapon, spun it between his hands and landed a crashing downward blow along the sallow man's body. His aim was perfect, snapping off every feeding spike on the right of the sallow man's pale torso. Kerrigan saw no humanity left in the thing that dropped to its knees in the dirt before him and in his heart he felt no mercy. He drew the tomahawk from his belt and swung it high over his head before bringing it down against the sallow man's neck and removing his head.

In the incandescent glow, another light sparked bright. It was the head of the tomahawk giving off a bright blue-white glare as it absorbed the fluids of the sallow man. Kerrigan replaced the weapon and strode to where the head lay, the eyes blinking in surprise and the mouth working without a sound.

He wasted no time. There were things he needed to know that only the sallow man could tell him. He held the head back against the earth to expose the wound and thrust his fingers deep into the dying creature's brain.

CHAPTER 33

He saw many things — past, present and future:

A child in a blanket stolen from a house in another valley. The child wept as it was taken into the forest and Kerrigan wept too, to behold it. They were the very same tears.

The sallow man, years younger, cutting himself with a worn-bladed knife and dripping his blood onto a huge flat rock.

The blood drying in the sun and him scraping it into a leather pouch. The sallow man mixing the dried blood with goat's milk and feeding it to the child. The look of hunger and absence on the poor child's face.

The nights, so many nights, when the sallow man had crept to the window of his childhood home or the threshold of his cabin and watched him sleeping. His voice as he instructed him in the ways of the Fugue Hunter while he slept. His voice was soothing, fatherly. He repeated his lessons over and over.

The sallow man stalking night after night through Hobson's Valley looking in at the windows of those who slept. The saliva on his chin.

The sallow man hungering in the forest and using a shattered stone to cut into the bark of a small tree in a tiny clearing. The sallow man drinking the sap of that tree and infecting it with Fugue.

The tree growing rapidly and its clearing becoming too

small for it. The trees and plants around it shrinking and dying as it sucked the life from them and grew into the spaces left when there was nothing left of them.

The sallow man feeding animals to the tree.

The sallow man stalking and feeding on the people of Hobson's Valley.

The sallow man feeding a live mountain lion to the tree.

The sallow man kidnapping and raping Gina Priestly and sharing her blood with the tree.

Carla held against the tree while a male Fugue, still gripped by the branches of the tree deflowered her and in so doing ejected not only his seed but the seed of the tree into her.

Beyond that last snippet, the sallow man had seen no further ahead and Kerrigan, the Fugue Hunter, had seen enough.

CHAPTER 34

Kerrigan removed his hand from the cooling mess within the dead creature's skull. He watched as the spark of life left the sallow man and his eyes took on a dull sheen. So ingrained in his cells and so long-lived was the Fugue within him that he did not return to human form even in death. What remained of him degraded into some fetid amalgam of ash and mucus. The stinging smell of decay made Kerrigan's eyes water and he backed away from his victim to look once more into the arbour.

The future was already unfolding.

Maria and Jose Jimenez had ceased their pretences with their daughter. They each held one of her hands and were dragging her backwards towards the tree. The looks on her parents' faces were set and blank. They could easily have been butchers about to slaughter a pig and their strength, much exaggerated by Fugue, was far more than Carla could resist. They pulled until she was stretched against the trunk of the tree, her arms wide and high above the level of her shoulders. As they pressed the backs of her hands against the luminescent bark, it parted and Carla's hands disappeared. The bark closed over them as far as the wrist and gripped her. The look of disgusted shock on Carla's face made Kerrigan nauseous. A moment later, whatever workings were inside the tree tightened and Carla's shoulders and chest were stretched to their very limit. She screamed, her agony laid bare.

Her parents—her guardians and carers no more—took hold of a kicking leg each and spread-eagled Carla by hauling her ankles back against the bark. Within seconds they'd been similarly 'swallowed', boots and all. The racking of her posture occurred again until she was stretched so tightly Kerrigan could see her pelvic bones pressing outward through her clothes. Carla gave up fighting for a moment, but must have decided that death or unconsciousness would be less painful than waiting out her fate. She began to smash the back of her head against the tree. Kerrigan didn't think she wanted to die until he saw the force with which she cracked her skull against the trunk. The third impact did seem to knock her into some half-dazed state because her head lolled a little and her screams and pleas stopped for a few seconds.

She didn't get another chance to kill herself. The tree responded immediately, not wanting her harmed, it appeared, only wanting her immobile. The bark behind her head became fluid for a moment and her long, dark hair sank into it as if into illuminated water. Then the surface hardened and once again the tree drew her tight towards it until she was no longer able to move anything but her eyes and mouth.

When she was safely bound into the flesh of the tree, her father stepped forward. He withdrew a clasp knife from the back pocket of his walking trousers and unfolded it. It had been well cared for and the blade flashed purple and silver in the tree's light.

Seeing it brought Carla back to full alertness.

'Papa?'

She stared in disbelief. When the blade touched her belly, she screamed.

'Papa, no. Please. Nooooo . . .'

He angled the knife upwards and split her clothing open. Once he'd made a cut, he tore her jacket and shirt the rest of the way open and pulled them wide so that her flawless skin was exposed. He put the knife through her bra between the cups and freed her breasts. She closed her eyes in shame as he exposed her chest to the night air. In the same way, her father removed her trousers and panties, leaving shredded clothing hanging all around her.

Even her crucifixion against the Fugue tree was not enough to prompt Kerrigan out of hiding.

Carla cried and could not even wipe away her own tears.

Behind her the bark of the tree undulated with each pulse of light. The bark was rough and hard but there was a warmth to its surface and a muscularity to its movement that revolted her. Her hands were held by living fibres that never stopped moving and yet maintained an unbreakable grip. The flesh of the tree rasped and sucked at her until it seemed the blood in her hands would burst from her fingertips.

Being in contact with the tree, Carla could sense its intentions to some degree. She knew the tree's plan was to propagate itself and that it wanted to use her body as a vehicle for its offspring. She also knew that the sallow man was dead, slain by Kerrigan. She knew because the tree knew. Instead of sending out Fugues to destroy him, it was waiting for him to enter the arbour where it was strongest and that had the most influence over the minds of its new minions.

The tree exuded an ecstatic confidence that terrified her. It seemed to know it could not be defeated and it would create a new race that very evening. Not even Kerrigan would be able prevent it.

Carla's parents turned away from her and walked out into the arbour. She knew she was acting like a child when she called out to them one last time but she couldn't stop herself.

'Mama, papa! Wait. Don't leave me here. Please? MAMA, PAPA.'

Neither of them flinched or hesitated at the sound of her voice. They abandoned her and were taken up to become yet more of the tree's strange fruit. Only one other person remained on the ground, a girl a little older than Carla. The one who had been dancing so lewdly for the tree's pleasure. She now approached, in a brazen swagger. She stood in front of Carla and appraised her body with a few up and down glances and a sneer of disgust.

'You can't be the one,' she said. 'You're too young. You should have bigger tits.'

She held one of Carla's breasts in her hand and as if weighing a fruit for value and ripeness. Then she let it go and slapped it.

'This is no good,' she said to herself before addressing the tree. 'She can't be the one. She's not woman enough to carry the seed. Look at her — she's weak and skinny. Take me instead.'

If the tree heard Gina's requests it made no response. Carla felt its unwillingness to take notice of the naked girl that was shouting to it. It had other desires. Understanding what those desires would result in, Carla began to shout.

'Jimmy! Jimmy Kerrigan,' she yelled. 'Help me. You've got to stop it.'

At the utterance of his name a ripple passed through the entire tree, starting deep in its roots, making the trunk shudder and sending shivers through to the leaves of every outer branch.

On the far side of the clearing a branch lowered itself to the ground, an ageing naked male fused to its tip. He walked towards her, the branch still fused into his spine.

Gina also turned to watch the man's approach, knowing the crucial moment had arrived. She moved in front of Carla, turning to face the inbound Fugue and began her pole dance routine all over again, calling to her intended lover as she moved in time to the tree's pulses.

'Hey, Randall. Remember me?' She stroked her palms upwards over her breasts, taking the nipples between her thumb and finger and rolling them for the old man. Randall stared through Gina, not even aware she was there. His eyes fixed on Carla's spread-eagled form. In fact, Randall's gaze was angled downwards. He wasn't even looking at *her* as such; he was intent on the vulnerability of her exposed sex.

Whatever ravages time had wrought on the man, Fugue had corrected at least some of them. The old man's penis was unnaturally swollen, its head the size of an apple. The whole appendage throbbed in time with the tree's rhythmic light show and some kind of evanescent sap already dribbled from its tip, pattering softly to the earth. There couldn't have been that much fluid in his ancient testicles; the sappy liquid was being produced by the tree and pumped right through him.

Gina stepped directly into the path of the Fugue that was once Randall Moore. He kept walking and she fell into the dirt when he barged her out of his way. Meanwhile, Carla felt the tree alter its shape. Her section of trunk levelled, thrusting her feet forward and causing her to recline until she was lying at forty-five degrees to the earth, ready for the Fugue to fertilise her.

Gina's eyes flashed purple fire. She jumped to her feet and placed herself once again between Carla and Randall Moore. This time she took the old man's penis in one hand, raised one leg up and climbed onto his dripping phallus. For a few moments Gina was successful, and she cried out as she impaled herself on him. A look of pleasure and distraction finally registered in Randall Moore's eyes and he turned his head towards Gina.

Carla felt the tree's response.

Its influence over Randall Moore intensified and his eyes widened, his body becoming taut. The tendons stood out on his neck and he threw Gina off as if she were no heavier than a cloth doll.

She never hit the ground. A branch reached down from overhead and caught her neck in a waiting crook formed at its tip. Carla expected Gina be hoisted upwards, joining the other Fugues but the tree held her a few inches above the ground while she kicked and fought to break free. Within moments Gina transformed from Fugue to Rage, her tongues flailing and beating at the branch that held her, her spikes tearing gouges in its bark. The tree squeezed, twisting more loops of the branch around Gina's neck until she was wearing a collar of mutated wood that almost obscured her lengthening head.

With a sound like gristle being ripped, her body separated from her head. It fell towards the ground but another branch swooped inwards and caught it. The two limbs then curled up towards the top of the tree's trunk and deposited the body parts where the first split in its trunk occurred.

Randall Moore was now only a couple of steps away from her—so close that his erection, which had seemed huge from a distance, now looked large enough to actually kill her if he used it. She screamed as he stepped forward to take her. The leak from his penis had become a torrent; he was oozing sap like blood from a breached vein. She felt the fluid splatter on the bark of the tree as he leaned over her and then she heard a strange sound. It took her attention totally for a brief moment. It was the hum of a single note struck perfectly or sung in a voice of crystal purity. It became louder and even Randall Moore paused before making the decisive thrust into her.

She recognised the sound a moment before the binder struck the back of Randall Moore's head and knocked him unconscious. The flash was so bright it left a huge, starry imprint on her retina, but she saw the damage it had done and choked out a sob of momentary relief. Randall came away from the vegetable apparatus that had penetrated his spine and slumped against her, his body covering hers completely. His erection lay pressed against the bare skin of her belly. There was nothing she could do to move him but she felt the monstrous prick he'd grown collapse rapidly until she felt no pressure from it at all.

Looking over the stunned man's shoulder she saw that Jimmy Kerrigan had entered the arbour. The tree was responding with extreme measures. It disconnected all its Fugues and passed them as rapidly as it could from branch to branch until all of them were near the entrance to the arbour. Once there the tree renewed its intimate bodily connections with each one and placed them either on the ground or in mid air until there were two rows of a dozen Fugues, one above the other.

CHAPTER 35

If Kerrigan could have killed Randall Moore from where he stood, he would have done it. He'd rather have saved any of the others that were in the tree that night but he was too far away to do anything more than bind the old man. As soon as Randall dropped, the tree responded and his decision was made for him. Kerrigan knew he would not be walking away from this. With that knowledge came the commitment that had escaped him up to that moment. He couldn't beat the tree and its Fugue warriors but he hoped he could at least free Carla before he was killed.

He watched the tree respond to his attack, ranging its remaining Fugues against him in two rows at the entrance to the arbour. It had no intention of letting him in. There among the Fugues he saw the Jimenez's with Luis between them. He saw the sheriff and the Priestlys. How they'd all been turned, he had no idea. Amy Cantrell, his ex lover was among them too and Maggie Fredericks, who had taken such good care of his adoptive parents. The worst of it was seeing Kath up there, ready to be used as a soldier in a war that yesterday she wouldn't even have known was taking place. Not far from her was Dingbat, faithful now to a new master.

Kerrigan had five binders left, not enough to save everyone dear to him. Not fifty yards away, one of the people he liked least in the valley, Randall Moore, was lying safely out of the action ready to be recovered if Kerrigan made it that far. He knew if Randall survived he'd hate him forever.

Kerrigan spun the first binder out at Kath. It hit her clean in the chest and she fell six feet or so from the clutches of the tree to the mercifully soft ground where she slumped into an undignified heap. The next one hit Luis Jimenez, the next his mother. The branches that had held them retracted their grip immediately and recoiled a short distance. He kept his eye on them as they waved threateningly behind the wall of Fugues.

It seemed then that the tree understood his intentions. It reached out with the branches that had held those he'd freed and began to whip their unconscious bodies. Somewhere behind the ranged lines of Fugues, Carla screamed as she saw what happened. It was no human punishment, ten lashes, a birching, the cat o' nine tails; these were huge branches, extensions of the gargantuan tree. Each blow broke bones. It was over before Kerrigan could even decide what to do to help them. The branches whipped down again and again so hard that the earth itself shook. Blood sprayed up from the bodies, and soon, severed chunks of flesh jumped and bounced as limbs and heads were shattered and separated by the force of the blows.

Knowing there was nothing he could do, but knowing he had to try, Kerrigan loosed the final two binders, the first at Dingbat and the second at José Jimenez. Both found their targets. The beating that the other branches were still dealing out, even though nothing lived in the pulped humanity they were attacking, had set up waves of motion in the other branches. When Dingbat came free he was thrown into the brush beyond the arbour's limit and out of the tree's reach. José Jimenez also fell beyond the boundary but he landed headfirst and Kerrigan heard the grinding crunch as his neck snapped. It was instinct that had caused him to throw those last binders, love and loyalty that dictated where he aimed them. Now there were no binders left and the task was far from over.

Kerrigan watched as the branch pounding his adoptive mother's body picked up her head. He was amazed to see that there was an expression of relief on Kath's face. Her eyes were still open, though he knew she was dead, and in that moment; the last he ever saw her, he felt all the love they'd shared push up from deep inside him. He acknowledged what she'd been to him — a true mother. Then the branch squeezed that wise and beautiful old head of hers and it cracked open.

Kerrigan heard someone screaming and realised it was him. The force of hatred flowed through him from the earth upwards. The Fury was upon him.

Carla watched the horrendous changes that overtook Kerrigan as he ran screaming into the arbour.

At first, because he was spinning and lashing out so fast, she assumed it was her imagination that he seemed to have grown larger or perhaps some trick of the unnatural lights throbbing from the tree. As Kerrigan hacked with his tomahawk, and thrust and struck with his staff, the tree responded by putting Fugue after Fugue in his way, manipulating them to defend itself.

It was no illusion, though; Kerrigan's body had almost doubled in size. His clothes split and the muscles in his forearms burst open his leather wristbands. Everything fell away in tatters except for his belt. Knifelike protrusions grew from him in the form of smooth, shiny bone. Ivory blades lined his back and chest in a similar pattern to the feeding tubes that had appeared on the Raging Fugues. Bone blades grew from his knees and thighs and from his shoulders and elbows.

He danced and screamed on the edge of the arbour as Fugues and tree branches surrounded him. He was not subdued. Carla saw limbs of Fugue and tree alike flying from the confused melee. She felt the shudders of pain run through the tree each time it or one of its protectors was wounded or destroyed. Snarls and howls of pain echoed around the arbour in the amethyst midnight. The wet sounds of stone slicing flesh and snapping bone and cries cut short by beheadings were the songs of Kerrigan's war. The tree itself began to make whistled cries of agony each time Kerrigan severed yet another of its combatant limbs.

The dismembered pieces of his enemies lay all around him but Kerrigan was not left unscathed. Many times he was caught by the flying, flailing branches and they knocked him hard to the ground. Carla saw several of his bone blades snapped off and huge cuts appeared on his back where the branches opened him up. Blood flew from him but still he twirled and hacked. One by one the Fugues were separated either from the tree or from their own heads and they fell, lifeless as broken marionettes, to the ground below the tree's monstrous canopy.

Carla felt a change in the tree's focus before it acted. It pulled one of the relatively undamaged males back from the fight and marched the man towards her. He was a tall, gangly man with bad skin. He wore an orange vest that hung on him as if it was two sizes too large. He wore a pair of large-lensed glasses that exaggerated the size of his eyes making him look like a skinny frog. Before he reached her, he stopped to take off his shoes and jeans. When he was naked from the waist down, his bony legs looked even more pathetic beside the penis that the tree had given him — its shaft was as thick as his calf. He walked towards her, his Adam's apple yo-yoing up and down as he swallowed in anticipation, his orange waistcoat flapping and his penis beating and dripping in time with the pulse of the tree.

Before he was within ten feet of her she heard an outraged war cry. In the next instant, the Fugue appeared to develop a second smaller penis in the region of his stomach but as Carla looked more closely she saw it was Kerrigan's staff impaling him. The Fugue blinked at her with his froggy eyes and tried to speak. Nothing came. He looked down at his abdomen and saw the new protrusion there without comprehending what it was. Only when he touched it did he understand that he was dead. He looked back at Carla, his eyes appealing to her but he fell to his knees and then onto his face and she saw the rest of the staff protruding from his back. The tree howled in frustration. It released the Fugue who collapsed forward onto the staff, sinking down onto it and forcing most of it back through the entry wound.

At the edge of the arbour the Fugues that weren't dead were now too wounded to be of any use in battle. The tree made them fight on even when they had lost both arms. One Fugue, now quadriplegic, was being used by a branch to batter the Fugue Hunter with its head. The only thing keeping it alive was the will of the tree. Kerrigan ended its life by separating it from the tree with one downward stroke of the tomahawk through the branch that held it. As it had with every successful contact, the head of the tomahawk glowed bright cobalt. So drenched was it now with the sap of the tree and the blood of dead Fugues that tiny stars of mica shone deep blue with piercing brightness; Kerrigan was a source of light to rival the tree. In fact, Carla could see that the tree had lost some of its brightness since the fighting had begun.

The surviving branches that had engaged him retracted now to hide among the healthier ones above.

The Fugue Hunter stood before her, his chest heaving. Blood and sap streaked his hulking body. Carla couldn't tell how much of it was his blood but she prayed he had some strength left. His eyes did not focus on her, but on some point high up the tree's trunk. His voice was unrecognisable, as if an animal was trying to speak, but she understood his words well enough.

'Let her go.'

Kerrigan raised his tomahawk, not at the tree as she'd expected, but above her head where it flamed and rained blue sparks upon her.

'Let her go and you live to try again. If you don't release her, I'll kill her.'

She saw in his eyes that he would do it.

'Jimmy, please don't do this. I . . . love you.'

'Shut up.' His voice was more the snarl of a beast than it was that of a human. He raised the tomahawk higher and tensed every muscle, ready to bring it down and divide her skull into two.

She felt the tree's grip give totally in that moment and she slipped to the ground. The pain of being released as her joints replaced themselves more neatly into their proper housings was worse than the original wrenching and she screamed.

The Fugue Hunter leaned down and picked her up carefully so that his bone blades did not wound her. He carried her to the edge of the arbour. With every step he took the tree rustled and shuddered its leaves and branches. A wailing began near the top of its trunk. Kerrigan laid Carla down beyond the entrance to the arbour and stroked her face with one enormous, clawed hand.

'You didn't do it.' She said.

'No. How could I?'

The pain in her limbs had lessened a little but she knew she could not sit up, let alone walk.

'It's over then. Are you going to leave me here?'

None of the humanity had returned to his voice but there was a sentiment behind his words.

'It's not over yet but when it is, I'll never leave you.'

Kerrigan the Fugue Hunter stood up. He strode back into the arbour. The tree's wailing became a yet more desperate keening at his return. Carla heard the fear in it. Though she could not see the incidents of the next hour she heard every single sound. The sound of Jimmy Kerrigan fighting off the branches that tried to prevent him entering the arbour a second time: she heard his response to each attack in the whoosh of his tomahawk and swish of his staff as he paralysed or cut every limb that advanced towards him. This advance and repulse must have gone on until the tree had no more limbs mobile enough to defend itself with.

The sound of fighting stopped for a short while and she heard only the sound of his footsteps as he walked towards the unprotected tree. Then came the hooted whistles of panic as he used his talons to climb the tree's trunk. By that time, he was too close to the centre of the tree for any branch to reach him and the hoots of panic became deep honks of terror. They made her think of some vast cathedral organ playing sharp and flat screams instead of notes. And in her mind she imagined a dismembered man, still alive and help-less while his attacker advanced with a gleaming blade and dark intent.

She heard the Fugue Hunter hack into the bark of the tree and was thankful she could no longer hear its thoughts. The hacking made a moist, fleshy squelch as he sliced through the bark and tore into the muscular tissue below. The echoes of butchery resounded across the arbour as Kerrigan bludg-eoned relentlessly into the body of the tree. Then Carla heard what she recognised as the sound of stone on bone and the agonised screams of the living tree reached a new and insane pitch. Not long after the chopping stopped she thought she could make out the ragged breathing of the tree as it tried to recover from the quartering it had been given.

Towards the end she heard the faint tinkle of smashing glass as the Fugue Hunter dashed his bottles of wellspring water against the exposed bones deep inside the tree's wounds and the hot roaring hiss that followed like steam being forced from the ground. Finally, the tree began to col-lapse. She heard limbs falling all over the arbour, higher ones crashing through lower ones as they fell, taking many more with them.

A moment later the Fugue Hunter was with her again and he lifted her up in time for her to see the trunk of the tree splitting in half and falling open. All the limbs that were still attached came down then with a creaking, thundering crash; the sound of a whole forest felled in a single cut.

MEXICO

One year later

When Carla told him she was pregnant Kerrigan was ecstatic.

They went down to Pepito's place on the beach and drank Coronas and tequila until they could hardly walk. They weren't married, but it would be easy enough to organise. For the time that the euphoria and alcohol held him in their thrall, he was the happiest man in Mexico.

That night, while Carla slept in something of a stupor, he dreamed of the forest below Bear Mountain. They were standing next to a heap of ash in the centre of what had been the arbour. The broad space was filled with light and saplings sprouted everywhere.

The sallow man fixed him in the glare of his dead eyes.

'You will destroy everything you fought to protect.'

'I'll never hurt her,' Kerrigan protested. 'And I'll never feed. I've kept up the rituals just like I always did.'

'You've spoken the words that every Fugue Hunter has uttered when they realise their destiny is to become a feeder. He searches for you even now.'

'Who does?'

'The boy you recovered. David Slater. He will find you and when he does you will initiate him or leave the world without protection.'

Kerrigan knew the sallow man was right. But was everything he said true?

'There's Fugue outside the valley?' he asked.

'Of course. It's a disease, foundling, and it can occur anywhere.'

'But surely there are other hunters.'

'You are the last,' he said. 'But that is not the worst of this. Let me show you something.'

Night fell across the arbour and where the pile of ash had been, now the Fugue tree had returned in all its pulsing glory. The sallow man pointed and Kerrigan saw himself in fury, fighting the Fugues that hung from the tree's branches. He'd never witnessed such brutality, but that was not what the sallow man wanted him to see. He brought the scene closer and showed him the wounds he sustained and the places where the tree's sap splashed into his cuts.

'The tree won that night. It lives on in you, foundling, and now you've fulfilled your lust, it lives in the belly of my great granddaughter—the place it always wanted to be. She bears its seed.'

Kerrigan heard the tree laughing, the piped hoots of its voice making him scream and cover his ears.

'Trees thrive on light, foundling, and so too will her child.'

He woke up then, sweating hard with his heart near to bursting in his chest.

Carla slept on.

ACKNOWLEDGEMENTS

Late in 2011, in a reversal of conventional publishing methods, an editor asked me to submit work to his imprint. That editor was Steven Haynes and *Blood Fugue* is the result.

'Just needs a bit of a tweak,' he said, sharpening his instruments and strapping the manuscript down. Though I shudder at the recollection, I adore the surgically enhanced result. And so, Hacker Haynes, Butcher of Bodmin, I salute you.

Heartfelt thanks to Adam Nevill and Will Hill for their unflinching support and to Donna Condon for advice when prospects were bleak. To every reader who's taken a moment to write in support of my stories, a hug.

Finally, and most importantly, so much love to my family, nuclear and extended, who weather the uncertainties of my 'job' with more grace and stoicism than I ever seem to manage.